ELIJAH IN JERUSALEM

Michael D. O'Brien

ELIJAH IN JERUSALEM

A Novel

IGNATIUS PRESS   SAN FRANCISCO

Cover art:
Elijah Sleeping by Michael D. O'Brien

Cover design by Roxanne Mei Lum

© 2015 by Ignatius Press, San Francisco
All rights reserved
ISBN 978-1-58617-946-5
Library of Congress Control Number 2015939068
Printed in the United States of America ∞

O Jerusalem, Jerusalem, killing the prophets and stoning those who are sent to you! How often would I have gathered your children together as a hen gathers her brood under her wings, and you would not!
—Matthew 23:37

*

Haec uenena potentius
detrahunt hominem sibi
dira quae penitus meant
nec nocentia corpori
mentis uulnere saeuiunt.

These poisons more potently
Usurp a man's true self,
Which penetrate deep within,
And, harming not the body,
Rage in a wound of the mind.

—Boethius

CONTENTS

PREFACE

Christ calls us in every generation to "stay awake and watch." God desires, above all, that we have faith in his coming victory and be attentive to the "still small voice" of the Holy Spirit, as did the prophet Elijah. In this way we will come to know what we need to know, *when* we need to know it.

To presume that we have received in advance a precise decryption of the symbolic prophecies in the book of Revelation—a route map or survivalist manual, as it were—is to weaken our faculty of discernment and our openness to the guidance of the Holy Spirit and the angels. This weakness can lead us to the tyranny of unholy fears on one hand or to self-reliance on the other, and both reactions will bring about increased vulnerability to the adversary's deceptions.

There is a grave admonition in the final lines of Revelation:

> I warn every one who hears the words of the prophecy of this book: if any one adds to them, God will add to him the plagues described in this book, and if any one takes away from the words of the book of this prophecy, God will take away his share in the tree of life and in the holy city, which are described in this book.

Here is an exhortation that one cannot read without fear and trembling. It is not merely a caution to careless scribes and publishers. It applies to all those who seek to know the mind of Christ and to follow him wholeheartedly through times of tribulation. Indeed, it applies with special urgency to those who claim to be messengers of private revelation, who would use Revelation and other sacred Scripture to reinforce their personal interpretations and theories—sometimes impelled by unruly imagination, sometimes "inspired" by untested spirits—and thus, in the context of our present culture where a proliferation of writings and films offer wildly contradictory apocalyptic scenarios, contribute to an ever-growing confusion among believers and unbelievers alike.

What, then, is the role of Christian fiction in this regard? If it is to be an authentic contribution to faith, its primary *missio* must be to awaken the reader's imagination in such a way that he is recalled to the basic principles of life in Christ. It does not attempt to predict the future, but rather, in the sense of Tolkien's concept of "sub-creation", it offers an imaginative possibility for the purpose of stimulating reflection. Such fiction makes no claims whatsoever to foretell the details of how the actual apocalypse will unfold. It asks, "What if?" Most importantly, it asks, "Am I awake?" and "Am I spiritually prepared, if indeed our times prove to be the ones toward which Jesus pointed?"

The spirit of Antichrist is already among us—it has been present since the beginning. As in every generation, Christians anticipate the coming of an actual Antichrist, one who will personify that diabolical spirit and wage total war against all those who follow Jesus.

Is the "Man of Sin, the Son of Perdition" among us now, not yet fully revealed? When he manifests himself, will he arise from the kingdoms of the former Roman Empire, which is what Blessed John Henry Newman and a number of Church Fathers believed? The empire, we should keep in mind, was vast, covering much of Europe,

Asia Minor, and North Africa. It embraced numerous races and religions. Will the Antichrist, when he comes, reveal his true origins? Will he be an unbelieving Jew, as some Church Fathers thought? Will he be an apostate Christian or an offspring of militant Islam? Will he step forth from the darkest corners of resurgent paganism? Will he come from Russia or China, as some commentators have proposed? And how prescient was G. K. Chesterton when he said the Antichrist would more likely come from Manhattan than from Moscow?

We would do well to remember Saint John's warning that "many antichrists have come.... Who is the liar but he who denies that Jesus is the Christ? This is the antichrist, he who denies the Father and the Son" (1 Jn 2:18, 22–23). Many of the major forces presently at work in the world will likely play crucial roles in the rise of the definitive Antichrist. They will do so by further destabilizing civilization, creating the external conditions and the internal psychological cosmos that make men receptive to a new "messiah". Through lies, flattery, and unceasing propaganda, men will be seduced into believing their salvation can come from sources other than God.

The *Catechism of the Catholic Church* (675–677) teaches that before Christ's second coming, the Church must pass through a final trial that will radically test the faith of many believers:

> The persecution that accompanies her pilgrimage on earth (cf. Lk 21:12; Jn 15:19–20) will unveil the "mystery of iniquity" in the form of a religious deception offering men an apparent solution to their problems at the price of apostasy from the truth. The supreme religious deception is that of the Antichrist, a pseudo-messianism by which man glorifies himself in place of God and of his Messiah come

in the flesh (cf. 2 Thess 2:4–12; 1 Thess 5:2–3; 2 Jn 7;
1 Jn 2:18, 22).

The Antichrist's deception already begins to take shape
in the world every time the claim is made to realize within
history that messianic hope which can only be realized
beyond history through the eschatological judgment. The
Church has rejected even modified forms of this falsifi-
cation of the kingdom to come under the name mille-
narianism (cf. *Enchiridion Symbolorum*, 3839) especially the
"intrinsically perverse" political form of a secular messianism (cf. *Divini Redemptoris*; *Gaudium et Spes*, 20–21).

The Church will enter the glory of the kingdom only
through this final Passover, when she will follow her Lord
in his death and Resurrection (cf. Rev 19:1–9).

Twenty years have passed since I wrote *Father Elijah: An
Apocalypse*. When I first composed it, the story was set in
the "near future". Though the date was never specified, I
had imagined it as the late 1990s—with numerous details
of character and geopolitical configurations befitting that
decade and extrapolated a little beyond it in anticipation
of the third millennium. Since then, the Church and the
world have experienced momentous changes. Nevertheless, the essential architecture, if you will, of the struggle
between good and evil in our times has grown ever more
intense, and the warnings I sought to convey through the
novel remain no less urgent. So, too, the role of God's
messengers is unchanged: their call to proclaim words of
exhortation and encouragement in the midst of a darkening
age. In the truest sense of the prophetic, such souls do not
so much predict the future as testify with their lives to the
message they bear—as living words, as signs of contradiction and of consolation. It is my hope that my fictional
Elijah embodies this truth.

In *Sophia House*, the first volume of the Father Elijah Trilogy, the young Elijah suffers under a blatant manifestation of evil, the Nazi occupation of Warsaw, where he as a Jew is saved by the sacrifices of a Christian and much about his character is formed. The second volume, *Father Elijah: An Apocalypse*, depicts a world further darkened and confused by another mask of materialism, the seemingly benign global revolution from which the Antichrist arises. The novel concludes with the arrival of Father Elijah and Brother Enoch in Jerusalem on the eve of their final confrontation with the long-prophesied Man of Sin. This third volume, *Elijah in Jerusalem*, takes up the narrative of their mission on the following morning. Thus I depend on the forbearance of readers to overlook the gap of twenty years and to see it as the merest blink of an eye—or as a watch in the night.

It is also my concern that readers of the trilogy do not bring away from these stories any thought that they have been given a neo-gnostic key to the Apocalypse—in other words, a hermeneutic for survival. It is my earnest desire that they return to daily life with refreshed eyes and hunger for the living word of God in sacred Scripture. And that we might cry out with renewed fervor, with the entire Church:

"Come, Lord Jesus!"

Michael D. O'Brien
Memorial of Our Lady Seat of Wisdom
June 8, 2015

PROLOGUE

Look closely. Here is the ocean of mankind. See the depths and the surface waves, the currents converging or parting, swift and silent or turbulent. There are riptides and calm, and monsters from which all recoil, and the marvels of beauty that draw us toward themselves, and every rank of complexity between the two. Among them are beautiful perils and virtues with repellant features. All of these are present, dwelling together within these waters, each in its place and depth. Each strives for mastery of microscopic realms or for sufficiency in the larger ones, a few of them sure of their right to be, others uncertain, many more indifferent.

Of man, the creature most blessed, most beautiful, and yet most capable of destroying, there is much to say. That he fell, and fell most grievously in a headlong plunge toward the bottomless dark, is now known by few. That he is rising of his own accord, in inexorable ascent to power and glory, is believed by many and is a feature of his continued descent.

Little remains to enact. The consequences of his self-belief are hidden from his eyes. He will declare defeats victories. He will call darkness light, and depths heights. He will gain nothing and call it everything. He will lose everything and call it nothing. He will worship, as all created things must worship. Yet as he strains to worship himself he will come, without knowing it, to worship the father of lies.

I

Jerusalem the Golden

Before sunrise on a fine September morning, two men awoke on a hilltop overlooking Jerusalem. They had slept among the rubble of a barren ridge not far from the Mount of Olives and Hebrew University. Theirs had been an exhausted and dreamless sleep, for they had walked the previous day from the Hajalah ford on the river Jordan. Dressed as laborers, impoverished and travel stained, they had made their way from the wilderness of Moab by indirect paths, only occasionally walking alongside Highway 1 when the route had climbed the narrow passes east of the city. They had hiked cross-country when the security barriers appeared to be too daunting. For several hours they had accompanied a flock of sheep and their West Bank shepherds, though mostly they traveled alone. At no point along the way had any officials been suspicious about their identity papers, and they were passed through the final checkpoint without undue difficulty.

Now they arose and prayed. Afterward they drank a little water and ate from the bag of dried food they had brought with them, figs and dates and flatbread. Presently they stood and gazed down at Jerusalem, golden in the dawn.

The elder, an old man, Jewish in appearance, was a bishop. He was called Elijah, his name in the Carmelite Order of the Catholic Church. The younger, a middle-aged

Palestinian, was also a Christian, a professed brother in the same order. He was called Enoch.

By temperament, Brother Enoch was light-hearted though profoundly devout and eager for their mission. Elijah, on the other hand, was solemn. A man of brilliant intellect, his spirituality was steady, though in rare moments he was afflicted by temptations to self-doubt.

As the sun rose behind them, Elijah saw the confusion of mind spread by the Man of Sin and the spirit that accompanied him. Throughout his long life, Elijah had engaged in combat with that spirit in its many manifestations. He knew that it changed its shape and its mask whenever it lost headway, retreating a little only to strike with renewed vigor against everything that was true and good. It desired above all to be worshipped as God. Hidden within its self-exaltation and its transitory exaltation of man was the relentless objective: to destroy the image and likeness of God in any way possible. Thus, for generations it had vomited a cloud of blinding smoke and a fog of drugging pleasures upon mankind, to seduce the mind, to enthrall the senses, to disguise through flattery and deception its true intention. Most of the world had been deceived.

Such were Elijah's thoughts as he pondered the city, knowing that the Man had arrived there before him and was already at work.

As a childless father, Elijah opened his arms to embrace the millions who had gathered here, though they did not know him and would not notice his presence. The city was full of lives held to be insignificant. His embrace was a poor man's gesture, an old man's lament for all that might have been. *O Jerusalem, Jerusalem, how little you have learned; still less have you remembered. Seething with your hatreds and your myths, chewing on the raw meat of your victims, you were to have been the Bride and you became the harlot.*

He felt suddenly alone with the impossible task before him.

"My feeble voice and my own wounds inhibit me," Elijah whispered, closing his eyes. "I cannot do it."

You are not alone, said the unseen angel.

"I am alone," he answered.

You are not alone, though you feel alone, the angel replied.

"Enoch is simple."

Your brother is simple, yet the light in him is great. Have you forgotten?

Elijah bowed his head, for he had forgotten. Throughout his life he had been pursued by the subtlest of demons, which told him that he would always be alone, that the light of the world would desert him. He knew well enough that this fear was due, in part, to the formation of his character in a ghetto destined to burn at the hands of conquerors, evil or blind. Early had he learned that the foundations of the world may collapse without warning, that love would be murdered in any form he attempted to know it. He understood that this lesson was a distortion. He knew that the adversary probed his wound at crucial moments, seeking to prevent any work that God had given him to do.

Knowing the truth about his enemy did not dispel its force. Only prayer and fasting cast out this particular demon.

Elijah, Elijah, he admonished himself, *you have been called to this task by apostles and saints. You have obeyed. And in the long journey that has brought you here at last, you have learned and relearned that your weakness is strength.*

And it is my weakness that I fear, he thought.

"The city is waking up," said Brother Enoch, a little anxious, tugging at Elijah's sleeve. "We should go down."

Elijah turned to look at the brother's guileless face, with its one good eye and its one damaged eye, now healed. He opened his right hand—the hand through which the Lord had healed Enoch's eye—and looked at the cross-shaped scar in the palm. He shuddered with the memory of his previous encounter with the Man of Sin.

He has chosen, thought Elijah. *And I, should I now turn away from my choosing?*

You are not alone, said the angel once more. *Will you come?*

To him and the One who sent him, Elijah gave his silent assent.

To the small man standing beside him, he said, "Yes, Brother, let us go down."

Picking their way slowly through rocks and weeds they went downhill until they struck Martin Buber Street, which bordered the grounds of the Mount Scopus campus of Hebrew University. On this long sloping drive they descended into the Kidron Valley. Arriving at the junction of an avenue that headed west toward the mount of the Old City, they turned onto it and proceeded at a steady pace. Most of the human traffic they met was in cars and buses, but occasionally there were men and women and children on foot, variously dressed, mainly Palestinian, some Jewish, some Druze, and from time to time groups of scantily clad tourists carrying backpacks, maps, and cameras. It seemed to the two visitors that there was less tension in faces than usual—both men knew Jerusalem well—and among the clusters of people gathered around news kiosks there was animation, indeed almost a festive air. Passing one such gathering, Elijah noted photographs of the President staring at him from the covers of magazines and newspapers. The headlines shouted in Hebrew and Arabic, Russian and English: "Peace!"

The face of the Man of Sin had not greatly changed since Elijah last met him on Capri. There was no hint of the diabolical malice that had contorted his distinguished visage, however. There was no evidence of the murderer or of the world-master to come. If anything, he seemed more benign than ever, his eyes emanating kindness and wisdom undergirded by determination—an adamantine resolve to build a civilization free from discord. *Unitas* was his catchphrase, his rallying banner, and his aim. Yet his concept of unity, Elijah knew, employed manipulation and would require, in the end, the use of force. For now, the main portion of mankind considered him to be a kind of secular saint—and a messiah.

Enoch met Elijah's eyes, clicked his tongue, and gestured that they should move on. When they were out of earshot, he said, "We should go to Sheikh Jarrah and find the people who will help us." He pointed to an intersection ahead. "We should turn there."

"Not yet, Brother," said Elijah. "I wish to go to Golgotha first, to pray for our work."

Enoch tilted his head inquisitively and then smiled. "Yes, it is best."

Instead of turning north on 417, the wide boulevard that would have taken them directly to Al Sheikh Jarrah, the Arab neighborhood in East Jerusalem where they hoped to spend the night, they continued toward the northwest side of the Old City. Elijah determined to enter the ancient city walls through the Damascus Gate, which was close to the Church of the Holy Sepulcher, the traditional site of Calvary and the cathedral of the Latin Catholic patriarch. After progressing along Sultan Suleiman Street for a time, they came to the gate. Here, half a dozen policemen stood by the open wooden doors, carrying automatic weapons and surveying the many pedestrians entering and leaving the Old City. Occasionally they stopped a person and demanded papers. Elijah carried his passport and his credentials as an archaeologist, but no visa. Enoch was an Israeli citizen, and though Palestinian he was categorized as a laborer from Haifa and would arouse no particular interest. It might be otherwise for Elijah, who was also an Israeli citizen but whose name on the passport he now carried was an assumed one—Davide Pastore—and issued by the Vatican. The Church in recent months had become the object of increased hostility. Even the Israelis were cooperating with the President's agenda.

Much depended on how suspicious the guards were, how vulnerable they were to unseen promptings. No doubt the evil spirits knew who Elijah was, but they could not know his purpose in coming to the city, nor, presumably, could they speak into the guards' ears. He prayed this would be so. Despite his apprehension, he and Enoch passed through the gate without being stopped. Now they entered Beit HaBad Street and went along it toward the Church of the Holy Sepulcher. Arriving in the small square before the main entrance, they found, to their disappointment, that the shrine was not open. Tacked to the door was a poster that read, "Closed for Renovations". From a larger poster beside it smiled the benevolent face of the President. Beneath were the dates of his state visit to Israel with the times and locations of his major public events.

Enoch groaned audibly and betrayed some physical agitation.

"Calm, Brother," said Elijah.

"It is a sacrilege!" declared the other. "This evil man is putting Jesus aside."

"We have known from the beginning that this is his intention. But I had expected Israel to preserve a modicum of respect for the holy places. Even if only to prop up the image of democracy."

"And tourist money."

Elijah nodded.

"This is the place of the skull," he said. "The precise locations of our Lord's death and burial are not known with absolute certainty, yet we are close, perhaps only a few steps away from his sacrifice."

They knelt on the cobblestones, facing the eucharistic presence of Christ within the church, and prayed wholeheartedly, though briefly, for the fruitful outcome of their mission. Rising to their feet, they walked briskly back toward the city gate, went through it into a crowd of people entering, and retraced their steps a short way along Suleiman. A few backward glances reassured them that they were not being followed.

"Now we will go to meet your friends," said Elijah.

"Brother Ass will lead the way," declared Enoch, striding ahead.

At the bottom end of Al Sheikh Jarrah, Elijah and Enoch came to a corner café and grocery store. Enoch went inside, leaving Elijah to stand on the sidewalk, trying to ignore the silent attention of coffee drinkers staring through the front window at the old man with the Jewish features lingering outside their precincts. Presently Enoch reappeared, holding two paper cups of steaming coffee.

"I have telephoned," he said in a low voice. "They are sending someone."

Glancing uneasily at the surrounding streets, they sipped their coffee and waited. And waited.

A young woman wearing a black pantsuit and a pink hijab walked slowly toward them and stopped half a block up the street, beyond the café's line of sight. She nodded at them, turned, and walked in the opposite direction. The two men followed at a distance.

She led them on a circuitous path through a maze of
streets that housed a few consulates of foreign nations,
an American hotel, Saint John's Eye Hospital, numerous
small homes, and a few expensive, recently constructed
residences. Within twenty minutes they approached an
older apartment building, six stories high, a few blocks
from the hospital. The girl paused, nodded toward the
entrance, and continued on at a brisk pace.

Elijah and Enoch entered the lobby, where they found
a middle-aged Palestinian man appraising them with
intelligent eyes through gold-rimmed spectacles. He
wore a tailored business suit and carried a leather valise.
After shaking their hands somberly, without a word, he
beckoned them to follow him up a staircase to the fourth
floor. There he unlocked one of the doors in the hallway,
and they entered an apartment. This space appeared to
be someone's home—the man's, Elijah supposed. It
had a single bedroom, a kitchenette, and a comfortably
furnished living room that gave onto a narrow balcony
offering a view of the immediate quarter. Beyond it were
the rooftops of the Old City, with the Temple Mount and
the domes of churches. There were full bookshelves
and original paintings, and there was also a crucifix above
the sofa. Elijah looked more closely at their host.

"It is good to see you, Brother Enoch," said the man.

"And you too, Doctor. You are so kind to take us in."

The doctor turned to Elijah.

"I am Dr. Tarek Abbas."

"I am—"

"It is best that I do not know your name," the man
interrupted with an upheld hand and an apologetic look.
"Come, please sit down; let us have chai."

While their host busied himself in the kitchen, opening
cupboards and setting a copper kettle to boil on a propane
burner, Elijah and Enoch sat down and observed him.

"You were not followed?" the man asked over his shoulder, as if unconcerned.

"No, I don't think so," Elijah replied. "The young Muslim woman was careful."

He paused, wondering over the coordinated activities of a Muslim and a Christian.

"She is not a Muslim," said the doctor, pouring water through a sieve in which spices and black tea swirled.

"It's his daughter," Enoch contributed. The doctor shot the latter a look of reprimand.

"You are Christian Palestinians," Elijah said.

The man nodded.

"A small minority."

"Yes, a small minority."

"She wore a head covering."

"The hijab is helpful in this district—in fact, in many places."

"Enoch has explained nothing to me, Dr. Abbas."

"That is good."

"Why are you helping us ... in this manner?"

"You mean the clandestine manner? It is because you are very unusual visitors."

"Are we? What do you know about us?" Elijah asked quietly.

"Well, I have known our friend here since he was a young man with a bad eye, a religious brother from Stella Maris Monastery, which is now vacated and most of the community dead. About you, I know nothing, and it is better to remain that way."

"Even so, you surely know something. Can we not speak plainly?"

The doctor brought a loaded tray to the coffee table and poured tea from a brass carafe into three small cups, each of which contained rather too much sugar. He offered a plate of honey pastries.

ease, do not hesitate." The host paused, ...te of one of the delicacies and closed his ...t. He took a sip of tea.

...plainly is to venture into territory from which one may not return," he said.

Elijah was at a loss for further questions. He sampled the tea, uncertain, yet noting the peace in the room. He felt now that the situation was part of God's plan, though much of it, perhaps rightly, would be hidden from his eyes.

"I know you have work to do in the city," said the doctor. "Important work for the Lord."

"To know this is no small thing," murmured Elijah.

"I have news for you. I will relate it all in good time. But first you must relax and later take a rest. Then we may speak. This will be your home for the coming week."

"You are very generous to open your home to a stranger."

"Are you a stranger?" the other replied with a smile and a look into his eyes. "You are not a stranger. And I should mention that this is not my home. The apartment belongs to a friend who is away at a conference in England. He has given permission for us to use it since he understands the lack of dwelling spaces for visitors while another important guest of Israel is here. The city is packed with visitors because of that guest." He took another sip of tea. "My friend is a generous person. He is also in the communion."

"I see."

"Would you like to rest now?"

"I would prefer to hear about what you have to tell me."

The doctor looked intensely at Elijah, then lowered his eyes.

"I am a Melkite Catholic," he said. "Our patriarch here in Jerusalem has disappeared. So too has my own pastor from Saint George's parish in Haifa, along with the archbishop of Akko, Nazareth, and all Galilee. My archbishop is a just man who ministers to people of any race or religion. He has often led peaceful protests against violence done to our people—some of the violence committed by Israeli military, some by agents of the Palestinian Authority. Many Jews and Christians joined him in his protest marches. Because of his work he was labeled a terrorist three months ago. The world would be a better place if it had many such terrorists."

"Do you think he has been arrested?"

"Yes, I think so. It's the only explanation, since he would never desert his flock in time of trouble. Do you know that the Catholic religious orders have been placed under house arrest during the President's visit to Jerusalem? The Carmelites here in the city were taken away in a police bus three days ago. Other priests and abbots have simply disappeared." He tightened his lips. "Perhaps they will be returned safely when the visitor has gone."

"We must pray it will be so. Do you know the situation of the Roman Catholic patriarch?"

"Of this I am not certain. But I am worried. This concerns you directly, so I must now tell you what I know. A week ago I received a call from the patriarch's secretary, a man I know personally. We studied together at the French University of Saint Joseph in Beirut when we were young. He phoned with a specific request. He told me that two men would arrive in Jerusalem within days. They would be a Palestinian Catholic and another man. This other man, he told me, would be involved in a private mission from the Holy Father in Rome. He would be a person maligned in the media as the murderer of an Italian judge and hunted by the police and security services of more than one nation. He is innocent, said the secretary." Now the doctor peered at Elijah closely, his face betraying no emotion. "Is he innocent?"

"He is innocent," Elijah answered.

"I believe you," the other said.

"You should believe him!" Brother Enoch declared with feeling. "Tarek, you saved my bad eye years ago when they wanted to take it out, but this man here, he put the vision back into it. He covered my eye with his hand, he prayed, and now I see."

The doctor looked from one to the other, his brow furrowing. He glanced at Elijah's hands, his rough clothing, his face.

"The secretary told me that the two men would come out of the desert, from Jordan," he continued. "He said they would need help, and he asked me to give it. He further informed me that the Palestinian was from the Carmelites at Haifa and that most of his community had been killed in an incident of racial or religious hatred. I suspected it was you, Brother Enoch."

"Me? Brother Ass?"

"Who else could it be, I thought. News had reached us that a one-eyed brother had pulled one or two of the friars from the ruins. That rather narrows it down."

Now Elijah smiled for the first time, a fleeting expression. "Our friend the ass sees farther than most men," he said and put a hand on Enoch's shoulder. The small one blushed and reached for a piece of baklava.

"What I do not understand, Enoch," said the doctor, "is how you knew you should contact me."

"I knew," Enoch shrugged. "I just knew. After the attack on Stella Maris, I got the prior's address book from his office and brought it with me because we needed to find someone to hide us. Later, after he recovered, he gave me your cell phone number. They tried to kill him, you know. They left him for dead."

"Who did it?" asked the doctor.

"Father Prior said they were masked."

"That does not rule out an operation by Israeli police or military."

"The New World Cleansing claimed responsibility," said Elijah.

"They may be a front of Hamas," said the doctor, "or an Islamic State kill squad. Possibly Tanzim, an affiliate of Al-Qaida. Hezbollah and others funded by Iran also have their many arms. Nor can we rule out the Righteous Warriors of Zion."

"Father Prior said they spoke Arabic," Enoch interjected. "I don't know who they were because I was down in the city shopping for the community and visiting a father in the hospital. When I heard gunshots on the mountain, I ran all the way up. But the killers were gone when I got there, and I found only Father Prior. He's in our new monastery near—"

Elijah raised a hand abruptly to silence him. Between the doctor and Elijah there now passed an understanding: the less they knew about certain particulars the better. That way, if either of them were captured, he would have less to betray if he broke under torture. *Torture? Would it come to that?*

"In any event, you are here," said Dr. Abbas. "Let me convey to you the little I know. This morning the Latin patriarch himself telephoned me. He confirmed the message his secretary had given me a week ago, that two men were coming to the city at the bidding of the Pope. A monk in Turkey had contacted him yesterday to say that these men would try to contact me. Would I help them? the patriarch asked me. I told him I would help in any way possible."

Enoch and Elijah glanced at each other. The "monk" in Turkey must be their father prior at the little monastery they had made in the wilderness beyond Ephesus.

"The patriarch also asked me to convey a message to you. A man named Sidi Ayif would also try to come

to Jerusalem to meet you here. If he is prevented from
entering the city, you are to proceed in your mission
without him. The patriarch spoke with Sidi Ayif as well
as the monk."

Elijah puzzled a moment over who this Sidi Ayif might
be and then realized he was CDF, the cardinal prefect of
the Congregation for the Doctrine of the Faith.

"The patriarch's conversation with you was a great
risk," Elijah said. "How secure is his telephone line? I
would expect state security to monitor every call throughout the city because of the President's visit."

"I think they monitor his communications all the time,
visit or no visit. However, he told me he was using an
encrypted cell, a friend's, a person unrelated to the patriarchate. My cell is also encrypted."

"Let us hope that no one has appropriated the encryp-
tion keys."

"It is a risk, I know," the doctor shrugged. "But what
else can we do?"

"To meet with him face-to-face would have been safer."

"Perhaps, but time is running out for us. I would
guess that every visitor to the patriarch's office is marked
and followed. That he has not disappeared or been arrested is only because he is internationally respected as
a humanitarian—there is still some goodwill left in the
world. Malice does not yet control everything."

"The Pope is being maligned everywhere," Elijah
pointed out.

The doctor grimaced. "Yes, an extraordinary propaganda campaign. Why are they doing it?"

"Because the Church stands as the only block in their
path to world domination, *worldpower*, and thus we must
be absolutely discredited in the eyes of the world." He
paused. "Did the patriarch say anything else?"

"He said his conversation with Sidi Ayif was cut off suddenly in midsentence. That call was through his office lines, you see, and he thought it indicated some kind of interference, which is why he contacted me this morning through the more private cell."

"And that was all he said?"

The doctor paused before answering. "As I told you, it was a broken sentence. It probably means little, but apparently this Sidi Ayif told him there are others."

"Others? What did he mean?"

"I don't know, and neither did the patriarch. Sidi said only, 'There are others.' Then the connection was broken. He never called again."

"On what day was the call from Turkey?"

"Yesterday."

Elijah pondered all of this. His chief concern was that if an agency or agencies were running surveillance on the patriarch's office, they had learned that two men had been sent by the Pope to Jerusalem and that one of them was a fugitive from justice, a supposed assassin. It would demand little effort on the part of intelligence or police to identify him, to spread photos of him throughout the city and to apprehend him the moment he showed his face.

And yet he and Enoch had passed security guards and entered the Old City only a few hours ago without trouble. Their safe passage could indicate that the first call from the secretary a week ago had not been tapped, or alternatively, if it was subject to routine automated surveillance, human intelligence had not yet analyzed the recording. Yesterday's call from Turkey to the patriarch may have been tapped by auditing since it was broken off in midtransmission. On the other hand, the interruption might have been no more than a technical problem; Turkish satellite inefficiency, a cell phone battery losing its charge, or possibly Jerusalem's communication systems overloaded with high traffic during the impending presidential visit. This morning's call from the patriarch himself was probably safe.

The doctor now rose to his feet and explained that he must go to his hospital and then to his home in another part of the city. He would return in the evening. There was enough food in the apartment for more than a week. He bid Elijah and Enoch rest, to sleep if they could. He would pray for them.

"Dr. Abbas," Elijah said, "we cannot presume that the three telephone calls have been immune to surveillance. I suggest that you be attentive to unusual patterns of behavior around you, such as vans or cars parked near your home with people sitting in them. Try to detect whether you are followed wherever you go, on foot or in vehicles. Also, please make no verbal or electronic communications regarding my presence in the city, not even in private conversations with your family. You are the link to my whereabouts, you see."

"I do see. And foresaw," he said, smiling. "Do not worry overmuch."

At the door to the outer hall, he turned back and said to Elijah, "You look Jewish, and your accent sounds Eastern European."

"I am a Jew, and I was born in Poland."

"But you're a priest, aren't you? I can sense it. Yes, you are a priest."

"I am a priest of our Lord Jesus and a son of the Church. Thank you for your help, Dr. Abbas."

Almost immediately after the doctor left, Elijah fell asleep sitting up in an armchair, his chin on his chest. So exhausted was he that he did not dream, nor did he stir for some hours. When he awoke he noticed that the light had changed. Enoch lay snoring on the rug, his back to the room. Through the billowing curtain of the front window came the sounds of motor traffic and the shouts of children playing a game on the sidewalk below. The sun was striking the balcony at an angle, and under its rays a potted juniper bush exhaled perfume.

The shouts and laughter ended; the roar of vehicles declined. Elijah, who had spent more than forty years in the quiet of Mount Carmel, now gratefully savored the relative silence. He prayed the Divine Office, using the volume he had brought in his knapsack. Then he continued to pray wordlessly. Mainly his prayer took the form of offering his poverty—his weaknesses and age. He sensed, as he had for the thousandth time since leaving Rome, his frailty, his inadequacy for what lay ahead. He understood that his limitations were fully within the ways of God, for he was best glorified by those who had little or nothing of their own to inhibit the flow of the Holy Spirit. On this truth his confidence was based. And yet his faith in it, his hope in it, needed to be renewed again and again.

On the mountain near Ephesus he had passed through a dark test. There, in a cave in the wilderness, he had undergone a form of purgation. During that period he had become like a child; in another way he felt more ancient than ever, with a deepened love for mankind—a love mixed with grief, for the children made in God's image and likeness no longer believed in their own Father-Creator. A remnant still believed, though many of them had been confused by relentless propaganda and torrential distractions. Some had even been brutalized into apostasy. Moreover, Satan had struck the shepherd, and the sheep were scattering. And he would strike again and again, harder and harder, in his passion to destroy anything that remained of the Son's realm on earth.

Elijah recalled his meeting with the Pope two years ago, before he was smuggled out of Italy into Turkey and the anonymity of the desert.

"Holy Father," he had asked, as he had asked himself numerous times before, "are these the times Jesus and the prophets foretold?"

"The Antichrist reaches deeper into man than ever before," the Pope had replied, with sorrow in his eyes.

"You believe, then, that the tribulation Jesus speaks about in Matthew and Luke is to come in our time?"

His answer was simply, "Yes."

For the present, the Antichrist had not yet revealed his nature, his identity in biblical terms, as the Savior and the prophets had foreseen. The President was marshaling the several dimensions of his influence and power, building alliances between former enemies, doing the seemingly impossible in the political sphere—performing "signs and wonders that could deceive even the elect". He was bringing peace into so many hopeless conflicts, though it was not, and never could be, a lasting peace. For the moment, he continued to rise in prominence in the minds of men everywhere. Among Muslims he was being seriously considered as the long-expected great prophet, Imam Mahdi. Among the Jews, learned men and spiritual leaders were saying he was the Messiah come at last. Many Hindus believed he was Krishna, in a new and foretold incarnation of their supreme god, Vishnu. Some Buddhists quoted their master's teaching that another would come after him who would be worth ten thousand Buddhas. For post-Christian New Age devotees he was the coming of the Cosmic Christ. For secularists he was the greatest human being in the history of the species, the self-actualized catalyst and facilitator of the evolution of man.

During their final meeting in Rome, the Pope had told Elijah, "You must go out into the desert, my son, and feed the flock of the Lord amid many tribulations."

"Your Holiness, I do not understand. I am to be a shepherd who feeds a flock where there is no flock?"

"The Holy Spirit will reveal your flock to you. From this time forward, God's people will be ravaged by wolves. Confusion will cover everything. Doors will be locked, and others will open. Foundations will be shaken. Things now standing will fall. Yet in the end, the great shall be cast down and the lowly shall be raised up, so that wisdom may be justified and the reign of evil cease."

They had last spoken together two years ago—it seemed a lifetime. Since then, as a newly consecrated bishop, Elijah had met fewer than a hundred souls who clung wholeheartedly to Christ in his Church. A very small flock indeed. Yet he knew that the particular was often a preparation for the universal, the small task a training for the greater. As if in answer to his doubt about his readiness for what lay ahead, the past returned to him in fragments, showing him other moments of preparation, other encounters with evil when the light had overcome the darkness. He had escaped the Nazis as a boy solely because a friend had sacrificed his life for him. The death of his wife and child, when he was a young lawyer, had humbled him and led him to conversion. His struggle against despair had taught him much about the tyranny of perception and emotion, and about the relationship between grace and nature. Later, his struggle for the soul of Count Smokrev in Warsaw had shown him the power of mercy. Then came his encounters with the President and the unseen forces that accompanied the man. The duplicity of Cardinal Vettore. The death of Anna Benedetti, who had tried to unmask the President and his inner circle. The false accusation that he—Elijah—had murdered her. His anointing as a bishop *in pectore* and his flight into exile. The graces of the mountain and the cave near Ephesus. And now this most impossible mission. *Impossibility heaped upon impossibility.*

Elijah gently caught himself, recognizing the first probing of temptation. He quieted his thoughts, turned to the presence of Christ, and prayed in this manner until he felt himself to be a child again, resting on the breast of the Lord, listening to the great heart of Love beating within.

Dr. Abbas returned shortly after sunset. His knock on the door woke Enoch, who, refreshed from his several hours' nap, jumped up to answer it.

"I am not being followed," said the doctor on entering. "There was nothing unusual at home or during my drive there and back. I waited in the lobby downstairs for fifteen minutes before coming up. The street was empty."

The three men shared a light supper, and afterward Enoch washed dishes while the two others went onto the balcony to watch an extraordinary display of fireworks.

"The city is celebrating," said the doctor with a tone of irony. "This afternoon he addressed the Knesset and received a standing ovation from all parties, some of which are usually deadlocked against each other. Fifty thousand people gathered on the grounds, hundreds of thousands more lined the roads to cheer the motorcade."

"And the general mood was positive?"

"Positive? Deliriously happy, I would say. No, *euphoric* would be the more descriptive word. There was a small demonstration by a branch of the Haredim shouting that the visitor could not be the Messiah because he is not a practicing Jew. He is not one of *them*, you see. They were attacked by a larger group from another branch of Haredim, who shouted louder and longer that the visitor *is* the long-expected one. Shoving became fistfights, very ugly, but a small flaw in the general rejoicing. The police dragged the protesters away, but they did not touch the pro-President Haredim."

"I was raised in the Hasidic tradition," Elijah said quietly.

At first, the doctor did not reply. He gazed at Elijah solemnly, absorbing what he had just learned.

"Voices carry," he said. "Let us go inside."

With the door to the balcony closed, they continued their discussion in the living room.

"What is the possibility of electronic surveillance in this space?" Elijah asked in a low voice.

"It is swept," said Dr. Abbas. "Regularly it is swept most professionally because the man who lives here is a junior diplomat of a nation I think we will not specify. It was done the day before you arrived."

"Then others know about my presence here?"

"My friend and possibly one or two more, all of them reliable people. They know only that a guest is here, not who he is or why he is here. If anyone bothers to question, they will presume you are an admirer come to see the historic event."

"Well, I am no admirer, but the other part is true."

The doctor removed a folded sheet of paper from his breast pocket and handed it to Elijah. Penned on it in Hebrew was the following:

President's Itinerary

Day 1 (today): He addresses Knesset—official state visit.

Day 2 (tomorrow): He visits the Temple Wall, major symbolic event for media and Israeli people, and the world.

Day 3: He flies to Lebanon to officiate at formal peace agreement between factions. Announcement of new unified government for the country.

Day 4: He flies to Tehran, where he meets leaders of Iran and America. Cessation of atomic weapons project and disarmament of all terrorist groups will be announced. Normalization of relations between the two nations.

Day 5: He flies back to Jerusalem early in the morning. By helicopter he visits communities and refugee camps in West Bank and Jordan. In the day's major ceremony he will receive an olive branch from the president of the Palestinian Authority—the de jure or de facto state of Palestine. The PM and president of Israel will be present to deliver formal apologies and to declare immediate demolition of 200 km of the Barrier, with incremental demolition of remaining portions of it.

Day 6: He visits Golan Heights with PM and president of Israel—meets Syrian president on the Golan Heights for ratification of permanent peace treaty, with mutual agreement on realigned border.

Day 7: Day of rest for the President.

Day 8: The so-called "Eighth Day"—climax of the visit. President attends the Temple Mount rally by the Dome of the Rock. Many world religious and political leaders will join in the event.

Elijah looked up at his host. "Thank you," he said.

The other shrugged. "It is nothing. All these events are advertised throughout the city."

"But none of the public postings describe what this man is going to announce at the events or the momentous changes that will be enacted there. What you have given me is most helpful."

Elijah reread the itinerary and then pondered for a few moments before returning his gaze to Dr. Abbas.

"How have you come by these details?"

The doctor again shrugged.

"And I wonder why you thought it vital to give them to me. It seems you know my mission very well."

The doctor pursed his lips, smiled, and said nothing.

"Do you?"

"Things may be known in the heart of the soul, Father."

"He's a bishop, Tarek," Enoch broke in for the first time. Elijah frowned.

"I have not been able to attend Divine Liturgy the past three weeks," said the doctor. "Is it possible that you will be offering your Mass soon?"

"I will offer it now, if you wish to attend."

Tears sprang to the doctor's eyes, and he nodded in mute affirmation.

"We can celebrate the Liturgy of Saint John Chrysostom, Dr. Abbas. I have been granted liturgical faculties for more than one rite."

He did not mention that it was the Pope himself who had given him this privilege during their final meeting.

The portable Mass kit he had brought in his knapsack was a very small one, but it would be enough. There were plenty of unconsecrated hosts. He had no vestments other than his long white linen shirt, which would have to stand duty as an alb, and his threadbare purple stole, which he had found crumpled in the debris of a sacked Armenian Catholic church in Anatolia.

Elijah offered the Liturgy at the kitchenette table, singing the ancient words in Greek, from memory. After receiving Communion, the three men observed a period of silence, measureless it seemed. Later, as Elijah was removing his stole, Enoch asked if he could go out to buy a packet of Turkish coffee for tomorrow. He fingered a few coins, frowning at them dubiously. The doctor brought out of his pockets an assortment of paper currency that he forced on the brother. He also gave Enoch and Elijah duplicate lobby and apartment keys.

After the brother left on his errand, Dr. Abbas mixed a pitcher of mineral water with mint and lemon slices.

Though the day's heat had declined, the room was still very warm, so he and Elijah brought their glasses onto the balcony to try to catch some breeze and the first hint of September coolness. They sat on plastic chairs, listening to the sounds of the city, watching more fireworks.

"Thank you for the Holy Mass," said Dr. Abbas.

"I am grateful to *you*," said Elijah. "I hope you understand the risk you have taken."

"I am aware of the risks."

"If I may speak frankly . . ."

"Please."

"In time of peril most men seek first to protect themselves. I know in a general sense that you are a man of goodwill, you are a member of the Church and would sacrifice much for her, but I wonder if your motives in helping us are political."

"Political?" the doctor replied, lowering his voice. "No, not in the usual meaning of the word—or I should say, no longer is this the case with me. I have been involved in the complex and apparently irresolvable chaos of this land since my youth. Always it was nonviolent initiatives." He paused. "I do not think you are here to assassinate the President, if that is what you are asking, and I would not help you if you were."

"Why *do* you think I am here?"

"I do not know precisely. I do not need to know."

"You are a rare kind of person," said Elijah.

The praise was met with a smile and a shrug.

"I can tell you this, Doctor: I am a courier. I bear a message of warning to the man who desires to rule the world."

Dr. Abbas pondered this, not taking his eyes from Elijah's.

"Truth has political consequences," he said at last, "consequences one may not foresee."

"It always has a cost. To accept unforeseen consequences is surely part of the cost."

"I agree. But what about failure, Bishop? What if your words fall on deaf ears or never reach those ears?"

"That is really none of my business," Elijah said, turning his gaze to the Dome of the Rock, luminous against the night sky.

Dr. Abbas shook his head. "An enormous investment for an uncertain end," he said with a sigh.

They lapsed into silence. Dr. Abbas refilled their glasses from the sweating pitcher

Suddenly Elijah turned to the other and said, "I believe you know what it is to give everything without likelihood of success. Though we have never met before, I feel certain that your whole life embodies this."

"Does it? I hope it does now. But it was not always so." He hesitated, bowed his head a little, and asked, "May I tell you a story?"

2

Gabriel's Sign

The doctor closed his eyes, as if gathering memory, and told this story.

I was born and raised in the northern city of Akko, an ancient Roman port and a crusader fortress. The majority of its people were Jews, and I was part of the Arab minority—my grandfather relocated there after the 1948 war. At the time he was a refugee from Nablus in the West Bank. My grandmother was also Palestinian, from Nazareth. Both were nominally Muslim, not very devout. They met and married in Akko and settled down in the predominantly Muslim section of the Old City.

During the war, most of the Arabs were displaced from the city, which was taken over by Jewish immigrants and new building projects. Yes, just as Arabs were leaving, my grandparents arrived. So you see, our family has always swum against the tide.

My father attended a technical college for a time but was forced to leave his studies for economic reasons. He married my mother, a girl from the city, and within a year I came along. I was born in the middle of the Six-Day War. I grew up in an atmosphere of terrible tension—you know the history—PLO terrorist attacks on Jews, sometimes killing our own people too. Government reprisals. More and more rootlessness, migrations, new borders. Confusion. Increased control and suspicion on every side.

I learned to hate while very young. Hatred was in the atmosphere because injustice could be seen at every turn. People did not forgive. My whole family did not forgive. We were forcibly evicted from our apartment in the early seventies, to make way for Jewish immigrants from Morocco. We moved into a run-down, low-rent place a few blocks away. I remember how the police treated us that day, the contempt in their eyes. I remember the rats crawling over me the first night in our new home. My mother's tears. My father's rage.

My parents wanted something better for me. They had an exalted admiration for engineers, and from childhood onward they were very hard on me, making me study without rest so that I could graduate and one day go on to a technical college and become an engineer. Then everything would go well with us, they were sure. Because of the situation in Israel, they thought it would be better if I studied at a university in Lebanon, where they had some relations who were exiles from Palestine. So I studied French intensively as I grew up, and after high school I went to live with these people in Beirut. I applied at the engineering faculty of Université Saint-Joseph and passed the entrance exam with the highest marks. In fact, I received a scholarship. I spoke Arabic and French fluently, was studying English on my own, and knew some Hebrew from the streets in Akko and a few courses in high school.

During the first semester, I learned that I had many qualities that ensured popularity. I became, to put it simply, a wild man. I was devilishly witty and drank prodigiously, ever ready for mischief with like-minded individuals, capable of punching any fellow student who slighted my pride and of making several girls fall in love with me at once. I sailed through my courses effortlessly, it seemed, though my new way of life lowered my marks somewhat, for I had discovered the pleasure of laziness as well. Above all, I felt released from the prison of my homeland. I was assured of a glorious future.

And so it might have been, had it not been for a providential encounter.

There was a film club on the Damascus Road campus, and that year they were having public screenings of films by the Russian director Andrei Tarkovsky. I went to see them all. I was fascinated by his work, first of all by *Stalker* and later by *The Sacrifice*. Between these two films I watched *Andrei Rublev*, a film about a medieval icon painter, but I was bored by this one. Nevertheless, I was thunderstruck by the intelligence behind the works—an intelligence that evoked undiscovered dimensions of reality, broadened the universe by dramatizing various unusual mental conditions, sometimes in symbolic forms. Strangest of all, Tarkovsky was a Christian making films in the Soviet Union. That was before his exile to the West. His films did not preach, they weren't explicitly Christian, yet they were haunted by a sense of the metaphysical. *Solaris* especially disturbed me. It was about conscience and memory. About forgiveness, really. I didn't like that. But I kept going back for more Tarkovsky because I had developed a taste for his kind of intrigue, mystery, and the thrill of existential illuminations.

At the first screening, there were maybe thirty or forty people. Among them was a young man about my own age—a university student, I thought. He sat very still with his head tilted forward, listening to the Russian dialogue and music with one ear and the whispering of a girl beside him with the other. At the end of the film he rose to his feet carefully, shook hands with the girl, and made his way alone toward the exit, feeling his way forward with a white cane. I passed him on the way out and shot a glance at his face. He was a handsome, tall Arab, but his eyes stared forward sightlessly. The girl, clearly, had been reciting the French subtitles for him.

On the steps outside the building I lit up a home-rolled cigarette that I had laced with crumbled hashish. Sucking on it, I walked to the street, playing with images of myself as the Stalker, the man with preternatural faculties, the guide, the revealer of men's inner states, and, in a sense, a savior. If you can imagine this—an eighteen-year-old, dark-skinned boy with bristling black hair and a thin moustache, wearing tight Wrangler jeans, red running shoes, and an orange T-shirt with a rock-band logo on it, bent forward as if he were fighting a headwind, lithe and muscled and trying to look dangerous while at the same time pretending he was very much the material that saviors are made of.

Waiting at the bus stop I heard the tap-tap of the blind fellow coming toward me. I grew still and held my breath, hoping he would pass, since if he spoke with me, I would have to struggle with feelings of pity and pretend that all was normal with him when he was obviously a walking tragedy. Besides, I did not like Lebanese Arabs. They were too sophisticated, intensely political, and liked to think of themselves as Phoenicians.

He stopped beside me and spoke to a space somewhere a few inches to the right of my face.

"Excuse me, sir," he said in French. A quiet, deep voice, oddly accented. "Can you please tell me where is the bus stop?"

"You are standing beside it," I said abruptly without warmth, not wanting to encourage conversation.

"Ah, yes, I thought I was close to it." He tapped his cane against the side of his head. "Everything is from memory. But one must reverse the map in the mind for return journeys."

I grunted in reply.

"Will this bus go along Malek to Saint George Hospital?" he asked.

"It should, if it's running."

"Did you enjoy the Tarkovsky film?" he inquired with a smile, still staring at a spot beyond my head.

"How do you know I saw the film?" I growled.

"I am blessed with an enhanced sense of smell. The smoke, you see."

"You followed my trail?"

"Not intentionally. But for a person such as myself, you are hard to miss. Did you find the film thought provoking?"

I shrugged. "It was Tarkovsky. But how did *you* enjoy seeing it?"

"Immensely," he replied, his face becoming studious. "*Stalker* dramatizes the alienation of the gifted—the central character steps beyond the normal categories of perception. He sees with other eyes."

At that point I decided to end the conversation.

"Your bus is coming now. *Ma salaam.* Good-bye."

I had intended to take that bus too. Now I determined to go on foot, which was dangerous on these night streets but less dangerous than encounters with lonely hearts. Puffing smoke, I walked slowly backward a few paces, watching him tap-tap his way up the bus steps. Then I forgot him.

At the next screening, there he was again. Afterward, feeling a little remorseful, I approached him silently to see if the smoke detector in his brain was turned on.

"Ah, my friend!" he erupted with a genuine look of delight and thrust out his right hand for a shake. I shook it uneasily. He was not my friend. This was too much enthusiasm. The hungry heart again. The kind who could easily eat up your time and get in the way of your fun with normal people.

In order to reassure myself that I was not entirely heartless, I suggested we walk together to the bus stop. I just wanted to see him safely off.

"Did you sense Tarkovsky's understanding of human nature?" he asked as we picked our way carefully toward the street. "Even the holy monk is blinded by his pride, until his pride is broken."

"It's a Christian film," I said indifferently. "I lost interest several times throughout. But I liked the torture scene where the Tartars use boiling oil."

"I missed that part," he replied with a frown. "Though my helper described it. You are from Akko."

"How do you know that?" I exclaimed.

"I too am from Akko. I study languages here at an institute. You speak French with an Akko accent."

"I did not know there was such a thing. There must be only two of us in Beirut."

"There are several," he said. "Most of us attend the Melkite church of Saint Anthony. And you?"

And me? I thought. *And me what?*

"I am a Muslim," I said in a hard voice.

"I'm Gabriel," he replied with a smile. It was the kind of smile that seemed to exclude no one, without becoming abstract philanthropy. I had seen many blind people staggering around our quarter in Akko, young and old. But in Gabriel's face there was something unique, a rare kind of goodness, an innocence, really. It frightened me, and at the same time it drew me in.

We got on the bus together and talked all the way eastward to his stop. *Just this once*, I thought to myself during a pause between his prodigious insights and his questions. When he was let off near the hospital, I realized that my own stop was only a few blocks farther along.

So began a dialogue that stretched throughout the academic year. This story is becoming too long, so I will not tell you everything about how our friendship developed. It was a fine relationship. It was interesting. I had never known a Christian personally before. He made me think, and perhaps I also made him think in ways he had not until then. But I continued to be disturbed by the fact that he was a Christian Arab and I was a Muslim. He would not, or could not, share my rants against the Jews—against the state of Israel, to be more precise. Whenever I was in one of those moods, he merely listened.

He told me he had lost his eyesight at age seven. It was due to trachoma, a disease rampant among Palestinians, especially those from the districts beyond the cities where hygiene and clean water were often lacking. His parents had no money for a specialist and instead had taken him to one of the field clinics run by Saint John's Eye Hospital. But they arrived too late to limit the damage done by the disease.

"I have such beautiful memories from my first seven years!" he declared once. "I am so grateful for this!" He described what he remembered best, what he loved most. Never was there a hint of bitterness in him.

Dr. Abbas paused to clear his throat. He then resumed his story.

What is love, Bishop? I have pondered this question a lot, all my life since then. Do we not love most what is best in another but lacking in ourselves? To see in someone else what we should be? That is part of it. Another part is to have one's eyes opened to the gift that each person is. Subtract him from existence, and the world is poorer. When he is present, the world is richer—full of wonder, really, if we can sustain that vision. I had glimpses of this, but only when I was around Gabriel. He gave me something that Tarkovsky, great as he was, could not.

That summer we met occasionally in Akko, since his family lived in the Christian quarter in the southwest corner of the Old City, while our flat was several blocks east, near the Al-Raml Mosque. We did not visit each other's homes but agreed to meet on Saturday mornings by the harbor. We took strolls back and forth from one end of the waterfront esplanade to the other, arguing about art and politics and atheism and sex, licking ice cream cones as we went along. I eyed the girls, and he, with chin raised high, listened to the surf, children's laughter, and the cries of seabirds.

"You should see these women," I murmured.

"I wish I could," he said with a smile.

"Have you ever loved a girl, or been loved by one?" I asked, curious about this splendidly good-looking nineteen-year-old celibate.

"Yes," he replied.

"Me, I am absolutely in love with all of them."

"So am I."

In our discussions Gabriel was fond of quoting Tarkovsky. "What is art?" was a favorite topic.

He now quoted:

"Art is like a declaration of love, the consciousness of our dependence on each other. A confession. An unconscious act that nonetheless reflects the true meaning of life—love and sacrifice."

"Nice," I replied, falling precipitously, as I so often did, into one of my moods. "Very grand. But such words do not alleviate the agony of parents who find their child bleeding to death in the street."

"Words do not, and cannot, relieve such agony," he replied thoughtfully. "Still, what hardly anyone understands is that the best love is always unrequited."

"How does that apply to anything I've said?" I snapped back. "The best love is unrequited? That's nonsense."

"Not so, Tarek. The highest love is given without thought of cost or reward—anything less is not love."

"Not love? Ha!"

"I should correct myself: at its best, anything less is training for the real thing. At its worst, it is destructive illusion."

"You are an idealist!" I shouted, throwing my arms around emphatically, a gesture he could not see. "You hide behind beautiful words! You are all theory!"

He laughed, which made me angrier.

"You are genuinely, authentically, ingeniously *stupid*, Jibril," I said, using the Arabic form of his name, shaking my head in disbelief.

On another occasion, a day of overcast and high winds off the sea, of unstable human emotions as well, we stood on the tower overlooking the marina. There were local Arab youths walking along the top of the wall, arms out for balance. Most of them attended the mosque where my family went. I had been to school with some of them, played soccer with them. I knew all their names, and they knew mine. They stopped their acrobatics as we walked past and stared at me coldly. Then they turned their backs on me. Gabriel, of course, was oblivious to this.

At the time, I believed my friendship with him was no more than a pleasant distraction, a relief from summer boredom, a slaking of mild curiosity about "them". It was based in Lebanon, not in the world of Akko, and would undoubtedly continue the following autumn when we returned to Beirut for our studies. But I felt that it was not permanent and, ultimately, not important for me. But what did it mean to Gabriel? I was a bit of companionship for a handicapped fellow, I thought. This poor solitary was unable to sustain relationships at the speed and in the style that his peers needed. He would always be treated kindly, I knew, and always left behind.

"It is good that you no longer smoke that poison," he declared as we walked on.

"How do you know I quit?"

"I know."

"Ah, yes, your famous nose."

"Actually, I know because your mind is always clear now, and there is more of *you* present when we speak."

Looking back over my shoulder, I saw my mosque brothers staring after us. They quickly turned away.

"You are a good person," said Gabriel.

"I am not a good person, Jibril. Beware of projection."

"I am being objective."

I snorted and gave myself the liberty of rolling my eyes.

"You take risks, Tarek. Am I not a risk for you?"

"You're no problem. I can handle any problem that comes up."

"Why are you a friend to me? Is it an exercise in charity? Or do you merely wish to rebel, in an adolescent manner, against the social and religious norms of your community?"

"What?"

He chuckled to himself, and I learned anew that he had a sense of humor somewhere deep inside all that gravity.

"No," I said, "I'm doing research on the psychological problems of Christian Arabs."

That made him laugh. He tripped on a cobblestone, but I caught him.

"So, why are you my friend?" he pressed.

"I don't know. Why are you *my* friend?"

"I don't know either. Isn't this fascinating?"

"Oh, yes, very fascinating," I shot back sarcastically.

"I am coming to believe that if you share your life with a person, if you give and receive openly, you begin to live in a larger universe."

"Larger than what?"

"Than the inner cosmos. The tyranny within us—what pushes us in the direction of the beast."

"The beast?"

"The beast within us. And the more we know each other, the more we understand that this is the fundamental human struggle—for everyone. In this land we breathe a certain atmosphere from birth—it tells us that everything depends on the political. But in reality, nothing is political."

"I disagree. *Everything* is political."

"Is your mother's kiss political? Is the warmth of a girl's hand in yours political? Is the peace that comes when you pray political?"

"Yes, they can be. Yes, yes, they are!" I said adamantly. "About the praying business—I don't pray, but if I did, it would be political too."

Gabriel shook his head back and forth, frowning mightily.

"You don't believe that."

"I do."

"You think you do, but you don't."

I did something I had never done before. Impulsively I punched him on the bicep. He looked startled for a moment, and then shot a retaliatory punch at me, missing my arm by a hair. He drew back his fist to try again. I shifted my body so he could hit the target.

"Ay-ach, that really hurt!" I yowled.

Now he began to laugh uncontrollably. I laughed too, though not with the same output of energy.

After that, we climbed onto the seawall and listened for a while to the surf hitting the stones.

"We're like rats in a cage," I said. "That's why we keep killing each other. The real problem is the cage."

"And the cage in men's minds," he added.

"The cage in men's minds?"

"Fear and hatred—the political manipulation of fear and hatred," he said.

"So, you do admit the existence of politics."

"As a form of delusional activity based on arbitrary assumptions."

"Politics are a tool that can unlock the gates of the cage," I argued.

"There are other ways."

"What ways?"

"We can simply refuse to live like rats snarling and biting each other."

"So, just like that, the rats decide to start treating each other with good manners, and the cage master is so impressed, he just opens the gates for our little friends—is that what you're saying?"

"It would be a start. We need a beginning."

"Jibril," I said in my most condescending, pontificating tone, "*You* are unfit for this world."

He did not respond. Instead, he invited me to his birthday party, which would be celebrated in his home on the following Sunday. He gave me the time and address, and we parted ways.

I remember stomping toward the Christian quarter on the day of his birthday. I was seething with angry questions: Why couldn't Gabriel have been a Muslim? Then we could have been real friends, had some real fun.

Why did he have to be blind? Why did he evoke my admiration combined with a stew of other feelings such as pity, dismay, helplessness, and loathing of fate? Why did he have to be so damn deep and so damn cheery all the time? He made me feel wretched, immature, and selfish. So why was I going to this birthday party anyway? Because I couldn't bear to disappoint him? If so, what had brought me to this kind of loyalty without my permission being given?

I approached the staircase to his apartment building with some trepidation. This was the first time in my life I would enter a Christian home. Doubtless the family would despise me, or fear me, or both. They would tolerate me only for the sake of their beloved son, who surely had no other friends.

I knocked on the door of the second-floor apartment.

A short, round lady, much like my own mother, opened the door. Her face lit up, and she clamped my arm and drew me inside.

"Gabi, Gabi," she called to another room, "your friend is here."

"Tarek!" was the happy cry in reply.

The mother dragged me deeper into their flat, which was smaller than ours and poorly furnished. There were books and religious icons everywhere. In a tiny living room a long table had been set up, covered with an oriental rug and candles, plates of decorated cakes, bottles of fruit drinks and liqueurs. At the head of the table, Gabriel was rising to his feet, with a red paper crown tipsy on his head. He was grinning, and his face beamed a light at me, a joy so strong it hit me like a blow. I could not respond. I could not say hello. I could not speak at all. Around the table there were other young men and women his age and a few small children. His father, I presumed, was the mustached man standing near the kitchen door, a carafe in hand, looking a lot like my own father. He said, "*As-salam alaykom*, peace be upon you!" The others in the room also turned looks of welcome toward me. I knew their faces. I had seen them around town, the young Christians. We had never bothered each other, just lived our separate lives in close proximity, as if none of us really existed outside our enclosures. Now, here they were, smiling at me, some extending a hand for a shake.

I looked into Gabriel's unseeing eyes, and I was paralyzed with fear. What was this fear? Fear of these people gathered here? No. Fear of the implications and repercussions for me, a Muslim crossing the social barriers? Perhaps, but this alone could not explain the terror I suddenly felt.

"Tarek, Tarek, don't be shy," his mother chided me, with little pats and squeezes on my arm. "Come, sit down now, sit, sit. See, you have the place of honor beside the Prince for a Day." I glanced down at the one unoccupied chair, which was at Gabriel's right hand. On the placemat before it was my name on a little card, penned in Arabic, along with a small wrapped present for me and a folded green party hat.

I choked, overcome by an emotion that even now I cannot understand. It was due in part to my terror of the open hearts before me, but the greater part was composed of shame and self-loathing.

"I am feeling very sick," I stammered and fled from the apartment.

I did not sleep much that night, though toward dawn I slipped into miserable dreams. Sometime around mid-morning, I awoke to the sound of gunfire. It was coming from the direction of the old caravanserai, the Khan al-Umdan, which surrounded a square a few blocks away. I leaned as far out of my bedroom window as possible, straining to see what was happening, just as my father burst into my room, gasping for breath.

"Get down!" he shouted, pulling me inside. I hastily dressed myself while he explained. He had just come from the square. An argument had broken out between Jews and Muslims, with name-calling. Then came pushing and shoving and shouting, which quickly became fistfights and stone throwing and slashing with broken bottles. More people arrived from surrounding streets, and the situation grew into a small riot. The police broke into the crowd, weapons were fired into the air; then someone fired a shot at a policeman, and the chaos spread. Different factions retreated to the covered porticoes and were now shooting at each other from the upper levels. It was uncertain who was shooting at whom. Along with ordinary people losing their tempers, my father was sure that some Lebanese Falangists were involved, and also the PLO, or they might have joined in the fighting after it had started. It was hard to say who had sparked the conflagration.

I stood at the open front door, listening. The gunfire would die down for a minute only to resume with greater ferocity.

To my astonishment I saw Gabriel tapping his way toward me from a side street that came from the southwest quarter.

"Come inside, quickly!" I shouted. "This thing could spread."

Pausing on the front step, Gabriel stood before me with an anxious face and heaving chest. He was wearing a crucifix on a cord about his neck.

"Come with me, Tarek. We have to stop it."

"We can't stop it," I said.

"We can show them there's another way. We'll be an example of brotherhood."

"No one is interested in your examples, Gabriel. No one. They *want* to do this."

"I cannot believe they truly want it. But we have to give them a reason to listen. They are blinded by their anger."

"Right. So let's stay out of their line of fire until they cool down."

"I'll be a symbol. I'm their blind man. We're all blind, you see."

"You may turn out to be a blind man with a lot of bruises," I warned him. "Maybe you would like to be blind *and* crippled "

"Come with me, Tarek," he pleaded.

"No."

"You and I, we'll walk arm in arm across the square. You wear your checkered head scarf; I'll wear my crucifix. We'll part the waves of violence like Moses at the Red Sea."

"Are you insane?" I said.

"No," he answered very quietly. "The world of hatred is insane. Let us show them a better way—we'll be a sign."

Our heads jerked up as gunfire reechoed in the streets nearby.

"You may become a dead sign if you go through with it," I roared above the din.

"Come with me, Tarek, please. It's our chance. We can unlock the cage together, but we cannot do it alone."

"I said *no*, you idiot! Now go home!"

Even as I shouted it, I slapped him hard on the cheek. I was infuriated by his naïveté and was also trying to wake him up. It was not then in my conscious mind, but I think I was trying to tell him: "This is what pain feels like. This is how worried I am about you. This is how much I love you . . . and hate you for your absurd goodness."

When I hit him, his face grew confused for a moment, and tears came to his unseeing eyes. I felt horror over what

I had done, but I could not take it back. He bowed slightly toward me, turned, and walked slowly away, tapping.

"Go home!" I shouted after him one more time.

Seeing his crucifix, a few children picked up stones and threw them as he rounded the corner and disappeared from my sight. He was heading in the direction of the Khan al-Umdan.

I struggled with myself for some minutes, wrestling with my fear—fear for myself, fear for him. Finally I leaped from the steps and ran toward the square, hoping to stop him before he entered it. But I was too late. I ran through the gate to see the square deserted, except for people cowering behind pillars in the lower porticoes. The gunfight continued on the upper levels. And before me, in the middle of the square, lay Gabriel in a pool of blood. Heedless now, I ran to him, intending to drag him to safety. But he was dead. His body had many bullet holes, some large, some small. His blood was all poured out. Part of his face was destroyed. I pulled off my shirt and covered it. His hands still clutched the crucifix.

I don't know why I was not killed along with him. Maybe because people were coming to their senses. Maybe they were stunned by the realization that they had shot a blind man. His white cane was plainly visible on the cobblestones. Not long after, the shooters crawled away over rooftops and soldiers rushed in. An ambulance came. They let me ride in it with his body. "My brother is dead," I said over and over. "My brother. They have killed him."

The newspaper accounts reported that there were no arrests because the perpetrators had fled. Gabriel's killers were never found.

I stood outside on the street during his funeral. It was held at Saint Andrew's, the white church with the red steeples on the seawall, close by the place where we used to eat ice cream and argue. I could not bear to go in. I followed the coffin to the cemetery and waited outside for hours until all the mourners had gone. Then I went in and knelt beside the raw soil, looking at the cross they had planted over his body. I felt numb. I felt nothing. I did not speak to him as mourners do. I did not cry. But I did not leave, and only in the night did my father find me and make me come home.

Dr. Abbas had recounted the final part of his story with his shoulders hunched, a hand covering his eyes. He said nothing more after that.

Elijah waited a while and then said, "You are a Christian now."

The man nodded, straightening. "Yes. For nearly thirty years I have loved the Lord Jesus. I was baptized in Beirut and studied medicine there. Then I returned to open a practice in Akko, where I lived for some years. It's where I met my wife and where our children were born. Later we moved to Haifa, which is now our home, though I am often in Jerusalem for surgeries."

"You are a physician of the eyes."

Again he nodded. "It would take a great deal of time to describe how all this has come to pass."

"There is no need. The story is visible in your life."

Dr. Abbas looked out across the quarter to Mount Zion.

"Not long after his burial I had a dream about him— about Gabriel. In it, he was walking toward me across the water, from the sea. I was on the fortress walls, reaching out my arms to him, angry at him and yet longing to see him again. When he was about ten meters away I climbed across the stone barrier and stepped onto the water. With each step I marveled that I was not sinking. When we stood face-to-face on top of the waves, he looked me straight in the eyes. He was *seeing* through his eyes. His face was totally restored, radiant, almost as bright as the sun. He said, 'I am happy now, Tarek. I want you to come where I am going, and then you will be happy too.' With that, I woke up."

"A beautiful gift from God, this dream," said Elijah.

"Yes, it is. In a way, I am still—always—strolling along the seawall, waiting for his return. And every day of my life I remember his final words: 'We can unlock the cage together, but we cannot do it alone.'"

After Dr. Abbas departed, Elijah prepared for sleep. Both he and Enoch preferred the floor to bed or sofa, and indeed the brother was already asleep by the time Elijah had completed praying Compline. He blessed the room with holy water, invoked the protection of the angels, and stretched out on the cool marble floor. Beyond the half-open door to the balcony, the city was growing quiet.

Elijah was aware of the momentous work that would be his tomorrow. He tried not to think about it other than in general terms. It was enough to know that he would be brought to an encounter where he would be free to speak. What the words would be specifically, he did not know. They would be given when they were needed.

In the cave he had learned to listen to the "still small voice" in the whispering breeze that had spoken to Elijah the prophet. In the cave he had also learned that he was called to Jerusalem to bear witness against the Man of Sin, who sought to usurp the throne of God.

To bear witness, he thought. *In what form do you want me to bear witness, O Lord? Are you now offering him one more opportunity to accept your mercy?*

Though Elijah heard no answers to his questions, he felt peace. He reminded himself that the presence of Christ's supernatural consolation was an answer—was *the* answer. In a language beyond all words it said, *I am with you.*

Fragments stirred in his memory as he closed his eyes and drifted.

"Your task is to obey, Elijah. The words will be given to you from above," said the cardinal prefect during their last conversation in the monastery near Ephesus.

"Salvation and glory and honor belong to you alone, O Lord!" Enoch had cried with arms raised as they stood on the hill overlooking Jerusalem. "You are the Alpha and the Omega, the First and the Last, the Morning Star shining bright. The Spirit and the Bride say 'Come!' Be with us as we face our foe, that we might stand firm and strengthen the things that remain."

Now, as Elijah sank into sleep he heard another word:

Go down without fear, my son, into the darkness of men's hearts; listen to their cries and bring them forth into the light.

3

The Woman Inviolate

Elijah and Enoch rose at five in the morning. They prayed their Divine Office together, and then Elijah offered the Holy Sacrifice. Afterward they continued to pray.

Enoch appeared to be blessed with an unusual (for him) state of recollection, kneeling for more than an hour facing the crucifix. Elijah prayed alongside him, kneeling for a short period until the aches in his back and joints forced him into a chair. As he rested in a state of attention before the presence of Christ, silence gazing upon Silence, the peace he had felt the night before was still with him; indeed, it had increased. When both he and Enoch stirred, they noticed that more than two hours had passed.

Shortly after nine o'clock, Dr. Abbas unlocked the apartment door and entered. He greeted them and offered Elijah a large plastic shopping bag. While Enoch made coffee and a light breakfast, the two other men sat in the living room, where Elijah opened the bag with some interest.

"It's Hasidic garb," said the doctor. "I thought it might help you get farther into the Old City, even as far as the Western Wall plaza. I have just come from an early morning stroll around the area. I must warn you that security is extraordinarily tight today."

Elijah unfolded a long white *tallith*, a prayer shawl. It was a beautiful garment and evoked a world of memories for him. Its black stripes were more numerous and the knotted tassels more elaborate than the one he had worn as a boy in Warsaw. It was woven from fine linen, not the coarser cloth he had known. There was also a small black velvet cap, the *kippah* that many kinds of Jews wore. He placed it on his head with a feeling of nostalgia. He would have preferred to wear a *spodik*, the round black fur hat traditional with Polish Hasids, but he was unbearded and had no *payot* sidelocks and would have appeared in the city as an anomaly. The objective was to blend in. He would go as a conservative Jew with Orthodox leanings, which was perhaps safer, considering the divisions within the branches of the ultra-Orthodox Haredim.

"You look very much the part," said Dr. Abbas.

"It once was my true self," Elijah said.

"Is it always the case that, as one grows and a larger self emerges, we do not lose what we once were?"

"Are you thinking of your own past?"

"Yes, in a way. I do not forget what was good in it, the *islam*, the surrender to the infinite God. Yet it was only a beginning. There was much error in it, and, as we know, those root errors have become aberrations in our world, with dangerous consequences."

"The man I hope to confront today would erase those consequences by erasing all differences."

"To bring an end to violence is a good thing, I will grant you. But what else would be erased if the differences between us were removed by force?"

"That is the question. The President seeks to eliminate the differences that divide men by positing that all religions are imperfect prefigurements. And he will point mankind to a single new source of transcendence."

"Through himself, of course," Dr. Abbas scowled.

"Yes, and if you read the sacred Scriptures with attentiveness you will see that it does not end with him."

"It ends in *Shaytan*."

Elijah nodded. "Can you tell me what he said in his speech to the Knesset, Doctor?"

"I watched it on television last night. He did not exhort his audience to fall on their knees and worship the devil."

"Of course."

"It was really quite a masterpiece of rhetoric. Touching actually. I frequently felt myself moved. He offers great hope to mankind. As I listened to him I thought, 'Is it possible, after all, that we can make happen what Gabriel sacrificed himself for?' "

Elijah studied the other's face.

Dr. Abbas smiled. "Do not worry, Bishop. He has extraordinary power to sway minds but not so much that he can dissolve all defenses. Besides, he was only laying out broad principles for reconciliation."

"These will be articulated more specifically in the days to come."

"In the most sincere and magnificent language, I expect."

"He is a brilliant man," said Elijah.

"And dangerous."

Dr. Abbas checked his wristwatch.

"In two hours the motorcade will bring him from an undisclosed location to the plaza. He and the chief rabbi of Israel, along with other religious dignitaries, will meet at the wall for prayers and a short speech by the President. They probably won't be entering through one of the main gates, since the maze of the Old City is a nightmare for security. Already the area is surrounded by military and police in great numbers, with lines of them at every gate. The closer one gets to the site, the more plainclothes security one sees everywhere, with buttons in their ears."

"You were able to get that close?"

"It is early yet, and crowds are only beginning to gather. But as I was leaving through the arches at the Dung

Gate, police had begun checking the papers of everyone entering. There is a new arch with a body scanner and metal detector. Dogs were sniffing for explosives, and I saw a lot of armed men on rooftops. Do you have papers that would let you through the barriers?"

"A Vatican passport—not in my name."

"A Jew from the Vatican? It is incongruous and may draw attention."

"My face is known to police in Europe, but my appearance is somewhat different now. The tallith and kippah may also help prevent too close an examination or prevent connections from being made. The faces of old men are rather indistinct. The young are bored by us and do not look closely."

"Israeli security are masters of observation," Dr. Abbas murmured. "Forgive me for asking, but what do you hope to accomplish? Will you try to speak with him personally, to give him your warning?"

"If the visible and invisible gates guarding him are unlocked by a miracle of providence, I will be ready. Though he seems set on his course, it may not be too late. He rejected the message the last time we met, but we must leave room for a final grace, here at the threshold of his great step toward worldpower."

"You've spoken with him before?" asked the doctor with raised eyebrows.

"Yes. It was a dramatic encounter."

"But now, in a crowd? It does not seem sensible to me, much less possible."

"The ways of God are not always sensible, and they seldom seem possible. I am merely obeying."

Enoch loved his *djellaba*, for the brown robe permitted him easier passage among different peoples. With a knotted white cord about his waist, he looked like a Franciscan;

with the addition of a black and white scarf, he was a peasant Palestinian. Today he would wear neither. With his loose robe and sandals, his squint and guileless face, not to mention the sweat and dust of the desert that he had not yet washed off, he looked completely harmless, with nothing of the *fedayeen*, the anti-Israeli commandos, about him.

Immediately before setting out for the Old City, they knelt and prayed for divine protection on the mission. Elijah blessed Enoch and Dr. Abbas. Each of the three kissed the feet of the crucifix on the wall.

The doctor would drive them as close to the city gates as the congested traffic would permit and leave them to walk the rest of the way. He had wanted to go with them, but Elijah insisted that he not risk association with them in any aspect of what lay ahead.

Dr. Abbas dropped them five blocks from the Damascus Gate, as the police had set up barriers across streets and avenues, prohibiting vehicle traffic from moving beyond that point. Pedestrian traffic toward the gate was heavy, with people of various races dressed in ethnic or religious clothing, along with a larger number of tourists than usual. Empty tour buses were parked everywhere.

Close by the gate, Elijah and Enoch stopped and prepared to bid each other farewell. As agreed, they would enter the Old City by different ways, which could help reduce scrutiny if security agencies were looking for two men. When they reunited in the square, they would stand side by side and approach the President if an opportunity presented itself. Their mission could be frustrated by one means or another. If this turned out to be the case, they would consider alternatives when they returned to the apartment later in the day, after walking the return routes they had carefully planned, which would enable them to avoid surveillance. If, however, what God intended was a success and they were able to accomplish it without being apprehended, they would rejoice and return to Ephesus as soon as they were able. On the other hand, even successful delivery of the message might mean arrest for one or both of them, in which case all their provisional plans would be futile.

"Everything is in his hands," said Enoch.

"Fear nothing," Elijah replied.

"To the glory of the Lamb who was slain!"

"And lives again!"

After watching Enoch pass through the security barrier at the Damascus Gate, Elijah set out among streams of pedestrians heading west and south around the walls of the Old City. When he arrived at the Beit Shalom Garden, leading to the Dung Gate, he felt his heart beating rapidly. He sensed also the first touches of consolation—the strengthening, he called it. The pattern of reassurances was familiar to him. There were no words in Elijah's thoughts, no rehearsal of a message that he must deliver. For the moment, he did not know what the message would be.

Though scrutinized by security people standing watch at the gate, he passed through without being stopped and entered the short street leading to the arches, beyond which was the walkway to the Western Wall. The street was crammed with dozens of parked cars, all of them expensive models, all guarded by chauffeurs who stood beside them, smoking and chatting with each other. Among them were silent individuals with grave expressions on their faces and listening devices in their ears. Although well dressed, their jackets were open, presumably for quick access to weapons. The long lines of people on foot eyed the vehicles with interest as they headed toward the main security barrier. The crowd's animation was similar to what Elijah had noticed among pilgrims whenever he had stood in Saint Peter's Square for papal events. But the heightened sense of adulation was something more than the excitement of seeing a world figure and beloved father close at hand. There were several elderly men in talliths and fedoras scattered along the line, a larger number wearing kippahs, about an equal number of Muslims, and many men and women without identifiable garb. Elijah inched toward the security barrier behind a man dressed much like him. After what seemed interminable progress, he waited while the man ahead of him had his papers checked, was sniffed by dogs, and was directed to the arch of the scanner and metal detector. Now Elijah stepped forward, passport in hand.

The Israeli military guard frowned as he opened the document and slowly turned its pages.

"Vatican?" he said, looking up. "Why are you a citizen of the Vatican State?"

"I am an archaeologist," Elijah explained. "I am permanently assigned to Vatican City."

"But you are a Jew."

"Yes, there are a number of us who work there."

The guard beckoned with a hand, and two policemen came over. He showed them the document. Each in turn went through the passport carefully, without expression, page by page. Other guards were now letting people through the scanner.

"These are entry and exit stamps for Turkey," one said with a probing look at Elijah's face.

"Yes, I have been engaged in excavations at the ruins of a fortress built by the Seljuk Turks, very ancient. It was built in the eleventh century at—"

"Stand over here, please," one of the guards interrupted, pointing to the sidewalk ten paces from the entry.

A plainclothesman approached. The four now conferred with each other in low voices, and the military man went off on an errand, perhaps to seek guidance. The three others surrounded Elijah, one holding him firmly by the arm, all assessing him without comment. He feared that police or intelligence agencies had indeed intercepted the three telephone calls and that he would be identified within minutes as a fugitive from justice, the accused murderer of an Italian judge. And if that happened, the President's condemnation of him—or worse—would swiftly follow.

Elijah tried to take a step back, to make excuses and apologies, to leave by the way he had come, but they would not let him, and their scrutiny intensified.

Finally the military man returned, accompanied by a plainclothesman with an identification badge around his neck and an air of higher authority. Elijah could not quite hear their consultations, though the words "suspicious" and "detain for questioning" surfaced.

The two policemen tightened their grip and hustled him past limousines and chauffeured cars toward a waiting police van. With sinking heart, Elijah was about to be pushed into the back of the van when they were hailed by two well-dressed young men.

"You've made a mistake," said one, waving a paper as he approached. "Read this."

Without letting go of Elijah, the policemen carefully read the document and then relaxed their grip. They turned away indifferently and walked back to the security barrier.

Perplexed, and with some trepidation, Elijah now found himself facing the two interventionists. Who were they? Were they agents of the President's circle?

"For your own safety, sir, please come with us," said one in Hebrew.

"Who are you?" Elijah asked without moving.

"That will be explained," said the other in German. "Please, it would be better for you to leave now."

Without further discussion, without compelling him, they walked ahead to one of the parked cars and opened a rear door. Elijah followed. Hesitating, looking inside, he saw to his surprise a woman looking back at him with amusement. He got in.

"A wise choice," she said in a clear, deep voice—again it was German.

The two men took the front seats, and the driver began to maneuver the vehicle backward out of the street. Following the directions of traffic police, they turned left onto Ma'ale HaShalom and shortly were on Derech HaOfel, dropping into the Kidron Valley. As the car accelerated onto 417 North, Elijah glanced at the woman beside him. She was in her late fifties. It took no imagination to see that she had once been a remarkable beauty, and though now in decline, she was still striking. Elegant, graceful, she was slender and lightly tanned. She wore an ankle-length deep-violet dress, and her white hair shone with a youthful glow.

The woman continued to smile to herself with an ironic twist to her lips, as if she were enjoying an elaborate joke.

"Who are you?" he asked.

She grinned, baring perfect teeth, fingering a discreet chain of diamonds about her neck.

"The real question is, who are you?" she responded. "Though you need not pick and choose from the several versions of your identity. I know who you are."

He said nothing until the car turned onto Golda Me'ir Boulevard, which would take them farther north in the city, well beyond the Islamic quarter.

"I appreciate your assistance," he said. "Why did they let me go?"

"My bodyguard showed them the Presidential pass for me and anyone who accompanied me."

"Please ask your driver to stop here and let me out."

"I will, if you insist. However, I propose an excursion in the countryside."

"No, thank you. Please stop here."

She leaned forward and rapped on the window separating the rear from the men in front.

"The curb. Let him out."

After the car pulled over near a bus stop, the doors unlocked and Elijah opened his.

"A pity," said the woman. "So much waste."

"Thank you again," he muttered, preparing to step out.

"Don't you wish to know why I rescued you?" she said.

"If you wish to tell me."

"Though we have never met before, our connections reach into the past and most definitely continue in the present."

She was playing with him. She was a bored, wealthy woman engaged in an afternoon's diversion. He got out and was in the act of closing the door when she said, "Ruth."

Startled, he did not move.

"Yes, I knew Ruth," the woman said.

"I do not understand," he whispered, choking.

"We can discuss it. Your situation is precarious, is it not? I will help you."

He considered her offer in a flood of confused emotions. His wife had died many years ago. Her absence was an old wound that had never entirely healed. If this woman knew he had been married to a Ruth, she must surely know more. How much more?

He got back into the seat beside her. She knocked on the glass, and the driver knifed his way into traffic.

Without further conversation, Elijah and the woman observed the passing scenery. At an interchange, the car turned onto Route 1, the main east-west artery leading to Tel Aviv.

Elijah reassured himself that when Enoch failed to find him in the plaza, he would refrain from any precipitous actions. That was their agreement. They were called to give witness side by side; it would be together or not at all. Thus, Enoch would return to the apartment, and later they would discuss alternative ways to reach the President.

Within half an hour, the car turned off onto secondary roads and proceeded deeper into the forested heights of the Judean hills. There were numerous villages along the way, and in the bottomlands fields of vegetables were still irrigated by sprinklers, though the hillside vineyards were ripening on drier ground in preparation for the coming Sukkoth harvest festival. Finally, the route took them onto a gravel road that rose toward the summit of land, with a view of the line of blue sea in the west and the distant crenellations of Tel Aviv's skyline. Immediately below and beside them were ravines green with scrub brush. To the south, the hills receded in layers of amber haze.

When a private laneway appeared to the right of the road, the driver turned onto it, shifted gear, and climbed higher through stands of pine and a few wild olive trees. Within minutes they came to a halt in a tiled courtyard surrounded on three sides by groves of swaying cypress. On the open side of this clearing stood a substantial two-story white stone house roofed with red tile, facing the multiple convolutions of hill country to the north, in the West Bank.

"My home," said the woman. "Would you care for some refreshments?"

Disoriented by this pleasantry, above all by the unexpected turn of events, Elijah did not reply. He followed the others to the house's front entrance, bronze double doors in which a keypad security lock was embedded. One of the men punched the numbers, and the doors parted sideways, disappearing into the walls. The men gave slight bows to the woman, casually yet deferentially, and walked away toward an annex. She and Elijah entered a wide hallway, and the doors slid closed behind them.

The hall was an atrium rising up to the roof. It was walled and floored in pale green marble, illuminated by a row of skylights. The air-conditioned atmosphere was cool, scented with a mild perfume that could have been natural or artificial—it smelled like lemon verbena.

Beyond was a large open living room with wall-to-wall glass facing a patio and a descending terrace of ornamental trees and cacti. Flowering shrubs fountained from turquoise pots. The interior was appointed with hand-woven Scandinavian rugs and furniture upholstered in white brocade. Elijah noticed a few artifacts displayed on side tables: a small amphora, a Roman sword with a chipped blade, a pewter bowl of ancient coins. The few paintings were inoffensive nudes made by avant-garde German artists at the beginning of the twentieth century. There was also a freestanding bronze sculpture of a rampant horse with a life-size warrior running beside it, his arm drawn back, his spear poised to hurl. Its style was a synthesis of ancient Greek and neoabstract.

"Please sit down," said the woman, gesturing to an armchair facing the window. "I will bring us something, and then we can talk."

Elijah sat down and removed the kippah from his head. As he listened to cupboard doors being opened and tinkling glasses in a nearby kitchen, he wondered who this

woman was and, most of all, how she knew his identity—
if that was the case.

Presently she returned bearing a large tray, which she set
on the coffee table before him. There was a bottle of red
wine, glasses, plates, a basket containing varieties of artfully
designed breads, and a platter heaped with ham, thinly
sliced sausages, and cheeses.

"I don't think you need kosher," she said with the smile
of a gracious hostess, seating herself in an armchair at right
angles to him.

She poured the wine, and Elijah sipped from his. Tense,
churning with questions, he declined her offers of food.

"You said the name *Ruth*," he murmured.

She looked at him over the rim of her wineglass, drank,
and then set it down on the coffee table.

"Ruth Sonnenberg was one of my teachers at university
in Jerusalem."

Pain seared through Elijah at the sound of her name,
but he hid it.

"Ruth Sonnenberg," he said noncommittally.

"Your wife. Perhaps you remember her."

She watched his reaction, her smile intact. He said
nothing.

"You are David Schäfer. That is your real name. Of
course, when I was young you had a different name,
probably provided by the Haganah years before. You were
a lawyer then, a rising politician. I often read about you in
the news. So handsome, so intelligent, a hero, and married
to my professor."

"What did she teach you?"

The woman laughed. "In a formal sense she taught
me postwar European literature. In the human sense she
taught me invaluable lessons."

"Were you that close to her?"

"Not really. I wasn't one of her peers. I was a student. An arrogant one, and a Marxist at that stage of my life. Before Jerusalem I spent a little time in the RAF, bombing Berlin."

"You are hardly old enough for that," he said dubiously.

"The other RAF. Red Army Faction—or, to be less dramatic and more honest, it was one of the Baader-Meinhof-Gruppe's bastard children."

"And so," he said, trying to move her along, "you met Ruth."

"She taught me about a certain kind of humanism that Marxists usually don't understand. She listened to me. She didn't agree with me, but she didn't mock me either. She was genuinely interested in the person hiding inside all my camouflage. The interest was real, you see; it wasn't a technique for handling rebels."

"Yes, that was Ruth."

"I was very sorry when she died. I have loathed terrorism ever since, though I was once an enthusiastic advocate of it."

Unable to speak, Elijah gazed out the window at the valleys beyond.

She dropped her irritating smile and pondered him.

"You are really in a great deal of trouble," she said. "How can one man get himself entangled in so many calamities at once?"

"I do not know what you mean."

"Killing a Supreme Court judge, who just happened to be your lover. Shocking."

He swallowed hard and tried to quiet his breathing. "She was not my—"

"Oh, I know, I know," she went on, waving away his objection. "It is obviously disinformation. I haven't the slightest doubt that you are innocent of murder. Benedetti was an honest person, a real person, and in your own way you are also an honest person, quite dedicated in fact. How do I know this? Because after Ruth's death I followed your career, saw how you were about to become very influential and then suddenly walked away. In the public's eyes you became invisible, just another politician who faded into private life and was heard from no more. You returned to the name you had at birth, and you became a Catholic. Moreover, a priest. It took me years to track down these latter pieces of information."

"How did you?"

"I have friends in Israel."

"Are you an Israeli?"

"I am a citizen of Austria, the country of my birth. But I have honorary citizenship in other nations, including Israel. This is my getaway place, where I come to be alone in winter." She turned and looked out the window. "Sometimes it snows here," she said. "I love it when it snows. The world becomes pure."

She looked into the distance, as if remembering an interesting adventure. "I once attended a Mass at Stella Maris Monastery, just to observe you in your metamorphosis. It was fascinating. I saw that you weren't running away from grief or hiding in a hole. No, you sincerely believed in what you were doing."

"And you? What do you believe in?"

"When I am not writing critiques of pure reason in my mind or engaging in social manipulation, I just live. I enjoy my life very much."

"Your help, our conversation here. . . . Is this an exercise in social manipulation?"

"If it were, I would not admit it."

"Am I an entertainment? A puzzle to be solved?"

"You certainly aren't boring. I should say, rather, that your situation is not. And I must point out that you don't have a great deal of common sense. What on earth were you trying to do, a hunted man entering a place where every second person is watching like a ferret? The prayer shawl and the cap might have fooled most people, but not all."

"How did you recognize me?"

"I read newspapers. I saw you on a number of front pages. What a scandal! What a bad, bad Church you belong to! My, what a media event you were. Old history now—two years ago, was it? There are always fresh scandals, of course, and people have short attention spans. But I never forget significant faces."

"Why were you watching the crowds at the arches?"

"I like to observe the panorama of self-deception in its various manifestations."

"This does not explain why you helped me."

"Passive enjoyment of a drama is not as pleasurable as being a participant. Besides, your past is, in a small way, my past. Ruth changed my life too."

"How?"

"In her I met a genuinely happy woman, a woman who was.... Well, her qualities were outstanding, of course. Dignity and self-respect, and no egoism. Maybe she had the kind of thing you people call wisdom. But mainly it was the love in her, which she gave to everyone, to anyone. A person like that *is* the way she is because she is loved totally and beautifully by someone—someone in whom she has absolute confidence. Until then I didn't believe in such love. After meeting Ruth I began to think it was possible. Rare but possible. That's all. She didn't convince me of anything intellectually. She only raised a doubt in my mind, and she didn't know she was doing it. She was just herself. She showed me there were other ways to live."

"Yet you ..."

"Yet I did not make much effort to become like her? Exactly. She shifted my world a degree or two, enlarged it a little. As a result, I did not die in a hail of bullets from a Mossad assassin team, as I might have eventually if I had persisted on the route I had taken." She smiled pensively. "Or from the KGB, MI6, CIA."

Elijah wondered why the woman was painting herself in lurid colors. Was she trying to impress him with the implications of a mysterious past? If so, what was her purpose? He resolved not to be drawn into it.

"After Ruth's death what did you do?" he asked.

"I left university in midterm and returned to Vienna. There I lost myself with my horses and young men. I still, regularly, lose myself with young men. It is a form of therapy."

"Are you married?"

"Not at the moment. I have been married four times."

"Do you have children?"

"None, thankfully. Imagine what it would be like to be mothered by me."

Elijah now wondered if the woman were offering him opportunities to criticize her and in this way to confirm the widespread assessment of Catholicism as a religion for hypocrites and grim moralists. Well, he felt grim enough. Or was she trying to hurt herself? Perhaps she had a driving need to test men, to prove to herself some theory about them. Or was she just leading the conversation in circuitous routes for whatever her byzantine purpose might be?

"You have no family then?" he said with a note of sympathy.

"I am a woman inviolate," she declared with mock pride, in English.

"Yes, it is a very nice dress," Elijah said inanely, looking away, his thoughts turning elsewhere.

She burst out laughing, which made him stare at her curiously. He wondered if she was becoming a little drunk.

"Never mind, Father Elijah. Let me put it another way. I am a woman whom no one has ever touched. I mean touched at the core."

"Loved, you mean?"

"Oh, I have been loved, hated, scorned, used, lied to, cheated, bought, sold, traded. And I have done the same in return—more so, I should say. It has been a glorious game, and I have won most of the matches. I have had so many men that I cannot count them, or remember them, but I do know that every one of them—without exception— was an empty shell. Complex or simple, they were nothing more than walking, talking theater pieces. They were *lustful* actors, occasionally *romantic* actors, sometimes *clever* actors. Sometimes even *sincere* ones. Now and then there would be a lustful, romantic, clever, and sincere actor. But mannequins, all."

"Have you considered the possibility that you did not touch *them* 'at the core'? Did not know them?"

"I knew them, and I touched them extensively."

"I mean the soul."

"That is abstract theology," she smiled indulgently.

He sighed and shook his head, feeling the weight of the world's unbelief, man's endless wounds caused by lack of faith, of hope, of genuine love. He was burdened also by his inability to find healing words.

He knew that in a sense he *was* a word, as Ruth had been a word to this woman by simply being herself. A word of presence—I am with you. I feel your suffering. I hear your cries beneath your smiling face and your statements so cal- culated to shock. I grieve with you, and I grieve in your place, as you will not allow yourself to grieve, because you think there is nothing beyond grief.

"Would you care to hear an abstract story?" she asked.

Urgently desiring to return to Jerusalem, to disappear in its maze, he did not answer.

"Before I begin," she went on, "let me reassure you that you are not the captive of a madwoman." She leaned forward, refilling their wine glasses. She drank from hers. He ignored his.

"You are not a hostage to my whims, O man of many names. Tell me you want to go, and my driver will take you wherever you choose. No one will know you have been here."

He considered a moment and then said, "I would like to hear your story."

Leaning back in the armchair, holding her glass with some elegance, she crossed her legs at the knees, lifted her chin, and began.

I am one of the wealthiest women in the world. Forgive the cliché, but it is true. I wouldn't mention it if it didn't play a role in what I am about to tell you. When I was a child, our estate outside Vienna was like a palace in my eyes. In fact it was a real palace, an historic site. I felt it was a fairy castle in which we lived our fairytale lives, my mother, my father, and I. And our horses, of course. This was before the young men. I was adored and pampered by my parents, but not loved. I was the darling princess, a child figurine. I did not understand anything about my world. Nothing at all, other than my love for my first ponies and the deer in our family parks, the smaller summer house in Salzburg, our boat on the Danube, and so forth. I liked music too but had no talent. I was a romantic dreamer, as are so many young girls.

I also treasured my doll collection, which grew steadily as a result of unceasing gifts from my father whenever he traveled abroad, or from family friends and relations. Even our head gardener made a doll for me once, a little girl shape he constructed from straw and seeds and red ribbons. He gave me the doll when I was running about the flower-erbeds one afternoon, the only opportunity for him to encounter the princess. He was a genuinely kind person, though I took him and his gift for granted, as I took everything for granted. I think I was eight years old then. Some of the dolls my parents' friends gave me must have cost small fortunes. They were exquisite and unique, from all parts of the world, usually made by master craftsmen, by artists. None of them moved me the way the straw doll did, but all of them were my babies, my little children.

I am not a princess, by the way, though members of royal houses visited our home when I was young. Why they did I do not know, because my parents were not in any way extraordinary personalities or gifted with unusual talent. They were rich and had style, and to be their guest was to enter an enchanted world of social pleasures and ingenious luxuries. Each guest room had its private sauna and sunken bath. Breakfast would be brought to you in bed. Our houses were crossroads for the world's influential. I have no doubt that we provided unparalleled opportunities for people to meet, to advance their interests, and that they did not come for the pleasure of my parents' company. Later I came to understand that this was an unspoken social contract. No one disdained the motives; everyone used each other. For the most part, our guests were money people and political types, a few heads of state now and then, all on a first-name basis.

My father was a banker—actually he owned two banks. The large one was open to the public, and the smaller one was for a very select clientele. Detractors of my father and his brother, who co-owned the large Vienna bank, said that some of their wealth was from the Nazi era—assets sequestered by the Third Reich, gold teeth from the Jews, et cetera. During the collapse of Austria's financial sector after World War I, Germans recapitalized many Austrian banks. They owned large stakes in Austrian banks long before the Anschluss. My father's banks were no exception. If they had refused German investors, they would have been ruined.

After World War II the media habitually savaged my father and uncle with innuendo. With the private banking laws in Austria, circumstantial evidence that publishers considered to be investigative reporting was all they could get their hands on. Writers of paperback thrillers loved to insinuate us into their stories, subtly and not so subtly disguised. My father and uncle laughed it off. They were clean, they said, and besides, no one could touch them.

As a child, the accusations were nothing but smoke swirling above my head, though occasionally flakes of ash would drift down to me—things overheard in conversation when the adults didn't realize I was in the room.

Do you think I am now going to tell you that I discovered that my elders were Nazis who had a hoard of victims' gold in their coffers? Well, I won't, because they weren't. My father had been a Nazi sympathizer who welcomed the Anschluss, and his father had been a member of the DNSAP. However, so were lots of Austrians then. They loathed Hitler but desired Pan-German socialism, and at the same time, like all good bankers, were opposed to Stalinism insofar as it would mean any loss of revenue. They foresaw the world that would emerge after the war, and so they guarded themselves carefully during the upheavals and rebuilt during the fifties and sixties. Their successors built upon that foundation. After the fall of the Soviet regime they soared with their newfound access to Eastern Europe. Now they have offices everywhere—London, New York, Berlin, Moscow, Beijing, Frankfurt, Tokyo.

My family remains one of the largest shareholders of these banks, and I am unable to escape the annual revenues that come to me. I must say, however, that I know little about how the people in the clouds do what they do. I am a recipient only. As always, I am a china doll on a gilded shelf, living out her life with the illusion of independence.

I mentioned to you that I was a Communist during my student days. If you were to infer that it was my adolescent attempt to shake off my past, you would be, on the whole, correct. Needless to say, I was a girl having a fit, caused by the first stirrings of self-awareness combined with disgust over my origins and hatred of the dollhouse and the hormones. There was another factor, and I might tell you about it later.

It began with my doting parents giving me permission for an epic Wanderjahr. I was only nineteen, and at that point in my life I lived on continual successes— society tours in the capitals of Europe, medals for dressage, mountain climbing, snorkeling, skydiving, boys—all of which activities were carefully guarded by paid companions and a bodyguard. When it came to the Wanderjahr, which I insisted I wanted to do alone, my parents at first refused, terrified of my being kidnapped and held for ransom. But even then I had my special skills, so eventually they capitulated, letting me go as long as bodyguards tramped along behind me on the goat paths and slept outside my door in alpine hostels. But I slipped away from them a few days into the Alps. I crossed into Germany illegally and got to Munich, dyed my hair black—I was a blonde—dressed myself something like a punk rocker, and made my way north. I gravitated to the industrial cities, roamed about, enthralled by every new unprotected experience, loving being a bad girl on the loose. Along the route I kept hoping to make contact with anyone who seriously hated the "established order". My quest became more and more mysterious and exciting as I descended into the various subcultures. In a disco bar in Hamburg I met a boy who led me to someone in a Communist cell. When a member of the group heard my name and figured out my background, he welcomed me with enthusiasm.

That whole period was classic overreaction on my part—from the extreme of capitalist exploitation to the opposite extreme of revolution. Well, it was anarchism, actually. I longed to throw a bomb, or even just to plant one. The feel of a loaded gun in my hand was ecstasy, like a magic wand that would crack the illusions of civilization and take me into a new world. The group saw through me completely. They knew I was a baby with revolutionary infatuations; I was good only for the money I might bring in from the class enemy back home. My parents wouldn't for a moment have guessed that I would have shot them both if ordered to do so. I didn't shoot anyone, didn't throw any bombs. A lot of my time with the Communists was pretty boring. I listened to endless intense debates among them, read mountains of Hegel, Marx, and Lenin ... and Mao, and after a few months became a knowledgeable, earnest polemicist. My main contribution was serving in the kitchen and the bedroom.

My parents tried to find me by tracking where I tapped into the money supply, but their searchers were always a step behind. I would download thousands at a bank and within minutes would be running for a train that would take me to another city. They let the money flow, hoping I would make a mistake and they could find me. Eventually they gave up and cut off the supply, thinking it would make me come home. When the money source died, the gang threw me out. Without my knowing, they arranged for me to be arrested for petty theft while they disappeared. It was generous of them not to dispose of me in a canal. Probably they knew I wasn't a real threat. They were constantly moving from safe house to safe house all over Germany, and these were always changing, always different. Also, they used cadre names only, so there wasn't much I could have told the police, if I had wanted to, which I didn't. Most of my fellow gang members were later killed by West German state security. Well, enough said about that.

After a tearful reconciliation with *Mutti und Vati*, I pretended I was their little girl who had had her fling— they presumed it was no more than sex, drugs, and rock and roll. Secretly I determined to continue on the way I had chosen, but to do it more subtly. As a first step I would investigate all forms of communal ownership, various kinds of workers' paradises. I thought it wouldn't disturb my parents overmuch if I went to Israel, so I spent a year tending fields and picking fruit in a *moshav*. Then I moved around from kibbutz to kibbutz, leaving a trail of radical Marxist rhetoric along the way, until someone in authority realized I was unstable, neither a good socialist nor a capitalist, and should be expelled from the country. However, family money came to the rescue and guaranteed that Israel put up with me a while longer. That's when I went to Jerusalem to study political science. I also took courses in literature.

Did I mention that I seduced men all along this route through the Holy Land? Oh, yes, many. And there were a few abortions as a result. You Catholics don't approve of abortion, do you? Which proves that your religion is unrealistic.

I'm getting ahead of myself. Back to the fairy palace when I was a thirteen- or fourteen-year-old romantic superheiress. The wealth aspect of my life meant little to me then, because I had never known anything different. I never really thought about it until I was in my late teens and began to dabble in Marxist writings—another sort of romanticism.

As I said, a lot of people passed through our houses, especially in Vienna. The most intimate friends came to our place in Salzburg, for music festivals and wine mainly. But promenading through the Vienna house were financial royalty, political royalty, and, from time to time, blood royalty or at least nobility ... aging Habsburgs and Bourbons, even a fake Romanov who said she had escaped the executions at Ekaterinburg.

Among the regular summer visitors came a family to whom my father's brother was distantly related by marriage. They were financiers, not as wealthy as we were, but wealthy enough to make them our peers. They had horses too, which they bred on their estate at Klosterneuburg, near Vienna. Like us, they had properties all over Europe, and this was just their summer house, with fields, vineyards, wooded hills, and a fine old mansion beside the Danube. We began to visit them when I was thirteen, I think, or almost fourteen. I had eyes only for the horses at first. But it was not long before I noticed the family's son. He was an only child, twenty-one years old, handsome, suave toward his elders and guests, but somewhat supercilious whenever he spoke to lesser mortals. He was always meticulously polite and always strangely cold. Yes, I felt cold around him, though he could dance with passion, could discuss world issues with older people, and was an excellent rider. He had the most delicious charm, and whenever he chose to use it people melted. He was frightfully intelligent, and I was not a very bright girl. Little by little I began to think about him a great deal, never reflecting on the chill and soon obsessively interested in the external appearance of heat. He had an abundance of energy, which he controlled at all times, releasing it with intense focus in his various activities. He never looked at me after our first courteous introduction.

I longed for our visits to their home, and their visits to ours. These occasions were infrequent, but they were enough to keep the flame of ardor alive. I worshipped him. In my mind I began to call him *the Prince*. Even though I knew a romance would be impossible, I could dream. I was a good dreamer in those days. My father said that this young man was going to be a very important figure in time to come. He was already the CEO of a corporation largely owned by his father. He also had his own properties, ventures, and independent means. His main interest at this stage was in learning to use power.

More important than our tenuous family connection, the Prince's father did some kind of work with my father and uncle. And he had a hold on them, which I do not think was a financial one. I sensed it from my father's demeanor around him, his unaccountable deference towards the man. For his part, the man was gracious to me, but for no reason that I could discern I felt sick whenever I was in his presence. I cringed when he turned his eyes on me, though I was not shy by temperament. His mother was a frightful person too. She was elegant, ironic, self-controlled, and controlling. She had been a notorious courtesan when she was younger, the gossips said, with important people tied to her little finger. I overheard my mother once whisper to my father that the woman was a witch. "They're both witches," my father laughed in reply, though there was no humor in his voice. I thought it was a metaphor for their uncanny ability to make everything they touched go their way—and for the way their enemies suffered misfortunes. All of this I had learned by overhearing bits and pieces of private conversations.

The summer I turned fourteen, we went for a visit to Klosterneuburg and stayed for a week. The mistress of the house was away on a shopping trip to Paris, the men were in conference each night, and my mother went out every day visiting local historic sites. I spent my time riding mostly or swimming alone in their pool and, in the evenings, playing chess with a butler or reading the novels I had brought along from home. I saw no sign of the Prince and assumed he was away doing business in the city.

One sunny morning, I had the groom in the stables saddle up one of their valuable Arabian mares—one of three these people owned. I rode out of the main grounds and took a bridle path into a nearby wooded park that was part of their holdings. The trees grew thicker and became virgin forest—mature birches mostly. There was a good breeze, and the leaves were rustling loudly—so loudly that anyone upwind would not have heard me coming. And that is what happened. The path opened out into a little meadow surrounding a pond. White swans were paddling in the reeds, butterflies were flitting about, and a black horse stood grazing nearby, tethered to a tree. My heart swelled with pleasure when I saw the Prince kneeling by the edge of the water, intent on something he was doing with his hands. Deciding to surprise him, I dismounted and walked carefully through the grass. Stopping a few paces behind his bending back, I was confused at first, then froze.

He had captured a number of turtles, eight of them arranged in a circle around him. They all lay on their backs with legs and tails flailing, necks twisting this way and that. He was using a surgeon's scalpel with concentration, cutting away the under shell from one of the living bodies. Two others lay there with their organs exposed, mouths gasping. He was working on the third, holding it down with his left hand while he cut.

When I cried out he turned his head, and I saw that his face was without expression, neither startled nor ashamed. His eyes were like nothing I had seen before. They were human eyes, not like the eyes in a cheap horror film. There was merely—all these years later I cannot describe it—it was as if his eyes were wells of darkness that had no bottom.

Suddenly he smiled. And that smile was also like nothing I had seen before. It looked like an ordinary warm smile, but it was colder than anything I had ever felt from a human being. It seemed to choke me. I began to shake with fear.

He stood up with the wriggling turtle in his hand, stuck the scalpel deep into its flesh, and with his right hand now free, he seized me by the collar of my blouse. I began to pull away, to thrash, trying to run, but he was very strong. He dragged me kicking and whining to the edge of the pasture and threw me to the ground. He dropped the turtle, pulled out the scalpel and put it to my neck. I began to whimper. He slowly, carefully removed my clothes, and then he raped me. Throughout all of it— the rape itself, the degrading things he did, cutting the turtle to pieces and sprinkling the blood on my naked body—he said not a word. And all the while I could not scream, and I could not look away from those eyes.

After it was over, he fixed his clothing and calmly said, "What I did to these turtles I will do to you, if you tell anyone about this. Now, or in the future, I will know if you say anything. I will know, and I will find you."

He threw the turtles back into the pond, mounted his horse, and rode away.

A week later, two horses were delivered to our estate, a gift from the Prince. A pure white Arabian stallion and a jet black Österreich Warmblood mare. I never rode those horses. I was terrified of them because they had come from him. I let a few weeks go by, and at the age of fourteen and a half I secretly poisoned the Arabian. A month later I led the Warmblood into the forest and broke one of its legs with an axe. Both of the animals were put down, their deaths attributed to sickness and accident.

I was about sixteen when I got over the worst of my depressions, my suicidal thoughts. I decided to stop hurting myself and to take hold. So began a long career of seducing and discarding boys and men. I took special pleasure in tormenting them before throwing them back where they came from. I am not speaking of violence, you understand. I am speaking of small cruelties, manipulation, words, betrayals, and scorn.

I discovered Nietzsche in those years—a great consolation—especially *Ecce Homo*. Reading Marx and Mao came later, as I said. Somewhere along the way, it came to me that I would like to bring the whole thing down, the world that was the natural habitat of people like the Prince's family and my own.

Throughout all of the foregoing, Elijah had remained silent, listening. Toward the end of her story, he had looked down in anguish.

When she stopped speaking, she refilled her wineglass and drank slowly from it, looking out the window at the Judean hills, nodding and nodding as if she had just completed a majestic act.

Elijah breathed heavily for a few moments, feeling jabs of pain in his physical heart and a pall of depression over his emotions.

"Did you ever meet this man again?" he asked in a shaken voice.

"Now and then, over the years. We have had superficial discussions about all manner of topics. Neither of us has made the slightest reference to that day."

"Yet he threatened to kill you."

"Oh, yes, and I know he would. I believed him then, and I believe him now. You are the first person I have ever told."

"But why have you told me?"

"Because I know you despise me, and I am interested to see how I will handle it."

"I do not despise you."

"Then let me state the situation in more ladylike terms. You look upon me with distaste."

"I see a gifted woman who has suffered an intolerable injustice. She is deeply hurt, and she is bitter. But I do not believe her solutions have restored justice—they never could."

"My hurts were healed long ago."

"Were they?"

"And my bitterness has become amusement."

"Amusement over the follies of the human race?"

"Precisely. I manipulate, therefore I am."

"The victim of injustice becomes the master of injustice? The abused becomes the abuser in turn? Is this a victory over helplessness?"

"Do not impute too much righteousness to this wounded damozel."

"No, but there is a kind of honesty in you. You are not indifferent to the truth."

"Wrong. I am quite indifferent."

"You hate lies, unmasking even the lies that you employ."

"Do I? I hadn't noticed. I simply am what I am, and as I mentioned before, I enjoy my life very much."

He paused, wondering why she had told him this appalling story.

"I know you hunger for justice," Elijah said at last. "In part, that is why you helped me today."

"Are you so sure? What if this is just my game? What if I am a cat that lets the mouse escape for a time, only to trap it again beneath its paws?"

"Is that what you think you are?"

She laughed and refilled her wineglass.

"The President must hate you very much," she said, suddenly serious. "Why such effort to defame a little professor of theology?"

"He strikes against me because I spoke the truth to him, and because I was instrumental in gathering evidence that he is a criminal. He strikes at the universal Church because she would impede his progress toward power over the world. He is not what he seems to be."

"Is that so?"

"I do not expect you to believe me, but it was he who arranged the murder of Anna Benedetti. He was also involved in the kidnapping and murder of her husband years ago. Stefano Benedetti was tortured, and the President was there for some of it."

She averted her eyes for a moment, as if lost in a private struggle—perhaps debating whether or not to believe him. She seemed to age before his eyes. Finally she inhaled sharply and turned her attention back to him.

"I am giving a party for some influential people the day after tomorrow. Would you like to come?"

"No," he shook his head. "I have work to do."

"If your work involves your problem with the President, I can tell you that he will be in Tehran that day. So you would be free to come, wouldn't you?"

"Yes, but I see no purpose in attending a party."

"Ah, but I do see a purpose. Some of the people coming to the party are connected to the President. They could open doors for you."

She mentioned a few names, people whom she thought might help him obtain a meeting, if that is what he wanted.

"You don't intend to kill him, do you?" she asked, almost as an afterthought.

"No."

"What, then?"

"My work is on another level."

"Spiritual?"

"Yes, spiritual."

"That is beyond me," she said, waving a dismissive hand. "You say you have evidence proving he is a murderer?"

"The evidence is now gone. He ensured that it was destroyed."

"And also tried to destroy the detective. Obviously your identification papers are no longer in the name David Schäfer. What is the name on your passport?"

He hesitated and then took the risk: "Davide Pastore, professor and archaeologist."

"That would do nicely. You could circulate among us as a member of my interesting people collection, which is always growing. You would be one of the less interesting, being an old and dry academic, which offers a certain anonymity. Thirty or forty people will be attending. I have rented a house for the evening in Talbieh, the neighborhood near the Old City. Please consider my invitation."

"I really must go now," he replied, rising to his feet.

"All right," she said. "My driver will drop you anywhere. He will also give you the address for the party in case you change your mind."

"There is no need for it."

Her eyes became expressionless as her face strained with the effort to control an emotion. It was not anger at his rejection, he sensed—it had nothing to do with him.

Her voice just above a whisper, she said, "My name is Karin. The man who raped me is the one who wants to own the world."

Meeting her eyes, Elijah said, "If I am still at liberty the day after tomorrow, I will come to your party."

4

The Strategist

As promised, the driver took Elijah back to Jerusalem, dropping him off on the sidewalk by the King David Hotel. After the car disappeared up the street, he commenced the circuitous trek back to Al Sheikh Jarrah. The sun was low in the west by the time he reached the apartment building.

Enoch had not yet returned. Dr. Abbas had come and gone, leaving a selection of clothing draped over the back of an armchair: a black suit, a white dress shirt, and two ties, one black, the other red checkered. There was also a box containing socks and a pair of new shoes. On another chair lay a similar set of apparel, smaller in size and of humbler cloth, apparently for Brother Enoch.

Elijah found an envelope lying on the coffee table, addressed to *D. Pastore*. It contained paper currency: Israeli, Jordanian, and American. An accompanying note explained:

> Travelers from the desert will be in need of water, shade, and fresh clothing. I hope I have guessed your sizes correctly. I will try to see you this evening.
>   With prayers,
>   T. A.

After praying his office, Elijah tried to nap, but mental images from the woman's story would not let him rest.

He sat for a while on the balcony, inhaling the sweet-acrid scent of the juniper bush, watching the sky change from evening blue to green, to gold, red, and cobalt. Little children on the street below played games with a ball, lifting his heart although the vile images returned again and again. He supposed the recollection was his mind's way of processing what he had heard.

He recognized another factor that should not be under-estimated: The serpent mesmerizes. Whenever it cannot seduce, it attempts to overwhelm. It is like a cobra projecting an image of its power in order to paralyze its victim with fear, disabling its defenses without a struggle, before devouring it. In the victim's eyes the threat grows so large that it becomes everything and appears to be irresistible. So too Satan desires that we think him omnipotent and omniscient.

Elijah stared at the purple-blue berries in the prickly branches of the juniper. Then he gazed at the open palms of his empty hands. He corrected himself, remembering that his hands were not empty but were anointed with the authority of Christ. The cross that had burned into his flesh was no small emblem. The Man of Sin had quailed before it and fallen into temporary powerlessness. The devil's powers, though estimable, were limited.

Yes, Satan's time was drawing to an end, though he would rage in his fury and soon would reveal his true nature as the ancient enemy of mankind. And then the nature of the human instruments controlled by him would also be revealed.

Elijah looked out over the city, wondering where the President was at this moment and whom he was mesmerizing, flattering, devouring. There would be no visible fangs and venom, he supposed—no, not at this point. For the time being, the man would seek to conquer by illusion.

Elijah prayed for several hours, little by little feeling the return of peace. In the wake of the day's intense experiences, he still felt sorrow. In the foreground was the suffering of the woman named Karin. He sighed when he thought about the death of Anna, which opened the reservoir of his love for Ruth and for their child in the womb, dead by murder, as were so many people he had loved. Much about these old lamentations had been resolved on the mountain near Ephesus and in the cave. Yet, in the long, slow process of integrating his losses, his heart continued to grieve. He knew that this mingling of grief and hope, this peace and sorrow, was not a condition of unbelief. Within it was the longing for reunion and beyond it the eternal communion in the realm of love.

Later, he lay down on the sofa and slept.

The apartment slowly filled with the dawn, and Elijah arose feeling less exhausted. The images from Karin's story seemed to have found their proper place in his memory, for he was no longer trapped within their horror and could look upon them with a measure of detachment. As he offered Mass, he prayed for her. At the elevation of the Body and Blood, and again after Communion, he asked the crucified Lord to confound all the devices of the enemy. He begged for the graces he would need during the day ahead, and also for the safe return of Enoch, who had not returned.

There was no television or radio in the apartment. Neither was there a telephone. On a desk in the bedroom, however, there was a computer, which Elijah supposed was the portal to all such communications. He was one of the few people left on the planet who did not know how to access this kind of machine. He tapped a few buttons on the keyboard, hoping that the screen would

activate and offer a menu of services, particularly television. He wanted to see what the President had been doing.
He knew that the man would be flying to Beirut today
and that he would untangle one of the most snarled nests
of conflict in the world.

The computer lit up with the image of an old man in
a gray cloak, holding a staff before him, confronting an
enormous fiery monster. A text in Hebrew below said
merely, "You shall not pass." What this meant Elijah
could not begin to guess, though it looked as if the
symbology was approximate to his own concerns. There
was also a prompt demanding a password that would
permit him entrance into the machine's inner depths.
Thus, its mysteries were locked. Yes, it was best this way,
he thought. He had no need to watch the performance
that would be enacted in Lebanon; his *curiositas* would
add nothing to his understanding and could well prove
to be a distraction. Moreover, had he begun to presume
invulnerability to the eyes of the serpent? To believe that
he knew the facts of a situation—quantity over essence—
could precipitate reasoning and strategies that might not
be within the plans of God for his own mission. Always—
always—weakness had been his strength. Unknowingness.
Simplicity. Trust.

Throughout the day, Elijah rested in the silence. He
prayed the liturgical Hours at their appointed times,
drank water and ate a few pieces of flatbread, napped in
the afternoon, and as sunset approached he went onto the
balcony and observed the life of the street. The children
had returned. Their games, their hilarity, delighted him,
helped him to leave aside his habitual gravity. As he
watched their antics, he remembered little scenes from
his childhood in Warsaw: skipping along the walkways of
the Saski Gardens in summer; catching snowflakes on his

tongue in winter; singing in Yiddish with his arms raised to the sky as he teetered daringly on the lip of a fountain; his older brothers teaching him bounce-ball on the apartment steps, and in moments of disobedience, his glee at successfully kicking the ball between the wheels of a rattling Muranów tram. Now he imagined himself running about with these children below, though they were speaking Arabic. He also heard some Hebrew, which struck him as incongruous. Perhaps children were able to cross barriers of hatred in ways that adults could not, or would not.

Elijah stayed awake until close to midnight, hoping to hear a key in the lock. But there was nothing. He wondered why Dr. Abbas had not returned. His worry that Enoch had been arrested steadily increased, but in the end he had to entrust his brother to God's care. He lay down on the floor and slept fitfully until dawn.

That day passed in much the same manner. The President was in Tehran, where representatives of the Iranian government were scheduled to meet with him and envoys of the United States government. If Dr. Abbas' itinerary was correct, a bilateral treaty for normalization of relations between the two nations would be signed, including the disarming of all terrorist organizations sponsored by Iran and the dismantling of its nuclear weapons program.

As evening drew near, Elijah prepared to leave for the party. In the bathroom he first inspected his face, feeling some reservation. During the past two years his appearance had changed, but would it be enough? He had aged a little, of course, and he was more stooped; the desert sun had darkened his skin; the remaining hair on his head had all but disappeared. It was a wonder that the woman in violet had recognized him, but he attributed this to her unusual memory for faces and her longstanding interest in him. It also indicated a movement of providence.

He showered and then dressed himself in the new black suit, which fit him well. The fine cloth of the jacket and trousers, the white shirt and black tie, and the fresh socks and shining shoes seemed luxurious to him. Missing his Carmelite habit, he kissed his brown scapular and tucked it inside his shirt. After that, he put the kippah on his head.

A ten-minute walk brought him to the nearest main artery, where he boarded a crowded city bus that took him southward as far as Mandelbaum Square. There he caught a taxi. The taxi dropped him off at an intersection near the Wolfson Garden close to the Old City, and from that point onward he walked a few blocks deeper into the neighborhood of Talbieh. It was one of the most beautiful parts of the city, known for its fine architecture, old and new, the residences of high government officials and the town houses of some of the nation's wealthiest people. The streets were ample, the sidewalks cobbled, and the abundance of trees offered shade and a softening of the Jerusalem ambience, which for the most part lacked the refined grandeur of Europe's old cities.

Night fell as he made his way toward the address by an indirect route, backtracking twice to make sure he was not being followed. As far as he could tell, there was no activity on the streets that implied surveillance. He knew that these precautions might prove to be pathetically futile if the woman in violet was playing one of her games. It was possible that she had intended from the beginning to hand him over to the President or his servants and had chosen to do it in an elaborate social setting, for effect, for the drama. Would he be like a centerpiece for her party, a stuffed pheasant or a chipped ice swan?

But he thought not. During their conversation he had sensed a fugitive authenticity beneath her story. She had been by turns sly, offensive, condescending, and candid. None of it added up to transparency or reliability. She could have fabricated the story about the young Prince, though it had the ring of a horror endured and overcome—and remembered. And it was consistent with what Elijah knew about the man—what hardly anyone else in the world knew about him. No, she was not an enemy. It seemed she wanted to help him, if only to honor the memory of someone who had treated her decently in times past.

"Dovidl, my Dovidl," Ruth had murmured into his ear, long ago. "When will you learn to be more subtle?" Their discussion had been about a conflict at the Ministry during the Eichmann trial.

"What do you mean?" he had asked, quite puzzled. He believed himself to be a very subtle man.

"That you have to ask what I mean *is* exactly what I mean," she said fondly, shaking her head in wry amusement. "You can be less direct, and more discreet, and still the guileless man I love."

"Ruth," he said with rather too much conviction. "The only thing one can give to others—and to volatile situations—is what one truly is."

She had laughed and kissed him.

While not completely candid, his choice of attire was not treachery, Elijah now reminded himself, adjusting the kippah on his head.

As he turned onto the street of his destination, the house appeared, halfway down the block. Floodlights illumined the entire three-story building, which was made of pink stone and surrounded by a compound wall at least three meters high. Above the walls could be seen the tops of cypress and palm. The front entrance, an open wrought iron gate, was manned by armed security guards, one of whom carried an automatic rifle. Expensive automobiles stopped and let out passengers, then whisked away, only to be replaced by others of their kind.

He paused for a few moments in the deep shadow of a palm tree, beyond the reach of streetlamps. Closing his eyes, he became attentive to an inner sense: There was evil in the house. It was not a major diabolical presence like the one he had confronted on Capri, yet there were adverse spirits here. He knew they would be especially active as all forces were marshaled for the coming decisive events. Doubtless, among the guests he would meet with degrees of sinfulness, compromise, and traffic with demonic impulse and reward. Some of the people would be completely corrupt; others would be idealistic followers of the dream. There would be a variety of motivating factors, a variety of ambitions. Certainly he would find some goodness too. He remembered the President's parties he had attended in Rome and Warsaw, remembered especially Anna Benedetti.

He prayed, then stepped toward the gate.

He gave his name to the guards—Davide Pastore—and one of them checked it off a list. Another gestured politely that he should pass through into the front garden and follow the walkway leading to the house. A servant who stood waiting outside the double doors of the entrance greeted him graciously and conducted him into the ground-floor reception area.

Stringed instruments and a piano were being played in another room. The subdued lighting was provided mainly by numerous candles in a crystal chandelier hanging from the high ceiling. The floor was white marble and the walls pastel green. There were paintings, among them one that Elijah recognized as an early Picasso in realist style. Another was almost certainly an original Renoir. The party appeared to be well underway, with fashionably dressed men and women standing about the foyer in small groups, chatting, laughing, kissing cheeks. Circulating among them, waiters offered glasses of champagne.

Karin stepped out of a knot of people and approached him in an ankle-length golden dress, her ears glittering with diamonds, her teeth bared in a welcoming smile, her right arm extended.

"*Professore*," she declared in a voice loud enough for all to hear. "How very kind of you to come."

"It is a pleasure, madame," said Elijah with a little bow.

As she continued with innocuous hostess chatter, those who had overheard turned away to more interesting guests.

"I realize what a sacrifice it is for you to abandon your research," she said, "but the university can spare you for one evening."

He let this go unanswered as she put her arm through his and deftly conducted him into a large and tastefully opulent salon. On a low stage in a far corner of the room, the musicians ended the piece for stringed instruments, and a pianist began a solo on a white grand piano.

"I love modern classical romantic. Don't you?" she said. "That's Grigor Iliev's 'Remains from the Past'."

She continued to speak to him in this manner, occasionally greeting those who drifted by, flashing her eyes, touching hands, offering kisses, receiving kisses, but refraining from introducing Elijah.

In a brief island of quiet, she leaned over and whispered into his ear, "Well, Mister Remains of the Past, the people I want you to meet have not yet arrived, but they will be here. Oh, most surely they will be here."

She took a step away from him, laughing.

"Who are they?" Elijah asked.

"Turtles," she said and sipped from her champagne glass.

Observing his sudden consternation, she said, "You should relax" and signaled to a waiter.

Elijah declined the offer of a glass.

"I must circulate," she whispered in a mock conspiratorial tone, with a touch to his arm. "Try not to look like a stagnant mingler. It creates black holes in the festivities, and it makes you stand out in the wrong way. Move around a little; inspect the antiquities as a tedious old professor would do. When the time comes, I'll bring the right people to you."

Elijah gravitated to the end of the room, where the violinists were tuning their strings. A lovely Asian woman in a long peacock-blue dress carried a cello to the stage and took a seat beside the piano. As she turned pages on the music stand, the pianist stood up and diffidently announced the next piece, "Hungarian Rhapsody" by David Popper. As the opening strains began, most of those present listened attentively for a few moments, then returned to their conversations or wandered into other rooms. A few of the guests moved closer to listen.

Elijah had not heard the piece before. He found it moving. The cellist's personal beauty and her mastery of the emerging themes entranced him totally. He watched her dancing fingers and her face, so involved in the mystery of what she was creating. At one point her eyes glistened with tears. When the performance was over, and a smattering of applause came from the small crowd, she stood and bowed deeply before gracefully leaving the stage. The other musicians stretched and rose to their feet, preparing to take their break.

"Marvelous," said a man standing beside Elijah. "But the poor girl was so nervous."

Elijah turned to him. "It did not affect her playing," he said. "The music itself was her focus. She lived inside it."

"Indeed, she seemed to *become* the music."

Elijah looked at the man more closely. In his late fifties, he had spoken Hebrew with an odd accent. His round face shone with well-being, and his girth was impressive inside a tailored, iridescent-charcoal suit. A bow tie matched his lapel pin, which was an enameled planet Earth. He eyed Elijah's kippah with a small smile.

"Are you one of Karin's new friends?"

"Yes," Elijah said. "And you, sir?"

"I'm an old one. A cousin of hers, in fact. I live in New York."

A banker, Elijah thought.

"You were quite taken with the rhapsody, I noticed. Are you a musician, or are you an appreciator?"

"I'm an archaeologist."

"Ah, dear Karin. Mistress of so many interests. Archaeology, literature, music. She's one of the benefactors of the Jerusalem Philharmonic, you know, which is why she was able to borrow these artists for the evening."

"I see."

"A delightful party. Eclectic as always. Well, I must not keep you."

The man meandered away, engaging other people. Finding himself to be the only solitary in the room, Elijah slowly moved about, gazing at various artifacts in glass-enclosed cabinets. In a small annex to the right of the stage he came upon a wall of ancient war helmets—Greek from various periods, Persian, Roman, and a later Lombardian. Stopping before a Greek helmet of the classical age, he was startled by the sudden appearance of a human face gazing back at him from within it. He stepped away, and the face disappeared. He stepped forward, and the face materialized again. It was his own face. His heart skipped a beat until he realized that the lighting and the reflection of his face in the glass had combined to make an optical illusion. He wondered if it was accidental or intentional.

Returning to the main room, he found nothing changed other than the constant realigning of conversationalists.

These lives, he thought, these personal histories, are each unique. Each person dwells in his own psychological cosmos, formed by his experiences, through which he interprets reality. Is a person governed by his feelings or by his beliefs? Or by a combination of both? Do feelings condition beliefs? Do beliefs condition feelings?

How many of them have been badly hurt? Certainly some of them, like Karin. Possibly all of them, considering the selfishness of our times.

What words could he use to reach them, he asked himself, to open them to a universe larger and a power greater than themselves? Perhaps it was enough to plant a seed of hope, prompting them to look beyond their enclosed worlds, so full of pleasure, power, pride—and the unacknowledged emptiness of an interior void.

They are as I once was during my years of unbelief. They cannot conceive of anything beyond what they know, as I once could not. They cannot let go of their illusions of autonomy. They are blind as I once was blind.

Silently, he prayed for them all.

I love you, my Lord, for you have rescued me. Have mercy on these souls gathered here. Have mercy and bring them forth out of darkness into your wonderful light. Do not let the dragon devour everything.

As Elijah moved on to the next display case—ancient coins—he overheard a conversation nearby. An elderly man spoke in Spanish, surrounded by a cluster of avid listeners. An interpreter translated his words simultaneously into Hebrew; another into French.

"In what language did you read the novel? Ah, in French. That translation was good, but it lost something, as all translations do—even what I am saying now is losing something in translation. I speak seven languages and write in three, but how many languages are there in the world? Thousands. Published in less than a hundred of these, my books are barely scratching the surface with my message, and I have no absolute control over the artistic dimension of these works.

"Still, in all my little tales I recount the story of humanity, and I am confident this universal reality comes across in every language. We are searchers for immortal transcendence, though we are alone in the universe, and yet not alone, for we have each other. This is our true spirituality. Love, love is our destiny. Are we illuminated by tales of the *via negativa*—the plague of pessimism inhibiting the flowering of love? Or are we heartened by the *via positiva*? Love is passion, and we must be true to our passions. Is love more than a passing illusion, an *indispensable* illusion? Is obsession a form of fidelity? Is fidelity a form of madness? If we are faithful to our passions, we will learn the truth that divine insanity is not insanity!"

One of the listeners asked a question, but Elijah could not hear it.

"So many enigmas life presents to us," the author replied, "in the main inexplicable. So many stories, told and untold."

Again another question Elijah could not hear.

"You are correct. I have chosen to write in my own style, neither in the bleak minimalism of the early existentialists nor in lavish magic realism, which so influenced my generation of South American writers. I choose simple narrative while retaining the grand symphony of the magical. That is not mere stylistic background but a dimension saturating what we call *the ordinary*."

In answer to another question, the author continued, "Of course, they were true humanists, each in his way a forerunner. In my own work I strive to see further and deeper. Man is a phenomenon. In my novels I ask why this absolutely unique phenomenon tells stories and listens to stories. To what end, ultimately, are these stories pointing? Does humanity have a collective story? If so, *what* is our definitive story?"

"Are you here in Jerusalem at the invitation of the President?" asked a woman near Elijah.

"Yes," answered the author. "The President is the man who more than anyone else in this world understands culture. He personally asked me to give the opening address to the World Congress of Artists. I hope that some of you will be there tomorrow."

"I would say that the President *is* the new humanism," he said in response to a comment. "I agree entirely with your point. He is telling us that, here and now, we dwell in *la conciencia divina*, which is to say *le milieu divin*."

"Were you not a Catholic when you were young?" asked another woman.

"Yes, I was raised in that religion. It had fragments of the truth, as do all religions, and I value to this day what it gave me. It gave me a symbolism for the hungry imagination, of angels and demons, of fiery apocalypses and sublime *paradisos*. It was one of many avenues into larger truths, though it became corrupted by greed and power and repression. Its dualistic moralism weakened what was good in it, and, worse, it denied the fullness of our identity. Now humanity is coming into its own, and we must leave the dead to bury the dead. I wish no ill to those people who cling to the past. The President wishes them nothing but good. We merely say that their time has ended and their story no longer illumines the imagination, for it too was only a precursor. Ours is the era of the true story. You are living in the midst of great events—rather, *colossal* events unprecedented in the history of humankind.

"You will see it. You will tell of it to your children and your children's children. You will count yourselves blessed above all generations to have been part of it."

The author paused, and one of his listeners asked if he would sign a copy of his book.

"Of course, I would be delighted to sign the book. And would someone please bring me more champagne?"

Like a floating island, the great writer and his listeners drifted away. Elijah moved to the next display case.

It contained large gold and silver medallions hanging on ribbons, more than a dozen. Try as he might, he could not make out what they represented. One was embossed with a leaping horse, another had a crown, and a third some abstract design. He supposed they belonged to whoever owned the house and had rented it to Karin for the occasion. It seemed odd to him that she had not borrowed the home of a wealthy friend, since she must surely have several such friends.

As if in answer, Karin appeared suddenly at his side.

"Are you interested in these?" she asked.

"The owner of the house is an accomplished person," observed Elijah, "though I cannot discern what the accomplishments are. Is he or she here this evening?"

"She is here. Would you like to talk with her?"

"If you think it would be helpful."

"You are talking with her."

"You told me two days ago that you had rented the house."

"I *rented* it, metaphorically speaking, from my other self. My bad self. My powerful, famous self. This evening you are talking to my good self, who circulates, as do you, in disguise."

"What prevents you from reverting to your bad self?"

"Mine is not an automatist psychosis. I select my personas carefully and sustain them intelligently, in the same way I choose my dresses from the closet. You need not worry. I did not invite you here to have you bound and trussed and presented to the Prince as a prize or a bribe."

"Why did you invite me here? Do you hope I will bring harm to him?"

"I suppose there is a remote chance of that. Or perhaps you will only embarrass him at some point. I wanted at least to open up the possibilities. This evening's venue is not the place for confrontations, but it is a first step. These people are orbiting in an outer ring of influence. However, there are a few among us tonight who have access to inner rings. Not the innermost, you must understand, but closer to the center. Everyone wants access to him. After all, that's why you're here, isn't it?"

"In part, that is why I am here. But there is another reason, Karin, and though you do not trust words or motives, I will say it regardless. I am here because when we talked two days ago, I felt great sorrow over what happened to you."

"Please, no emotional dramatics," she said with a scolding look.

"You were degraded and utterly violated. I felt a terrible grief for you."

She pondered this without comment. His words seemed to make no impression whatsoever. She took his arm and turned him around to face the room. A few steps away stood a man who looked very much like Elijah himself. His suit was somewhat ill used, and his tie was clumsily knotted. The black kippah on his white hair was slightly askew. He was carrying a book, opening it and reading short passages, closing it, opening it again, absorbed in whatever it contained.

"A believer," Karin said sotto voce. "Old Testament variety. He's cautious about our Prince but interested enough to be here tonight, at my invitation. He won't get you into any other orbits, but he might keep you from running out the front door prematurely. He's a nice person. Politically neither right nor left. An independent thinker. Enjoy the brief respite. The monsters come later."

As they approached, the man looked up from his book and gazed at Elijah with curiosity. Karin made the introduction in her fashion.

"Gentlemen, you are twin brothers separated at birth. Please, examine each other through the looking glass. I leave you to untangle the details."

They watched her sail away toward other guests and then turned to face each other.

"*Shalom*," said the man in Hebrew, extending his hand for a shake.

"*Sholem aleykhem*," said Elijah, which made the other smile.

"You speak Yiddish. Shall we converse in that language ... yes?"

"Please, if you prefer."

"Excellent! I'm in history. Tel Aviv University."

"Archaeology," said Elijah.

They exchanged names.

"Nice to meet you, Professor. Italian, are you? But you look like any number of my uncles from circa 1941 to '42."

"As you resemble mine."

"I was born in Lodz."

"Warsaw was my home."

"The Shoah?"

Elijah nodded.

"We are a long way from the ghettos."

"Yes, a very long way."

"And now we are here in this most amazing and troubled nation, where I have spent most of my life trying to keep young *Sabras* honest. The present is always prologue, I tell them."

"So is the past."

"Yet the past is safer. More so the farther back one goes. I have sometimes wished I were like you, digging in the ruins of fallen kingdoms."

"Beneath the rubble, one occasionally discovers keys to understanding our identity."

"Ah, identity, identity. The insatiable appetite for self-discovery. Who are we? Why were we chosen? Are we still the chosen?"

"Your kippah indicates that you consider it a possibility, yes?"

"Yes. I keep an open mind. Unceasingly, I pray to the Most High for light. What is Jewish identity, I ask him? Is the Messiah coming soon? How will we know him when he arrives? Will we recognize him only after much interpretation, discernment, rabbinical discussions of great complexity, not to mention media commentary? Or will there be no doubt?"

"I believe there will be no doubt," said Elijah. "Many passages in the Torah tell us so."

"I agree," the man said, nodding with a detached smile.

"And yet we are here this evening, are we not, among numerous advocates of a certain messianism?"

"You are an interesting man," said the professor.

"It seems to me that you, sir, are an honest scholar with an inquiring mind."

"That is my hope. As I think you would agree, there is messianism and there is messianism. It depends on which school one follows. Did you know that a few years ago, Rabbi Yitzhak Kaduri, the greatest and oldest of all Torah scholars in Israel, wrote a note on his deathbed that he had received a visitation from the Messiah? No? Well, it seems the note, which is undoubtedly in his own hand, declares that in the vision the Messiah told the rabbi that he is coming soon and that his name is Yeshuah. As you can imagine, it created considerable consternation, this note. However, with the passage of time, learned commentators have concluded that it referred only to the name's literal meaning, *the Lord saves*."

"The Christians say that, in the end, the whole houschold of Israel will embrace Christ."

"You refer to Paul the Pharisee, who became an apostle. He too was an interesting man."

"Somewhere in his writings he claims prophetic vision. He anticipated a great apostasy from faith—as prologue to the coming of the Messiah."

"Yes, apostasy as catastrophic deception. And a false messiah preceding the true Messiah."

"I see you know the Christian scriptures," said Elijah.

"Yes, I read them. I ponder them. Also the Koran."

"An academic interest?"

"It is essential to my work."

They fell silent, regarding each other with attention, neither of them making any gesture that would imply the end of their discussion. At the same time, they seemed to have come to an impasse.

"The book of the prophet Daniel is still with us," said Elijah.

"Are you speaking in a twofold sense?" asked the professor, keeping his eyes locked on Elijah's.

"Yes," he answered without further elucidation.

"Do you interpret the passage about the king who exalts himself against the Lord Most High in strictly historical terms?"

"Partly historical. I would use our word *prologue* again. Antiochus Epiphanes, the Romans, the abomination of desolation, the abolition of the perpetual sacrifice, Titus, the Diaspora—only some of the prophecies were fulfilled, and these imperfectly."

"Hitler? And even more so, Stalin?"

"They were precursors."

"Daniel says that the false king will make war against all those who worship the Most High, for three and a half years."

"The Christian visionary John says the same in his Revelation. Have you read it?"

"I have read it." The man paused, lowering his eyes. "I reread it often."

"So do I."

The professor looked up, inhaled deeply, and straightened his kippah.

"Now I am thinking about something that surprises me. It comes into my mind without a connecting train of ideas. Without a reason, I see the courage of David, son of Jesse, as he goes by stealth into the camp of King Saul, even as the king searches throughout Israel in order to slay him."

Elijah said nothing in reply.

"The courage of David is immense, yet he is human; he is not without fear. He is willing to lose everything at every moment for the sake of the Lord, but his will and his capacity are not always the same. His confidence grows by the practice of an obedience that approaches folly."

"That is the way we grow in trust," Elijah murmured.

"It seems to me," said the professor, lowering his voice, "that you are a man who moves in the realm of mystery. You have forced yourself to grow in trust. But this place, this night, this city—they are not safe for you."

Elijah did not respond to this, though he leaned closer.

"I think you should leave the house quickly," the man added. "This king will not be moved as Saul was moved by your namesake. This king will not forgive."

"I will go soon," said Elijah. "Pray for me to the Most High."

"I will."

Taking a step back, the professor resumed his previous expression, pleasant, studious, friendly but detached.

"The twins reunited," he said with a smile.

"The looking glass is not as thick as we presumed," Elijah replied.

"The glass is within ourselves."

"And soon may be no more than a forgotten breath."

"All my family perished, and I alone was spared. How great a gift to meet a brother. Though I do not know him, I know him."

"It is the same with me. All were lost. And now a new brother is given."

"We are well met in a time of darkness."

"Though I do not think we will meet again in this world," said Elijah.

"Nor do I."

Karin returned as they were shaking hands in farewell. She appropriated Elijah and led him away toward a wide doorway opening onto a garden. Most of this area was flagged with old stones, softened by flowerbeds. Here and there, small lemon and orange trees sprouted from glazed pots. Cypress trees as slender as spears lined the high walls, interspersed with palmettos fanning their symmetrical crowns.

There were fewer people outside, clustering in groups of three or four, some seated on padded patio chairs, others standing, holding their drinks as they engaged in animated conversation. Candles in wall alcoves provided the light, in addition to a great number of tiny blue and white sparkles so small they appeared to be stars come down from the heavens, floating just above the people's heads. A fountain at the very back of the garden sent a jet of fine spray into the air, feeding a low rectangular pool, brightly lit from within.

"You are on your own for now," Karin said to Elijah. "That man over there is the British ambassador. He is a portal. The other portal is the man at the table talking with the violinist. He's an archbishop, a skilled negotiator valued by the Prince. These two revolve in an inner orbit, though as I mentioned before, not in one of the innermost orbits. Meeting them might bring you to the next circle, and there you might find other ways to get closer."

"Where are you situated in this solar system?"

"Superficially, socially, I revolve in an intermediate-to-outer ring, not far from the ambassador's and the archbishop's. I have no more influence than they do, and sometimes less, since I am part of a large number of random debris caught in his gravitational pull. He does not control me, but I am useful to him."

"That is how Anna Benedetti saw herself."

This gave her pause.

"I am not as honorable as was the estimable judge," said Karin with a whiff of bitterness. "I do not hurl myself upon the enemy's sword."

"Then you do consider him to be an enemy?"

"I am a Trojan horse."

"That too is how Anna thought of herself."

"I am more careful."

"It was careless of you to tell me your story."

"Only he and I know what happened those many years ago. It could be he doesn't even remember it. If he does remember, it is probably as part of a panorama of memories from his youth. It was so long ago, and doubtless he has had many kinds of victims since then. If it ever does come to his mind, his arrogance would presume that I either enjoyed it in some perverse way or have sloughed it off. I've never given him any reason to think otherwise. And of course, I gravitate so graciously."

"A dangerous game."

"Would you prefer me to learn tennis? Or collect antiques?"

"Who else knows about your connection with ... with the hidden side of the man? It would take little deduction for him and his circle to see you as a potential danger."

"I told a psychiatrist in Vienna once, during my suicidal period. Of course, the great friend of mankind was relatively unknown then. I told Ruth. And now you."

Elijah shook his head, puzzled.

"Why us?"

"Because I sensed you were absolutely reliable."

"Well, Ruth certainly was, because she never told me anything about you."

"The more important reason is that claustrophobia can be avoided by poking a little hole in the wall of the prison cell. There is no light in the cell, you understand; there are only walls, not even a locked door. So the beam of light, thin as a needle, tells the prisoner that there is a world beyond."

"Karin, there is a world beyond this world. Be careful. The enemy has other allies, invisible spirits that can inform him of things the mind alone cannot know. He is a man controlled by such spirits."

"Devils?" she chuckled. "*Professore, Professore*, he is a devil all right, but entirely the human kind."

"You have not seen what I have seen."

"Whatever you've seen you interpret according to your mythology. Come now, let me introduce you to the ambassador."

During the introductions, the ambassador examined Elijah with studied interest. His breeding and good manners did not permit him to show a hint of boredom. But bored he was. After Karin left them alone together, the man exercised a few exchanges in tortuous Hebrew. He had loved archaeology as an undergraduate at Cambridge, he said, and had worked on digs in Sumer during the summers. Mesopotamia was the birthplace of every significant historical development.

Elijah replied in English that while he understood the immense importance of Mesopotamia, his excavations in Turkey never failed to surprise him. Mankind's history was a strata of great complexity, and much of it had occurred in Asia Minor.

The ambassador replied as if he had not understood. He said that Turkey sounded interesting, but his chief love was for more ancient civilizations.

From that point onward it was all in the man's language. Indeed the meeting was all about the man. Accustomed to being listened to, he did not courteously intersperse his comments with questions about Elijah's life and work. He simply held forth.

"I am very concerned about the problems of contemporary Israel," he said. "Her position is unique. This very small nation grips the world's attention in a way that, say, Madagascar or Croatia does not, even though these nations are larger and are strategically important in geopolitical terms.

"Why, then, does the world breathlessly hang upon every event that occurs in Israel? If Israeli soldiers rough up a mob of rock-throwing Palestinian youths, maybe shoot a few, the world howls with outrage."

"I see your point," Elijah interrupted. "And if an Iraqi or Syrian or Egyptian mob burns down a Christian church and kills its congregation, the world more or less ignores it."

"Yes, well," said the ambassador uncomfortably, clearing his throat. "Or a Palestinian rocket kills ten Israelis, the Israelis retaliate, and the world media roars with condemnation against a nation that is simply defending itself. What else can Israel do when Islamic extremists use their own people as human shields? To do nothing is to encourage more of the same.

"Please do not misunderstand me. Both in my official capacity and personally, I abhor violence. It is the crudest possible political tool and a tragedy for everyone involved. My point is that the world's obsession with Israel is disproportionate to what happens here. Worse horrors, indeed genocides, occur daily in Asia and Africa, even in parts of Europe. Every year, more people die of traffic accidents and murders in Chicago or London than die in present-day Israel. So, why this obsession with Israel?

"I will tell you my opinion, though I ask you not to repeat it to the media—in my position, after all, it would not be helpful. One must articulate the situation carefully, because there are always diplomatic consequences to how one phrases things.

"Israel is the land of the Bible, and this story has given the Western world its basic narrative, or the lens through which it analyzes history and understands itself. Human consciousness is not a tabula rasa, a blank page, on which we can write whatever we wish; we are always—always—written upon. We inherit specific cultural origins, an account of chronological developments, and an identity. We are preconditioned by the world around us and the story we have been given. Now we stand at the threshold of a new story, the story of all mankind. It has been made possible, in part, because for two generations now, the basic story of the West has receded into the background as globalized culture has become reality. The old mythos sustained us for a time, but it grew moribund and self-defeating.

"This is not a loss, you see. It is a *necessary* phase of development, which will bring mankind to the next stage, where we will have a world culture and a world identity, and the hideous conflicts of our past will be left behind like a bad dream.

"Even so, the drama of the Second World War and its aftermath survives. The Holocaust was more than a terrible tragedy. It changed everything, in a way that Stalin's massacres of millions more did not. The Holocaust took place in Europe, the heart of Western civilization that had been shaped by the old story. The survivors— are you a survivor, Professor? Yes? You have my profound sympathies."

The man cast down his eyes, reflecting thoughtfully for the required minimum of respect. He took a sip of his scotch and continued.

"As I was saying, the survivors took hold of their own story and made a nation out of rubble and desert and the ghosts of their families. More Jews died under Hitler than presently live here. You are a heroic remnant of a martyred people, and out of the ashes you have done the impossible. The tale of David defeating Goliath is as fresh as this morning's headlines, and it is reenacted again and again and again as the nation continues to survive against all odds. Thus it becomes the new story in the imagination of all those now living on the earth. They may love you or they may hate you, but they cannot ignore you.

"Leaving aside one's political position on the matter of the Palestinians and the Jews, I am merely saying that this drama cannot be relegated to the archives of history. It continues to be high drama. It is tragedy and triumph, in which everyone, whether he lives in Rio de Janeiro or Brussels, Capetown or Los Angeles, has a personal investment. The investment is psychological, often subconscious. All men suffer injustice. Your people's sufferings embody in a vicarious way the sufferings of everyone. If the Jews can overcome annihilation, so can we.

"I know the objections. You will argue that this is not the consciousness of the Chinese commissar, the tribal chief in Africa, the information technologist in Tokyo. You would be right, but their indifference is temporary.

"Jerusalem is the psychological and spiritual hub of the world, and this present moment is the nexus through which history and consciousness will leap forward. Why do so many world religions have their base here? Why have so many wars been fought for this little scrap of territory? Why were the original Jewish people of biblical times— few in number and relatively powerless—so crucial to the development of mankind? What informed them that they were the chosen? What was meant by *chosen*?

"You see that modern Israel is not simply an extrapolation of the Israel of the biblical era. It is its own new story, and in a sense it is mankind's story, which has not yet been revealed in its fullness. In ancient days your people provided the foundation out of which the true and eternal revelation will come. The new covenant is near. Indeed it is coming now.

"That is why this phenomenal person, the best man humanity has ever seen, is here among us this week. *He* will give the new revelation. All nations of the earth will see him and hear him as he stands upon Mount Zion and breaks open the new heavens and the new earth."

The ambassador drew a deep breath, moved by his own words. He glanced at his wristwatch.

"Please excuse me. Our conversation has been a pleasure. Good-bye."

"Good-bye."

As Elijah watched the man walk away, he felt singularly empty-headed for a few moments. The monologue had been a mixture of truths and untruths, a malignant tumor intertwined with the cells of a healthy organ. He now felt that he should have made more effort to break the current of the man's speech. But he had been overwhelmed, held back by his own habits of courtesy, by his age and declining energy, the slowing of his thoughts.

At a loss for what to do next, he noticed that the arch-bishop and the violinist were in the process of thumbing data into their cell phones—an exchange of addresses or other contact information, Elijah supposed. Their dialogue continued with what appeared to be a good deal of mutual charm.

Glancing elsewhere, Elijah noticed the cellist standing alone by the pool. He walked across the garden toward her, navigating past the clusters of guests without anyone making eye contact. *Good*, he thought, *I am socially invisible*. As he approached the young woman, however, she glanced at him and smiled. There was sadness in her smile. Otherwise, her expression was entirely reserved.

"I wish to commend you for your very fine performance," he said in Hebrew.

She looked confused by this, so he repeated it in English.

"Thank you," she said. "The composer is most excellent."

She turned a degree and gazed into the pool, where several large carp were serenely swimming. They were white with a variety of red markings.

"The fish are enchanting," said Elijah.

"They are *nishikigoi*," she replied. "You would say *koi*."

"Are you with the Jerusalem Philharmonic?"

"Yes, I am."

"Have you been in Israel long?"

"Not long."

"Has it been a good experience for you?"

She did not answer. Instead she bent over the pool and crumbled a piece of bread upon the waters. The fishes swam to it and began lazily gulping. She wore a fine-link gold chain around her neck, and the ornament hanging on it was hidden within her modest dress. When she bent over to feed more bread to the fish, the ornament slid out, and Elijah saw that it was a tiny gold cross. Noticing his glance upon it, the woman hid it quickly from view.

"These *nishikigoi* are red and white," she said, straightening, "the colors of my country."

"Also the colors of martyrdom."

She turned to face him. "You know this word *martyrdom*, sir? Do you mean the fires of Hiroshima and Nagasaki?"

"I am thinking farther back in history—the crucifixions at Nagasaki."

Her face become still. She glanced at his kippah.

"Not everything is as it appears," he said.

"Please, sir, I do not understand."

"Are you alone here in this country?"

"Yes."

"You would prefer to be with your brothers and sisters?'

"I would be happy if it were possible."

"It is possible. This is a place of great darkness."

"I know. I am frightened."

"I think you will come to no harm. May I suggest that you return to your homeland soon?"

"I pray for it."

"I will pray for it also."

"Who are you?"

Elijah did not answer the question. Instead, he asked, "Are you from Akita?"

Startled, she said, "But how can you know this?"

"I knew it only when I said it."

"It is, maybe, *Seirei*—the Holy Spirit."

"I do not know any Japanese words. Yet another word is in my mind—*Kami*."

"Yes, it means God." She bowed and said, "I am Hanna Tsukino." He bowed in return. "I am Elijah."

"My surname means *field of the moon*. Do you know about the lady who stands on the moon with twelve stars around her head?"

"I know her and love her."

The woman smiled brightly. "Yes, I thought so. You are a kind man, Mr. Elijah. Thank you for speaking with me."

"I thank *you*, daughter. May the Lord be your light, strength, and consolation, always."

"May he be the same for you, sir."

"May the Mother of Akita carry you home safely."

"May she carry you also."

They bowed once again, and the woman left the garden.

Elijah watched the slow-motion ballet of the koi. He did not want to leave the pool, for it was a little sea of serenity, which at the moment he sorely needed. When he looked across the garden, he saw the archbishop sitting alone, staring at the glass tabletop, smiling as if enjoying a sweet secret. Elijah went to him.

"Good evening. May I sit down?" he asked in Hebrew.

The archbishop gestured with largesse. "Please join me." His Hebrew was correct, though more guttural than the diction of Israelis.

Elijah introduced himself, using his assumed name and situating himself in the other's mind as a Jew and an archae-ologist. He was both, of course, but the man did not need to know the qualifiers. He in turn gave his name and his city, a major one in Germany. The man mentioned that he was a Catholic archbishop, in fact a cardinal, though this detail was offered as incidental. His black suit and tie, with no pectoral cross, revealed nothing of his office, though there was a large gold ring on the fourth finger of his right hand, and on his head he wore a scarlet zucchetto.

"Have you visited my country?" the man asked.

"No, I haven't," Elijah said, resisting a silent eruption of conflicting emotions.

"If you ever do, you must take a boat trip down the Rhine. Our white wines are superb. Of course, Austrian wines are also excellent. Have you ever visited Austria?"

"Many years ago, I passed through Vienna," Elijah replied in German, remembering the year 1949, when he had been confronted by two Red Army intelligence agents in an alley near the Hofburg Palace. He had been in the city on a mission for the Zva Haganah, the newly formed Israel Defense Forces. The Russians were not satisfied with his forged papers and tried to arrest him. The ensuing struggle had been brutal; he had left them prone and unconscious, had refrained from killing them, and had walked away with a few bruises. He had swiftly left the country, never to return.

Seeming relieved to be speaking in German, the archbishop said with a smile, "Ah, and did you visit Klosterneuburg, to the north of Vienna?"

"No, I regret I didn't," said Elijah.

"It has some important historic sites, in particular a magnificent twelfth-century monastery, a functioning Augustinian community until only a year ago. Now it is a museum. It has a marvelous vineyard and a hospitality center for wine-tasting. You really must sample their wine if you are ever in the area."

From the first, the archbishop appeared to be an amiable personality, well accustomed to making all sorts of people feel at ease. His further remarks were about Israeli wines, the loveliness of the evening, Jerusalem's cool autumn weather, and the graciousness of their hostess, whom he knew personally. An old friend, he said. The music had been wonderfully selected; the musicians were world-class. He too was a trained musician, a pianist, of course not as talented as these professionals.

"Have you come to Jerusalem for the Presidential visit?" Elijah asked.

"Yes, like so many people from around the world. I know him well, as do several of my brother bishops. Our dialogues with him have moved the Church forward in an unprecedented way. Are you aware of the longstanding dialogues between the Church and leaders of the major religions—for example, Judaism?"

"Yes, I have followed them closely for years."

"There has been so much progress, it is heartening. And there are other dialogues, official and informal, between the Church and state and nongovernmental organizations, all of which are helping to move us beyond the horrors of the last century. One might say the previous millennium."

"Do all the hierarchs of the Church feel as you do?"

"No, sadly, not all of them." He shook his head, musing. "It takes time to detach some people from the psychology of rigid dogmatism. That is a process. Such processes are made possible only by courageous leadership."

"The Pope seems to be a courageous man."

"He has courage, yes, but the Church must not depend on only one man. We need other leaders too."

"Where does the Church find them?"

"The leaders of the new paradigm first emerge as voices crying out in the wilderness. Then they enter the temple as prophetic voices of the future. They are not always understood, but they persevere, and in the end they will prevail, for this is the course of history. Among us there are cardinals, bishops, gifted theologians …"

"I have read about your Cardinal Vettore."

"He is one of the lights in the new ecclesiology. A man of great vision."

"Do you know him?"

"He is a colleague and close friend. He arrives in Jerusalem tomorrow and will be one of the Vatican representatives at the interreligious liturgy to be held at the Western Wall. The President will also be there and will offer prayers."

"I have not read about it on the list of his public engagements. When will this happen?"

"In the afternoon of the seventh day of his visit. The event has not been publicized because everyone involved wishes to make it an experience shared intimately between like-minded people, without the crowds, the noise, and not least the danger of fanatics breaking into what will be one of the greatest spiritual watersheds in history. In Beirut, three million people gathered to hear him. In Tehran this afternoon there were five million."

"Do you think there is any real danger of fanatical acts?"

"Jerusalem is a unique psychological and spiritual zone. Religion, without a unified vision, breeds extremists who would do anything in the name of fostering their obsessions. It is a psychosis, a religious dementia. I fear it more than I fear political terrorism."

"Do you?" said Elijah in an inoffensive tone. "I lost my wife and child to a terrorist bomb many years ago."

"I am so very sorry," said the archbishop with a compassionate look. "You have suffered much, Dr. Pastore."

"Suffering is a great teacher. And a test."

"Yes, but we must never seek suffering."

"Of course. Though when it comes, we should understand that it is not the destruction of life's foundations. It can show us the measure of our character and how we must grow."

"But God does not want us to be unhappy."

"Human choices make happiness and unhappiness, and we live with the consequences."

"That is why the time has come for all men to lay aside their differences. Though it was not always so, it is my belief—a belief on which I now base my life—that the time for an overarching *unitas* has come, a convergence of all the spiritual streams within our histories, within our universal humanity."

"How does this *unitas* propose to cope with the tendency to evil in our nature?"

"It proposes a new integration in which all divisions, internal and external, will be revealed as illusion and then will fade away."

"Beyond good and evil?"

"Yes, but not in the sense that Nietzsche intended. With the alliance of Christianity, the new vision will redirect the will to power toward the will to love."

"Is that not what Christ also proposes? My understanding is that his teaching says the ground for love is internal and begins in the heart—including the struggles in the heart."

"Yet much of the struggle is caused by misplaced moralism. An alliance will raise mankind above moralism—"

"Do you mean above morality?"

"No, no, certainly not. I mean to say that Judeo-Christianity, and Islam to a degree, have imposed unrealistic norms of behavior on mankind. The internal conflicts generated by this make it difficult, if not impossible, to love."

"My belief is that our willingness to undertake the struggle within our damaged natures is the very thing that broadens and deepens our capacity to love. If all conflict is removed, if all suffering is removed, are we not left with sentiment and sensuality?"

"You make a point worth considering. Note, however, that in my religion we have tried to live by inhuman moralism for two millennia, and it has not worked. Human beings are more miserable than ever."

"Is this misery the result of Catholic morality or of sin?"

"I see you are a man of faith. I hope I have not offended you. I respect Judaism profoundly. One of my closest friends is the chief rabbi of ..." The archbishop paused, and then leaned forward with a warm smile. "Perhaps you would like to attend the gathering at the Wall. I can arrange a pass for you. Only a few hundred people will be in attendance, leaders of the world's organized religions and also many prominent figures from a multitude of spiritualties. There will be no exclusivity."

"I would very much like to attend."

"It will be an experience of intense and authentic *community*, I would call it. Of course, the media will be there to record the event for future generations, but they will not be intrusive."

"Surely a great number of people would desire to take part in it."

"The Wall is a prelude, an essential one. On the following day, the eighth day, the entire world will take part in it. The Temple Mount will become the foundation of the new Temple, as it were, so that all of mankind may be freed to worship in spirit and in truth."

"Yet, I would ask, what deity would be worshipped?"

The archbishop smiled congenially, his expression conveying the message that while he was privy to the most elite information, he must judiciously withhold it. Elijah read in the man's eyes his intention: he wished to be recognized as both very important and very humble.

"Be assured, my friend, what is about to occur is good news," said the archbishop. "It is good news of the highest order."

"The President will announce it?" Elijah asked.

"He will. Have you read his *Metasynthesis*?"

"I haven't," Elijah said.

"There has been some controversy regarding the metasynthesis among the devout of organized religions. A small minority, fundamentalists. Few people in the world are able to grasp everything in the book, and thus there are misinterpretations. Personally, I found his exegesis of the philosophical foundations of East and West to be on par with Plato and Averroës. He goes on to encompass Descartes and then surpasses him with a new epistemological sense."

"Having studied some philosophy, I can appreciate what an achievement it would be to surpass Descartes," Elijah said.

"An interesting combination, archaeology and philosophy. You must tell me more about it." The archbishop paused, his brow furrowing a little. "It seems to me, after all, that your attendance at the Wall would be premature."

"You do not wish to obtain a pass for me?"

"It would be better for you to participate at a later time, after the eighth day, when more will be revealed. The vision will then become accessible and understandable to everyone. You are a believing Jew, and you have raised honest questions with me and have been forthcoming about your reservations. When the President's vision is accepted universally, I trust that you will see that it takes nothing away from humanity while giving us the manifesto for our common future."

"It would change the world dramatically," said Elijah.

The archbishop nodded in affirmation, adding with gentle emphasis, "It will be entirely for the better."

Unable to contain himself any longer, Elijah rose to his feet and said, "The darkness he would spread over the world is beyond your fathoming. He is using you. And through him, Satan is using you."

The archbishop's mouth dropped open; his eyes widened with astonishment.

"You are a shepherd of the flock of the Lord," Elijah continued, raising the palms of his hands over the man. "On the Day of Judgment you will render an account for your every word and deed. I adjure you, leave the camp of the evil one immediately, return to your flock, and strengthen what remains!"

Jerking his head back, the archbishop gave a small laugh of incredulity. "You are insane," he muttered. Standing, he pushed back his chair and walked in the direction of a group of guests sharing drinks by the pool, where he began to talk and gesture with vehemence. The others turned and stared after Elijah as he went into the house. Unobtrusively, unnoticed, he left the party.

5

The Pebble War

As Elijah began the long walk back to Al Sheikh Jarrah, he ached with pain over the blindness he had encountered during his conversations. The archbishop's delusions were the worst, for the man had been given every advantage for knowing better. Elijah reminded himself that the Church had been afflicted from the beginning by those who compromised the truth. There had never been a lack of such strategists, especially during times of crisis for the Church. Whenever she had been attacked from the outside, there had arisen within her proponents of the lesser-evil argument— make peace with our oppressors, try to save what can be saved by cooperating with their unjust demands. How like the *Judenrat*, the Jewish council in the Warsaw ghetto, whose motives were good but through whom, little by little, everything was lost.

And there was Christ's mysterious choice to allow Judas to be in his company until the very end, when the betrayer made his ultimate choice. Had he been corrupted by greed alone? Or had he been a disappointed idealist? Had he been driven by political ambition, a distorted concept of the good, the salvation of Israel according to his own criteria? The theories about Judas varied widely—always guesswork and often projection. Elijah also recognized that in the ranks of the clergy there had always been careerists, men who were indifferent to the truth and sought a comfortable living as a priest or a bishop.

In the case of the archbishop, there had been no evident moral corruption in his face and manner. There was a softness about him, however, a gentleness that lacked real strength. In all likelihood the man had succumbed to one of Satan's more clever ploys, a subtle backdoor devil entering where the front-door devils of vice had not gained admittance. If the Judas syndrome had failed to corrupt, had the Caiaphas syndrome succeeded? When had the man begun to lose his bearings? Certainly a misplaced compassion was at work in the matrix of his thinking. Did the archbishop have friends and relatives whose lives violated the commandments? Perhaps in the beginning he had meant only to be kind, to evangelize with empathy. Then, because of the adamancy of God's laws, he had fallen into the dilemma of kindly men who lack courage to speak the truth in love. Their natural sympathies told them one thing, and their faith told them another.

Thus, internally divided, these pastors strained for a resolution. They were further weakened by long years of endless nuances, by reading disordered theology and feeling helpless whenever they were confronted by the tears and reproaches of those who found moral imperatives too hard. Add to this their discussions with like-minded peers, people they admired, clever people who chose to manipulate opinion as they sought to deconstruct the Church and rebuild it in their own image. These dynamics, combined with a hidden thread of pride, had led the archbishop to the conclusion that orthodox Catholicism was simply no longer feasible, could no longer function as it had for two millennia. Primitive Christianity, such men believed, must evolve into something inclusive, nonjudgmental, and nonconfrontational. Above all, it must never offend.

Elijah was most familiar with this tendency in German and Austrian bishops, though it could be found elsewhere.

It was particularly difficult for them to stand firm against a materialist social revolution and against dissent within their own dioceses. He had often wondered if they were still overreacting to the guilt of Nazism, whether or not their parents and grandparents had suffered under it or had endorsed it. For all of them it continued to be, three generations after the war, a factor in their identity and memory. Thus, all authority was suspect, even dangerous, equated with authoritarianism. Religious authority, therefore, should be collegial in an egalitarian sense. The authority of the papacy—the rule of one man, as they saw it—could not be tolerated, for that form of governance was undemocratic, and because it was undemocratic, it must surely tend in the direction of fascism.

Elijah's tired mind continued to fume.

The new Germans believed they had learned from their history. We are not the bad Germans, they proclaimed; we are the good Germans. Do not hate us, do not hold us collectively guilty, do not make us live in shame forever. We are the loving people. We want everyone to be happy. And if you won't be happy, we will *make* you happy.

Elijah sighed with a feeling of dismay. Could they not see it? Why did they not detect their own new fascism beneath their surface antifascism, as they enabled the imposition of social revolution, the violation of conscience, the dismantling of sovereignties, the indoctrination of the young, the spread of a tragically stunted anthropology?

Such men fell into the hands of the Antichrist like overripe plums. As long as the surface of his agenda was socially acceptable, they would applaud him. But what would they do when his underlying authoritarianism was manifested?

He had greatly loved Benedict XVI, a brilliant and holy man who had been a universal shepherd of souls and a lucid teacher of all who would listen. The prior at Stella Maris, now prior of their little foundation near Ephesus, was a wise superior and a friend. Elijah knew other Germanic bishops, true sons of Christ, but they were a minority held in contempt by their confreres. There were his spiritual directees as well, a layman in Berlin, a laywoman in Bavaria, both of them valiant journalists who had fought courageously against the totalitarian aspects of the emerging new European order. Invariably, they had been savaged in the media as "Nazis". During the past two years, they, and the few clear voices like them, had been eliminated from the public forum one by one.

In this manner Elijah silently vented his feelings as he journeyed back to the apartment. The evening had been a waste, he thought. He had learned little that he did not already know, and he had permitted his sorrow to become frustration and now anger. He had lost his peace. He needed very badly to find a quiet place where he could pray. Nearing the high walls along the west side of the Old City, he abruptly detoured and entered through the Jaffa Gate. Shops and bistros were still open, the streets full of jubilant people, discordant music contending with televisions in open shop windows replaying the day's events in Tehran. The streets grew less crowded as he neared the Church of the Holy Sepulcher, and in the small square before its main entrance there were three people bellowing into their cell phones. He stood quietly to the side, waiting. Finally the conversations ended and the people went away, leaving Elijah relatively alone.

The golden glow of spotlights illumined the ancient building with enough ambient light to dispel most of the shadows in the square. Now only a solitary figure remained, standing a few paces from the locked entrance and staring at the poster of the President. Elijah hoped that the man would soon leave so that he could kneel in privacy before the doors and ask for a return of interior peace. He waited in a shadowed place.

The man did not leave. He continued to stand there in a posture of stillness. Then, to Elijah's great surprise, he strode to the entrance and tore the poster of the President's face off the door. He further tore it into pieces and deposited it in a trash can. That done, he sat on the bottom step of the stone staircase to the right of the entrance and put his face in his hands. His chest heaved with what appeared to be a deep sigh.

Elijah stepped out of the shadows and approached.

"*Shalom*," he said.

The man's head jerked up, and he rose to his feet with fear in his eyes. Turning away without responding to the greeting, he took a step toward the exit onto Saint Helena Street.

"May we speak together?" Elijah asked in Hebrew.

"I don't know your language," the man murmured in English. "Sorry, I have to go."

"I understand how difficult it is to trust," said Elijah in English.

The other stopped and inspected him more closely. For his part, Elijah saw that the person before him was in his midtwenties and possessed an unusually fine face that was accustomed to openness. For the moment, the expression flickered back and forth between alarm and cautious interest.

"Trust?" the man said.

"You need not fear me. May we speak together?"

"You saw what I did?"

"Yes. If you had not been here, it is likely I would have done as you did."

"Even Jews have doubts about him?"

"Yes, some Jews."

Elijah continued to ponder the young man's face, noticing also that the tension in his body had eased a little, though his expression remained cautious. He thought that this person, hardly more than a boy, was one of those anomalies he encountered from time to time among the young generation. Here was an exemplar of courageous manhood—of what men should be. There was humble self-mastery, intelligence, and a great deal of goodness.

"Shall we sit for a minute?" Elijah asked. The other nodded, and they sat down side by side on the stone steps.

Speaking with a quiet voice, strong and clear, the young man said, "Sir, I don't expect you to believe me. But in my faith we have gifts—faculties, you could call them—that have warned us about this man's coming. For two thousand years we've been warned."

He glanced at Elijah uncertainly.

"For longer than that," said Elijah.

"You mean the Old Testament. Sorry, I should say the Torah."

"Have you studied sacred Scripture?"

"Yes, biblical theology."

"I have studied it also. And taught it."

"You're a rabbi."

"I am a Roman Catholic bishop."

This was greeted by stunned silence.

Elijah removed the kippah from his head. He opened his shirtfront and brought out the scapular on its cord. He kissed it.

"I am a Carmelite priest . . . and a bishop."

Still the other said nothing, staring, his lips parted as if to speak, his eyes perplexed. He rose to his feet, and Elijah stood with him.

As they faced each other, Elijah was now struck with a new awareness. He sensed that the young man before him was not only strong and wholesome; he was blessed with the rare quality of purity of heart. He said, "You are a priest."

The man startled. "Yes, I am. I was ordained five weeks ago."

"Why are you here in Jerusalem?"

"My bishop sent me to pray at the tomb of Christ. He believes a persecution is coming, and he wanted his youngest son, as he calls me, to pray for our diocese, to pray for souls."

"With the churches closed, where do you offer your Mass?"

"This morning, I offered the Holy Sacrifice in the room I rented in a hostel. Before that, I was staying with some people in Lod near Tel Aviv, and I have to go back to them. I can't stay here any longer."

"Why not?"

"The atmosphere is strangling me. There are evil spirits in the city, and I can sense them. They're trying to drag me down. I've learned that it's not good for Christians to try to do things alone. The Lord sent the disciples out two by two for a reason. Also, I need to return to the community because there's the risk of arrest."

"If you wish, you can stay with me and another Carmelite brother. We have a temporary shelter in the city."

"Thank you, but my friends are expecting me tonight. I have to catch the last bus about an hour from now. You said *temporary*. Why are you in Jerusalem? And why are you disguised as a Jew?"

"The explanation for this would take too much time. Also, my situation is complex, and parts of it would be difficult for you to believe. I can say only that my brother and I are in great need of prayers—for protection and for our mission to be fulfilled. Will you pray for us?"

"I will pray to our Lord for you. And to our holy Mother. Pray for me too, please. I'm feeling very discouraged."

"Why are you discouraged?"

"That man is swallowing the whole world bit by bit. And we, people like us who see what's really happening, we're all being slowly, deliberately herded into ghettos— isolated little ghettos everywhere."

"Ghettos without walls, you mean. Ghettos in the mind."

"Yes, like that. We try to resist, but it's just throwing pebbles at a Sherman tank."

"Prayer is more than useless pebbles."

"I know. I believe it. But I also know the Scriptures, and I listen to what the Holy Father has been saying the past few years, whenever his teaching reaches us."

"Whenever it reaches you? Surely the Church's Internet services still function."

"There are Internet sites that post our real daily news, but one by one they're going off-line, with no explanation. The Vatican site is still there, but I think it's being run by people who aren't giving us the real picture. There's a lot of distorted thinking in it."

"Is there a Cardinal Vettore involved?"

"Vettore? Yes, I read an interview with him. Poison mixed with feel-good theology and a few pious plati- tudes. Now and then, this site has extracts from the Holy Father's talks in Saint Peter's, but they weed out anything that goes against the popular tide—or anything prophetic. I know, because I was in the piazza for one of those talks. His handlers cut it short, claiming the Holy Father was ill. But he said enough for me to realize he's calling the whole Church to wake up. He told the crowd we're now living in the midst of the greatest crisis in history, and he kept quoting Revelation. That's when the handlers stepped in."

"And the Vatican website deleted it?"

"Yes. They left only the parts that would give people the impression he's a kindly old uncle with nothing much to say—except that we should be nice to each other."

" 'They will strike the shepherd, and the sheep will scatter.' "

The priest nodded grimly.

"Surely the crowd in the piazza heard it, and they would spread it," said Elijah.

"I hope so. I wrote down what he said, and I've spread it as far and wide as I can. But there were only a few hundred people there. Remember the days when hundreds of thousands would gather to listen to him? Now I wonder how many would be interested if they *had* heard the whole thing."

" 'Will there be any faith left on the earth when the Son of Man returns?' "

"Exactly."

Both men fell silent. During this pause, Elijah saw again, as vividly as if it had just occurred, his confrontation with the President on Capri.

"Though you would try to seize the throne of the Lamb of God," Elijah had proclaimed, "you will stand before his judgment seat, for he who was, who is, and who is to come is the First and the Last. He is Alpha and Omega. He comes swiftly, riding upon a white horse, and his name is Faithful and True. He has conquered you."

"Oh, you poor little man," the President had sneered. "Has he conquered me? He has no army left on this earth. Billions follow me."

"Your army is like the retreating German army at the end of the war. They were already defeated, though they could lash out as their empire crashed about them."

"My army grows daily, and we spread and spread across this planet. Leave him, you fool. He was a little Christ. He is dead. The Christ of *this* age stands before you, and you do not recognize him."

"You are not Christ. You never will be. Jesus Christ is the Light of the world! There is no other Christ. In him, everything in heaven and on earth was created, things visible and invisible, whether thrones, dominations, principalities or powers; all was created through him and for him."

"Silence!" the President had roared, and from his mouth there poured a stream of blasphemies. Elijah had averted his head and prayed the name of Jesus until the flow was stemmed and he could cut through it with the authority rising within him: "The Lamb is the firstborn and the height of everything. It is through him and by him that all creation is reconciled to the Father, by the merits of his sacred Blood!"

In retort, the President had shouted denial of the primary and singular sonship of the Lamb, denial that Jesus was the Christ, denial of the victory of the Cross, denial of the One who had come into the world.

"There is no light left in the world save one," he had concluded, "he who is the angel of light cast out by the jealousy of God. Lucifer is the light bringer, and now he rises!"

"He is darkness. He is *Satan*—the enemy!" Elijah had said.

"My lord will lead mankind to its highest truth."

"Your lord is *the devil*—the murderer from the beginning. May the Lord Most High rebuke him!"

And then Elijah had said prayers of exorcism, and the *diabolus* had manifested still further, with the President collapsing to the floor, writhing, and making bestial noises.

"You've studied the book of Revelation," the young priest said.

Elijah looked up, turning from the memory.

"Yes, of course you have," the priest continued. "It may sound extreme, Bishop, but I think we're in the middle of the eleventh chapter. You know, the part where Saint John says the inhabitants of the earth will rejoice and give gifts to one another when the beast kills the two prophets?"

"I know the passage well."

"More and more, that's what people are like. They hate anything that challenges their consciences. I mean real hatred. Words don't touch them because they don't want to hear anything that might make them feel their pain and emptiness. Then they would have to change, and they think it would cost them too much. Is *think* the right word? Maybe they just sense the cost in their subconscious, or in their souls, and they block it out."

"This is true of some," said Elijah. "For others it is simply ignorance, especially for the young who have never known anything else. The world in its present darkness *is* their reality."

"If only they could break out of *their* ghettos. I keep trying to reach them, in conversations, homilies, e-mail. I won't stop trying, but now I think that only something huge can break down their walls. It will have to be bigger than words. Real signs of God's power are needed now."

"Power?" said Elijah. "Yes, but it will be through the power of the Cross that each of us will bear witness—in the particular mission God has called us to."

"Well, I expect we're going to see it. We've never experienced such apostasy before."

"We have experienced much that is similar, but not as universal."

"I think parts of the twelfth chapter are close—very close. Pretty soon the enemy's going to make war on everyone who follows Jesus. I don't think it'll stop at silencing and removing non-profit status. There are going to be real martyrs. If it happens to me, I hope I can offer that, at least."

"Such an offering is no small thing, my son."

"You say *son*," the priest whispered. "I don't feel like much of a son at the moment. It turns out I don't have the stamina to stay calm and confident in the midst of"— he made a sweeping gesture—"in the midst of all this. So what kind of martyr material am I?"

"I see very clearly that you are a steadfast man."

"Am I? But when push comes to shove, will I cut and run? Maybe I'll turn out to be a betrayer."

"You are a true son, a beloved son."

"My name is David," he said in a shaken voice. "I'm Father David. And you, Bishop, who are you, really?"

"The name my parents gave me at birth was also David. The name given to me at my solemn profession was Elijah."

Father David sighed and covered his eyes with his right hand. When he looked up again, he saw that Elijah was standing before him with bowed head.

"Please give me your blessing, Father," said the old man.

Father David raised both arms and held the palms of his hands over Elijah's head. He closed his eyes, cleared his throat, and prayed aloud.

"O Lord God our Father, please bless your servant Bishop Elijah. May he console your grieved Heart. May he convert sinners and bring those to paradise who might not otherwise be there. May he confound the malice and devices of the enemy. May your holy angels protect him from Satan and from every other evil spirit."

He made the sign of the cross over Elijah and then with thumb and forefinger traced another cross on his forehead, saying "May Almighty God bless you, in the name of the Father, and of the Son, and of the Holy Spirit."

Father David now knelt before Elijah, who blessed him with formal prayers in Latin. In the man's native tongue he also invoked the protection of Saint Michael and all the holy angels.

"May you bear abundant fruit for eternity," said Elijah at the last. "If you are called to the cross, David, keep this truth alive in your heart: his love is within you, and you are in him. *This* is your power. Fear nothing."

When the young priest stood up, all tension seemed to have gone from his body. He squared his shoulders and lifted his chin.

"Thank you, Bishop. When you prayed over me I felt a black cloud lifting. Peace like a warm river flowed all over me, and through me. I don't know much about you, really, but I know you're in Christ. Somehow you're in his plans, and my guess is, what he wants you to do is very big."

"I am very small, my brother. That is why I am depending on you to pray for me."

"I will pray. Don't forget me either."

"How could I forget you? Our meeting has been a great consolation, more than you can imagine."

From his breast pocket, Father David took a pen and a small notepad. He wrote on it and tore off a page, which he handed to Elijah.

"Let me give you this. It's the address where I'm staying in Lod. If you need a place to go, to find shelter, please come to us. I might not be around because I have to leave for home a few days from now. But I'll tell my friends about you."

"Thank you."

Elijah in turn told Father David the address of the apartment in Sheikh Jarrah. It would be better, he said, not to write it down. If he needed a refuge, he should not hesitate to come.

Father David checked his wristwatch.

"If I go now, I can just make it to the bus station on time. I hope we meet again."

"I too hope we meet again. Go with God."

Father David turned left onto Saint Helena Street and calmly walked past two security police, who paid him no notice. Elijah read the Lod address. Realizing that if he were arrested, the paper would lead authorities to the priest and his friends, and almost certainly would result in their detention, he tore it into small pieces and sprinkled them into the trash can. He placed the kippah on his head, turned right onto the street, and reached the Jaffa Gate without interference.

It was close to midnight when Elijah unlocked the apartment door and went in. There were no signs that Enoch had returned in his absence.

After the long walk and the stress of his conversations with the diplomat and the archbishop, he felt suddenly overwhelmed with exhaustion. He sat on the sofa for a while, focusing on the blessings of the evening, the Jewish professor, the Japanese cellist, the young priest. Goodness was everywhere, he thought, and the indwelling of the Holy Trinity in the souls of believers was a power greater than the serpent now coiling itself around mankind, seeking to devour everything. He must be wary of the seduction of its eyes. It mesmerized. It sought to neutralize Christ's servants throughout the world by defamation, then isolation, and finally discouragement. It was deluging the earth with the lie that the Savior was an old myth that had lost its relevance and influence, a tired story soon to be forgotten by all but a pitiful remnant. The serpent would convince, if it could, even the believing remnant, by whispering, insinuating, and paralyzing, telling them they were forgotten, defeated, and that their Lord would remain eternally absent.

These were feelings, Elijah reminded himself, natural enough when one looked around at the pervading environment, where evil seemed to be spreading without impediment, where so many good souls grew weaker and those who were less than good sank deeper into bondage, all the while proclaiming their freedom. And such feelings were fertile ground for the tempter.

Elijah now felt some of this himself. He recognized it, for he knew the pattern well and had resisted it for most of his adult life. He had helped countless people in the confessional and in spiritual direction to understand the strategies of the enemy. Satan was not creative. There was no love in him, only lies and malice—brilliant Luciferian malice, subtle or blatant, but limited because he was no more than a creature. He could not invade souls unless they let him—or worse, knowingly invited him. Moreover, he was restrained by an unseen hand.

Yet a global persecution is coming, Elijah thought. *And men will call this evil good, and good they will call evil. Few will step forth to contradict the lies, for the word of the Lord will have been banished from the earth, and those who still bear this word in their hearts will be hunted and many pursued unto destruction.*

Elijah got up and drank water and ate a disk of flatbread. He went onto the balcony and looked out over the city. He pondered the beauty of two of the souls he had met this evening, Hanna Tsukino and Father David. They were like a fresh breeze from a distant promised land, or a damp and fragrant garden discovered by surprise in the middle of the desert. Each in his way was a living word. They were, as well, signs for him of all that he had lived for. They were his brother and sister, and they were his children.

Would they be martyred? For the present, the world appeared to be troubled but stabilizing. There were no outward dramatic signs that global persecution was coming. Only the swiftly growing "signs of the times", as Christ had warned, signs that could be understood only by those who sought truth wholeheartedly and pondered the eschatological prophecies of Scripture. Yes, the ultimate persecution was near. Would Father David and Hanna and countless souls like them fall victim to it? Or would they be spared as he had been spared from the flames of the Shoah, a branch pulled from the burning? He now prayed that they would not perish. That they would be the seeds of a new springtime. That they would grow old in grace and come peacefully to the eternal Promised Land. He hoped it would be so. He was free to ask for it, to beg for it. And so he did. Yet he knew that the path of each person in the world was known in its fullness to God alone. If these two held firm, they would be witnesses in one way or another.

Prompted by the young priest's remarks about the eleventh and twelfth chapters of Revelation and Hanna's uncanny reference to an image from one of these chapters, he reflected a little on the seeming coincidence. As he often had done in recent years, he wondered over the identity of the two witnesses. Saint John's prophetic vision gave no personal details about them, only that they were "olive trees" and "lampstands" who would exercise extraordinary spiritual authority as well as the power to keep rain from falling on the earth, to turn waters into blood, and to smite the world with plagues. Above all, they would prophesy against the Antichrist. They would be killed by him and their dead bodies would be left exposed for "three and a half days" in the streets of Jerusalem. Then God would raise them to life again and call them up into heaven in a cloud.

The symbolism—if symbolism it was—indicated that the witnesses were types of the Church herself. Would all those who truly followed the Lord enact with their lives what was described by these passages? Would the prayers of believers be the very instruments for bringing chastisements upon unbelieving mankind? Would the Church be apparently destroyed for three and a half years? Would she rise again as the breath of God entered her? And would she then be taken up into heaven?

Father David had likened the prayers of believers to pebbles thrown at a battle tank. In terms of the apparent disproportion of strength, he was correct. But from the perspective of the entire configuration of struggle between good and evil happening now, the nature of these pebbles must not be underestimated. One might call it a pebble war, a futile attempt to resist the irresistible, but that would describe the surface appearance only.

The interpretation of the passages was not an either-or choice. The unfolding of the apocalypse could very well prove to be both figurative *and* literal. If this were the case, one aspect of the vast, mysterious plans of God would take flesh in the form of two men sent to challenge the Antichrist openly in the streets of Jerusalem, just as the entire living Church would do so in a multitude of ways and places.

Elijah now reflected on his own mission.

Who am I in your eyes, O Lord? At Foligno, on the mountain above Anna's farm, you spoke to me in the heart of my soul. Yet now, here, in the center of the war you have been silent, O my Savior.

On the mountain the interior voice had said to him,

Little one, my son. Fear nothing. The beast that impersonates a lamb approaches the sanctuary in order to destroy it and to take the throne of Jesus, the true Lamb of God. He will succeed for a time in obscuring the light of heaven in many places.

You are to be a witness for Christ. You are to be a sign. Fear nothing. Speak only what shall be given to you, and it shall be for the salvation of many souls.

Then came the cave in the hills beyond Ephesus, where he had lived for forty days. Angels had been with him there, appearing visibly at crucial moments, though briefly, and saying little. Much of what had occurred during that period of purification was within his soul. How could it be otherwise? He was a Carmelite, and thus it was appropriate that he would be called farther on the path of unknowing. No details had been given, no specific instructions—only the essence of his task. The angel had said that he was to go to Jerusalem to give witness for Christ against the Man of Sin, who sought to usurp the throne of God.

Obedience. Simplicity. Trust. These would guide him.

Yet it was difficult not to wonder if he was one of the two witnesses prophesied by Saint John. Was this unhealthy *curiositas*? Did he desire such an exalted role? Or was he terrified by the possibility? At the moment he felt neither desire nor terror, but if he personally—he, David Shäfer of Warsaw; he, Father Elijah of Carmel—if his own small life were to become a prophecy fulfilled, he would accept everything that would be asked of him.

He remembered the long tradition in the Church that the two witnesses would be the prophets Enoch and Elijah returned. Scripture recounted that these two had been bodily taken up into heaven and not seen again. They had not died, said the Fathers and the saints, and they would return.

There was also the prophecy of Malachi, the final prophet of the Old Testament: "Behold, I will send you Elijah the prophet before the great and awesome day of the LORD comes. And he will turn the hearts of fathers to their children and the hearts of children to their fathers, lest I come and strike the land with a curse."

Then there was John the Baptist, of whom the angel spoke to his father, Zechariah: "He will go before him in the spirit and power of Elijah, to turn the hearts of the fathers to the children, and the disobedient to the wisdom of the just, to make ready for the Lord a people prepared."

Jesus himself spoke about this gift of the mantle of Elijah when referring to John: "Elijah has already come, and they did not know him."

Clearly, Jesus understood that the Old Testament prophecy was multidimensional, both literal-historical and spiritual. At the advent of the new covenant, the spirit of Elijah had been given to John. Even so, Malachi's prophecy was not fulfilled during the foundation period of the Church or during the two thousand years since then, for the great and terrible Day of the Lord had not yet come. And that day, as described in numerous Scripture passages of the Old and New Testaments, would be a day of unprecedented catastrophe for mankind, of judgment— and of liberation. Translations varied: the earth would be struck with "doom", a "curse", "anathema", but in essence the prophecy warned against a chastisement that would be utter destruction. In their epistles, both Peter and Paul taught that it would be destruction by fire.

The fire had not fallen on the world, and Elijah, the prophet reserved for the end, had not yet come. He would surely come, but was it conceivable that, like John, he would be a man given the spirit of Elijah? And by the same token, if the tradition was correct that the two witnesses of Revelation were Elijah and Enoch, was it possible that both of them would be men born in these times, who would be given the spirits of those prophets?

The thought of it now pierced him with an arrow of dread. He wondered over this abrupt change of mood. Where was his faith? Where was the confidence he had once felt in the face of other foes, most significantly during his confrontation with the Man of Sin on Capri? He had felt no fear then, only an inner calm and certainty.

He knew that extraordinary graces were given when they were needed, and not a moment before. The Holy Spirit never moved within believers as if they were puppet instruments, but rather in cocreative choices—Person and person working together in faith and freedom.

Elijah held his face in his hands and bowed over his knees. Trembling, groaning, he prayed:

"Is it possible, my Lord? Or is it only in my imagination? Has an intuition become a question, an apprehension building upon the similarities: my name, my life on Mount Carmel, the cave where you taught me as you taught the prophet, the forty days of purification, the companionship of my little brother Enoch? And is it also because of the convergence of my Jewish origins and my Catholic faith? Have I conflated the numerous strands of my life and interpreted them with too much subjectivity?

"I know that you have called me to bear witness against the Man of Sin. This much you have revealed to me. But to think of myself as one of the two witnesses? Is it temptation? Is it presumption? O my Lord, I dread it. I dread most of all to be deceived at this most crucial time of testing for your people."

Elijah sighed and sighed. He longed to find release in tears, but they would not come. Now he felt only the rising fear. He did not fear death. He had long ago accepted that in all probability martyrdom was coming for him. Until the moment of his death, if he lived long enough, he would have to deal with many assaults from the enemy, not least of which would be the invisible ones: the apparent triumph of evil, the paralysis of discouragement, and the temptation to despair. More than these, however, he feared to be misled in such a way that he would fail to feed the flock of the Lord and become instead an affliction to it.

"If I am deluded, I beg you to keep me from harming souls. Please speak to me, my Savior, for I am small and weak and do not know what I am doing."

Slowly, with aching limbs, Elijah went down on his knees. He remained in this position for some minutes, without forming any words of prayer, receiving neither light nor consolation. He felt as if he were adrift on a sea of uncertainties, as if it were impossible to act, for he did not know the way forward. Memories of his childhood returned: when he had escaped from the ghetto through the sewer; when he had been hidden away because he was a Jew destined for burning; when he ran from hiding place to hiding place across Europe; when he was beaten and humiliated; when he was treated as vermin; and later, during his years of unbelief, when he had nearly hurled himself off a cliff and had toyed with shooting himself.

After these memories passed like a wave of darkness, Elijah recalled other, better times when God had moved in his life, when grace and peace had been liberally given. Not once during all his long years had he been able to engineer these blessings of divine rescue. They had always been given by surprise, and often for reasons that did not become apparent until later. He knew that God saw him. And this had been enough.

Now he began quietly to shed the tears of abandonment, of grieving and acceptance, in which he knew his powerlessness and wordlessly thanked God for it. Peace returned and the Lord spoke to him at last. Only this:

My son, fulfill the task I have set before you.

6

Cities of the Plain

In his sleep that night, he had a recurring dream, the one he had dreamt before his departure from Ephesus to Jordan. Rather, it was two dreams.

In the first there was a violent storm. Like a shepherd, he was guiding a flock of children through a gloomy wasteland of sterile soil. He was disheartened by the enormity of his task.

Look up, said a voice.

He looked up and saw a distant city in the sky. It had twelve gates, and upon its walls millions of people were cheering, urging him to enter. He was some distance from the main gate, moving toward it at a creeping pace, for the children were crying, confused, and frightened, and he was delayed again and again when they scattered into the dark and he was forced to gather them together. He would not let the smallest of them lag behind and be lost. The storm was quickening in fury with howling wind and flashing lightning in the boiling clouds and in it the eyes of a serpent sought the children to devour them. The slowness of their flight toward sanctuary was at first a torment, but an angel came out of the gates and flew around the little flock with a golden cord, girding them and guiding them onward.

Then the dream melted into another. A skinny boy staggered through the rubble heaps of bombed ruins. He was naked, save for a tallith with which he wrapped his loins. He was sobbing for all that was lost in the world. "Everything is gone," he cried, "everything." He passed men and women who stopped and laughed at him.

"Repent!" he shouted at them.

"Repent? Repent of what?" they mocked.

"The fire is coming," he said.

"Fire?" they answered. "Look around. Everything is fine. There will be no fire."

"All is not fine," the boy sobbed.

"Peace," they shouted. "Peace!"

"There is no peace!" the boy cried out with great strength.

Then they threw stones at him, and he ran away. He fell and got up, fell again and crawled, cutting himself on broken glass. Through the ruins he went on hands and knees until he came to the edge of a bomb crater. In the bottom of the crater, lit by stubs of candles, was a priest saying Mass. His altar was a cardboard box, his chalice a tin cup, and his paten a cracked plate. The priest was the Pope, assisted by three bishops. Thirty or forty people knelt around the altar, dressed in rags. They were worshipping the Host the Pope lifted up. Its light was dazzling, and it pushed back the darkness for the space of two hours, and another hour, and a half hour. The people worshipped, but they were frightened. The Pope prayed, but his face streamed with tears.

Look up, said a voice.

Elijah was abruptly woken by the sound of rapping on the apartment door. When he opened it, he found a ten-year-old boy standing in the hallway. The child immediately began chattering in rapid-fire Arabic. Elijah had a fair grasp of the language, but the child's diction was impeded by a cleft palate. He heard "donkey" and "go to" and

"Ramallah"; the rest was unintelligible. Try as he might, Elijah could get nothing more from the boy, who laughed and laughed at the old man's inability to understand. Elijah tried Hebrew and English but elicited a blank look. In the end, the boy resorted to other means.

He made the sound of a braying donkey and covered one eye with his hand. Then he said, emphatically, "Ramallah, Ramallah", and pointed in the general direction of north. Then he pointed at Elijah's chest, made walking gestures with his fingers, and again pointed north. After that he skipped along the hallway and disappeared down the staircase.

Elijah stood in the open doorway, thinking. Brother Ass had gone to Ramallah, the city of Rachel. And today the President would be in the West Bank for the ceremony of reconciliation. No doubt it would take place in or near the city, because it was the Palestinian Authority's seat of government. Elijah was to walk there.

If the boy had been an angel in disguise, Elijah thought that he would have sensed it to some degree and would not have deliberated. But the lad had been no more than what he appeared, an Arab child with a message to deliver, his face full of eagerness and good humor. Clearly, Brother Enoch had sent him.

So he would go. If all went well, he would somehow connect with Enoch in the city, by providence, by other intermediaries, and they would consult about their next move. But should he literally walk? Perhaps the little fingers had meant only that he should go there. Ramallah was at least ten kilometers from Jerusalem. That would mean a thirty-minute drive by car, a little more by bus. It was a journey of several hours on foot, an arduous task for an old man in his condition. Nevertheless, he said, "I will walk."

It was still early when he left the apartment. The cool morning air and the clear skies in the light of the rising sun promised that the clement autumn weather would hold. He wore no distinctive clothing, only his white shirt and dark trousers, his old socks and shoes, his hidden scapular. His identity papers and money were pocketed, and for nourishment he carried a roll of bread and some dates. These and the water bottle fit easily into his small knapsack. The Mass kit and Divine Office remained in the apartment. On his head he wore a khaki cloth hat to ward off the sun.

Al Sheikh Jarrah was not far from Route 60, which would take him directly to Ramallah. The streets were already packed with vehicles heading north, in contrast to the inbound commuter traffic, which was lighter than usual. There were a lot of people on foot, most of them Arabs, some young tourists, and a few Jews. The squeal and roar of buses was deafening. A fleet of taxis was in motion, though their horns were quieter than usual.

Elijah was glad he had chosen to walk, because the vehicle traffic was verging on congestion, moving forward in fits and starts. Fortunately, the road to 60 offered sidewalks, and these continued for some kilometers along that main thoroughfare as well. Outside the city, the walkers were forced to keep to the paved shoulders.

The day grew warmer, and the route climbed higher into the hills. The people around Elijah were sweating, drinking from their water bottles—men with small children in back carriers, women pushing baby strollers, teenagers ambling with music plugs in their ears. There were many older people too, slower moving but determined. In general there was a festive mood among them all.

It took him three hours to reach the Qalandia checkpoint just south of Ramallah. He had expected to be delayed there as military or police inspected the papers of those entering the Palestinian territory. Security forces were indeed present at the bottleneck, intensely observing the passing crowds and glancing into vehicles, but the gates were wide open and the chief concern seemed to be to keep the people and the vehicles moving.

On the other side of the gate, Elijah slowed his pace for the final stage of the journey. Pausing on the edge of the crowd to refresh himself, he noted a Bedouin shepherd with a flock of about thirty sheep meandering along the roadside slope in the direction of Ramallah. The city's towers were visible in the valley ahead.

As Elijah finished the last of his water, three old women swept past him. Heavy in body and forcing their way through the crowd like a phalanx, they were holding each other's hands, swinging their arms and singing as they went past. They could have been sisters. Their brown faces were wrinkled with age and desert sun. They looked as though, without warning, they might either kiss you or snap at you. Their blouses were slightly open, revealing perspiring, spotted chests, and all three wore inexpensive chains about their necks. Hanging on one was a three-barred Byzantine cross, on another a small wooden crucifix, and on the third a Star of David.

Rachel's children, he thought.

Though her tomb was in Bethlehem, Rachel's home village of Ramah was held by tradition to be near or on the site of present-day Ramallah.

"A voice was heard in Ramah, wailing and loud lamentation. Rachel is weeping for her children; she refuses to be comforted for her children, because they are no more."

The prophet Jeremiah referred to Rachel's tears symbolically, because it was from Ramah that the Babylonian conquerors had deported the people of Israel into captivity.

The evangelist Matthew saw the slaughter of the innocents in Bethlehem as a fulfillment of Jeremiah's prophecy. In recent centuries, Ramallah had been a Christian town, and though it was now predominantly Muslim, it was still home for a substantial Christian minority.

By noon Elijah had arrived in the center of the city. It had prospered greatly since he had last seen it, when he had given a parish retreat just before the popular uprising, the first intifada. There were now many new apartment buildings and office towers. He went first to Holy Family Church, but it and its office were closed—with posters of the President and the day's events displayed on the door. Despite the fact that people were moving about nearby, Elijah tore the images off the door, and prayed for the protection of the church from further sacrilege.

Retracing his steps, he returned to the main road, where countless cars and buses had become immobilized in gridlock. Tens of thousands of people on foot were navigating through it in the direction of a hill on the eastern side of the city. Just as Elijah turned right to enter the streams of people, he clearly heard an interior voice say, *Turn left.*

Recognizing its authenticity, he turned left and began walking with no certain purpose. Leaving the congested streets behind, he came to an avenue and turned again, following the gentle instructions of the voice. Three blocks farther along, as he approached the entrance of a modern hotel, he heard, *Go inside.*

The lobby was a confection of marble and glass and gold. Elijah came to a stop a few steps from the reception desk, where a desk clerk gave him a professional look of inquiry.

"I am waiting," he said to her. She nodded and returned to reading her computer screen.

Hoping that Enoch would soon arrive, he waited and waited, presuming that he had heard the last of the voice. But it came one more time:

Enter the restaurant.

As he did so, an image flashed into his mind of a man seated alone at a table, smoking a cigarette and sipping from a brandy glass. He was deeply tanned, in his mid- to late forties, dressed in a shimmering silver suit and wearing jeweled rings and a gold wristwatch. A thin gold chain hung from his neck, and a gold ring circled one of his earlobes.

As Elijah went farther into the semideserted room, he turned into one of its wings, which was walled entirely with glass. It offered a view of the high place where the day's major event would occur. Seated at a table by the glass was the very man he had seen in his mind a minute before. The only difference between the inspiration and the reality was the three bodyguards who stood nearby, facing outward into the room. As Elijah took a step closer, they uncrossed their arms and opened their jackets. One of them stepped between Elijah and the man at the table. Another came forward and said, "This is a private dining room."

Elijah did not move.

The guard opened his jacket wide and put his hand on the butt of a pistol.

"Leave now," he said in Hebrew.

Another image flashed through Elijah's mind. He said, "Tell the man at the table 'black fish and blue dog'."

"Get out of here."

"Just tell him—'black fish and blue dog'—and let him decide. If he wishes me to go, I will go. You need not be afraid."

"Afraid," the guard snorted.

He signaled to another bodyguard. They conferred, and the second went to speak with the man at the table.

Then, after an inspection of his knapsack and a thorough patting of his body, Elijah was conducted to the table. A guard pulled out a chair for him, and he sat down facing the man across an expanse of white linen. On the table were an arrangement of flowers, a brandy bottle beside a half-full snifter, and an ashtray with a cigarette turning to ash at the end of a red alabaster holder.

The man laid down his knife and fork and pushed aside his plate of half-eaten rare steak. Sitting back, he examined Elijah with an expression that was both sour and amused. There was also curiosity.

"Black fish and blue dog," he rumbled in a deep voice, with an accent that Elijah could not place. His skin was dark, but his features appeared to be more Slavic than Arabian. His eyes were green.

Elijah said nothing, for he did not know what to say.

"Interesting," the man said, squinting as he lifted the cigarette holder. One of his attendants promptly refilled it with a fresh cigarette and held a lighter as the man inhaled a few puffs.

He exhaled the smoke above Elijah's head and asked him, "So, who sent you to me, messenger boy?"

Elijah shook his head.

"No one sent you? You came on your own initiative?"

"In a sense," Elijah murmured.

"And what is the meaning of your cryptic message?"

"I think you know its meaning. I do not."

With a slight frown, the man carefully tapped the ash from his cigarette, took a sip of brandy, and resumed his inspection of Elijah.

"You are just some old man who wanders in off the street to say 'fish and dog' to a stranger? Did you escape from a hospital?"

"No."

"Why these words?"

"They must be a key," said Elijah, "a key to understanding."

The man absorbed this and smiled humorlessly. "You wish to *understand* me?"

"The key is for your own understanding."

"*Zyd*?" the man asked with raised eyebrows.

Elijah nodded and asked, "What is your name?"

"My name? I have many names. And whoever sent you to me knows an older version. During the very brief duration of our relationship, you may call me Viktor. After all, that is my name for the present, the name of the man who owns this hotel. Everyone in Ramallah knows me—in Jerusalem too. Are you Mossad?"

"No," Elijah shook his head.

"Not even an extremely old agent, a *deceptively* old assassin?"

Elijah did not trouble to reply to this.

"Well, it would take little effort for anyone to discover that I own this magnificent enterprise. What else do you know?"

"Nothing."

Now the man jerked his head at the omnipresent guards. They stepped away and took up positions across the room, out of earshot.

In a lowered voice, their employer said, "But it seems you know I owned a nightclub in New York City by the name of the Blue Dog. Actually two blue dogs, with an ingenious neon sign, though I will not bore you with a description of what the dogs were doing. Then there was the Black Fish club in Moscow. That was a bad, bad place, though it made me a great deal of money. However, I am quite intrigued by you, because no one back then knew who really owned the clubs, you see. Or should I say that

the people who once knew are no longer with us in this
world. Where do you come from, America or Russia?"

"I am a citizen of Israel."

"May I see your papers?"

Elijah gave him his passport.

"Hmmm. *Pastore.* A Vatican passport. This is very
strange. Of course, it has happened countless times before
that the Vatican has been helpful to the hunted and the
haunted. Are you a banker? No? Well, if you are also an
Israeli citizen, as you claim, then we now know that you
have more than one identity. This means either one of
two things: Crime or espionage … or both."

"I am involved in neither."

"Very well, then let us return to the subject of the black
fish and the blue dog. How do you know about them?
And why do you wish to speak with me?"

"I do not know the purpose."

The man who called himself Viktor lifted his shoulders
in a distinctly Slavic shrug, as if to say, What can one do
with a fellow like this?

"Are you a shaman?" he asked.

"A shaman, no," Elijah replied with some revulsion.

"A pity. I am part owner of a major studio in Hollywood.
It's not a controlling interest but almost. We're making a
film called *The Shaman.* You seem to have some kind of
extrasensory perception, so I wonder if you dabble in magic
or that sort of thing? You don't? Oh, that's regrettable."

"Do you?"

"Do I what?"

"Do you dabble in it?"

"No. I'm fascinated but careful. I don't like anyone or
anything tinkering with my mind. Except, perhaps, for a
few well-crafted drugs, nothing and nobody gets to tinker
in my head. But it's a slow day, so go ahead and tinker."

"I would not know how," said Elijah.

He was beginning to understand Viktor in a way that even Viktor might not have understood. Without realizing it, the man was opening his thoughts in a manner that revealed his loneliness. And his unacknowledged craving for life to have meaning.

"All right. What else do you know about me? The hotels, the production companies, the fashion house in Paris, all these are public knowledge. Oh, and of course there's the Viktor line of designer pants and the Viktor cell phones in pastel colors."

As Viktor continued his list, Elijah looked through the pitiful skin of pride and vanity and into the vulnerable place where evil dwelt in the darkness—storing up acts and accusations stretching back to the man's childhood. But there was also something uncorrupted, the last remnant of innocence under siege.

Suddenly Viktor ceased speaking.

"Boys, why am I talking to this guy?" he shouted to his bodyguards.

"We don't know, sir," they called back.

"Does he look like a business associate?"

They chuckled dutifully.

Turning to Elijah, Viktor said, "They've never heard me talk so much. I don't talk. I say do this, do that. Shut up. Shoot him.... So what's your game, and why are you doing this to me?"

"I have no game."

"You told me you have a magic key."

"I told you that the words were a key to understanding. They are not magic, and I am not magic. I do not know for certain, but I think you named your club after a black fish because of what happened to you when you were a boy. And you named another club after a blue dog also because of what happened."

All semblance of pleasantness dropped from Viktor's face. "Who are you?" he said in a growl just above a whisper.

"As you say, a messenger."

"And I say again, from where?"

Elijah tried to form words of explanation, but he could not.

"Are you a Russian?"

"No," Elijah said.

Viktor laughed abruptly, leaned back, and gazed out the window at the mountain and the crowds climbing it.

"A swarm of ants," he said. "They've all come to see magic."

"Are you here to see him?" Elijah asked.

"I'm here because I'm here. Strictly business. But I can tell you that the magician on the hill is the greatest businessman of all time."

"Do you have business connections with him?"

"None. At least for the time being. Do you?"

"No, I am from a world that is antithetical to his."

"*Antithetical.* Now that's a big word. So, you are not an assassin, and you are not a mole from a competitor, and you are not a lackey of the magician. You could be simply crazy, or you might be a research librarian who examines the lives of public figures, or you might even be a biographer hoping to make money on a book about Israeli crime bosses, and you have connected a few dots and filled in a blank or two."

Elijah shook his head.

"You don't seem to be afraid of me. As a gesture of our friendship may I give you a bit of helpful advice? You really should be afraid. Possibly—no, probably—a few minutes from now I'm going to ask my executive assistants here to take you to a lonely spot in the hills and shoot you."

Elijah said, "If that is to happen, I forgive you."

"You forgive me?" he laughed.

"I do not know much," Elijah began in a slow voice, "very little, in fact. But I see what happened to you when you were young, the wound that will not heal."

Viktor's face settled into stillness. He leaned back in his seat, laced his fingers on his belly, and gazed at Elijah from under his brows.

"Continue."

"I see a little boy fishing in a river. There are birch trees all around."

"Birches, rivers, little boys," Viktor shrugged. "They're everywhere in Russia."

"It was not in Russia. You are not a Russian. You are Ukrainian."

For many years, Elijah had experienced the phenomenon of "reading souls", knowing things he had no natural way of knowing. It was infrequent and occurred mainly in confession and sometimes during counseling. It was usually mediated through interior images or very short scenes that appeared in his imagination and occasionally in specific words. Such lights from the Holy Spirit enabled him to advise those who had come to him for guidance and absolution. Rarely, perhaps only half a dozen times during his priestly life, had he been given an understanding or pure knowledge of someone who wanted none of his help. He thought that it was God's final effort to reach the invincibly unrepentant.

"Tell me more," said Viktor.

"Your father left your mother when you were seven or eight years old. You loved your mother and your baby sister, and you loved a dog that was precious to your family. Its name was Syniy, and you called it Syniyochka, Little Blue. It followed you everywhere. It gave you affection, and you loved it in return.

"Yet you were lonely and did not know why. You knew that your mother was a troubled woman and that your family was very poor. You thought that you should be the man of the family, to protect your mother and your sister, to provide for them, though this was not possible for one so young.

"You liked to fish. You felt like a man whenever you fished. At times you caught trout and small sturgeon. One day you hooked a large sturgeon, and after hours of fighting with it, you brought it in. You jumped into the water, and it cost all your strength to drag it onto the shore. It was a huge fish and seemed longer than you were tall, weighing even more than you. You felt so proud, so happy. Because you were often hungry, this catch was a boon to your body and your soul, above all to your family. There would be fish to cook, and there would be black caviar.

"On this river in the forest there was a *dacha* for privileged Russians. They too enjoyed fishing. On the day you caught your fish, they watched from the opposite shore, and they hailed you and saluted you and praised you. You felt very proud. These were fine men, you thought. They took you to their dacha. One of the men carried the fish for you, because it was too heavy for a boy. They gave you a sip of vodka to celebrate. Then more sips."

Elijah ceased speaking, his head bowed.

"What a magnificent imagination you have," Viktor whispered. "Go on, magician."

"They all became drunk. They shot your dog, and they took your fish. One of them raped you. They threw you naked and bleeding into the forest by the side of the road, and drove away with the fish."

Viktor jerked upright in his seat, his face flushing.

"You could know this only if you were the rapist," he said.

"I am not the rapist. There are other ways of knowing. I know that your name is Petro."

With a look of astonishment, the man stared at Elijah.

"No one knows this name," he said. "No one."

"Petro, you have never told anyone about what happened. You even managed to hide it from your mother. When you were twelve she became ill and died. You and your sister were sent to a state orphanage. You ran away from it to the city of Kiev."

"And then?"

"Are you sure you want to hear more?" Elijah asked.

"Sure, why not."

"In Kiev you starved on the streets, until you fell in with a band of young men who were prostitutes. You became a prostitute, and within a few years you were their leader. You were very beautiful in appearance, and you understood well the fallen part of human nature. Should I continue?"

"Yes," was the strangulated reply.

"Then there was the time of the lamb."

"A lamb?" said Viktor, obviously perplexed.

"You hated Russians—all Russians. It was like a black fire that burned ceaselessly within you. And then, one day, you stole a child from the street, a Russian child."

Now Viktor's face paled, and his mouth dropped open.

"You took him into the forest, and you slaughtered him on an altar."

"It was not an altar," Viktor breathed.

"The stone in the forest was as an altar, and upon it you made a covenant with evil."

The man seated across from Elijah now looked at him without expression.

"No one has ever known. No one *could* know about it," he said. "How do you know?"

"I see you, Petro. I see you as a small child. Do you remember how you loved your own name? Your grandmother told you stories about the apostle who was a fisherman. You were proud of your name because of this. She taught you prayers, the prayers of a child. On the day you caught the great fish, you knelt and prayed that God would send you a fish to feed your family. And God did send a fish. But the day of victory became a day of darkness when you were violated, and all faith was wiped away from your mind.

"Later, after you made the covenant, your power grew and grew. You made pornography—photographs and films. You made it and sold it, and with the profits you made more and more of it, and then came exports to the West and affiliation with crime syndicates. Ten thousand girls, thousands of boys, were your art."

"They were Russians."

"No, Petro, at first it was only Russians. Then came Ukrainians and others. Your world was full of young people with no work and no homes, no fathers to protect them."

"I fed them. Their art fed them."

"What died within them as their bodies were fed? Millions more were hooked by the evil appetite, and they too slowly died within themselves as they sank into that slavery."

"Would you prefer my artists to starve, old man?"

"I want them to live."

"How, then, should they live, if not by their art?"

"You are very wealthy. Could you not use this money to turn evil to good? Could you help them make a new start?"

Viktor—Petro—looked past the window, past the mountain, into the distance.

"Most of them are gone, lost in Europe or America. I cannot help them, even if I wanted to. The older ones go away, and there are always new ones to take their places."

"You could stop what you are doing. You could close the trap so no new ones fall into it."

"If I stop what I am doing, I will be awarded a bullet in the brain by my associates, and someone else will scoop up my territory."

"The covenant can be broken."

"It cannot be broken. I am what I am."

"At every moment the world can begin again, with grace."

"Grace?" he laughed humorlessly. "What is grace?"

"I am a priest of Jesus Christ. I can help you."

Petro looked long at Elijah, his face still expressionless. At one point his eyes flickered, and Elijah thought he saw regret, and within the regret a hope.

"The evil covenant can be broken," Elijah said again and waited for an answer. "You can be free."

Finally, the man called one of his bodyguards and whispered into his ear. With that, the guards surrounded Elijah and lifted him to his feet. Then two of them hustled him toward a door that took him out of the building by a back entrance. Behind him in the deserted restaurant, Petro sat without moving, his forehead in his hand, staring at the tabletop. He butted the ember of his cigarette in the uneaten meat.

They bound Elijah's wrists behind his back and pushed him into the rear of a black SUV with smoked windows. One of the guards sat beside him; the other drove. Because of blocked traffic, they took a series of back-streets, heading away from the mountain where the President was addressing an enormous crowd. Wave after wave of cheering could be heard through the vehicle's closed windows, thundering like the roars of a tsunami pouring through the city.

"You are a very stupid man," said the guard beside him.

"Don't waste your breath," said the driver.

"Did the boss say clean or wet?"

"Clean."

"But this guy could tell more with a little encouragement."

"He said clean, so clean it will be. He doesn't make mistakes. And he doesn't like mistakes."

"Back of the head?"

"No, in one ear and out the other."

"I forgive you for what you are about to do," said Elijah.

"Shut up, old man."

The guard forced Elijah's mouth open and rammed a black rubber ball into it. Then he bound it with a silk scarf. Elijah did not resist.

Knowing that his life was now coming to an end, he felt little fear for himself. But with a sinking heart he realized that he would not be able to fulfill his mission. Wordlessly he prayed throughout the remainder of the journey. The car climbed a short way into the western side of the hills surrounding Ramallah, following the route of a dry wadi. The driver turned onto a gravel road and stopped at a deserted spot. The two men dragged Elijah from the car and threw him to the ground.

Into your hands I commend my spirit, O Lord.

One of the guards unholstered his pistol and put the barrel to Elijah's ear.

The name of Jesus in several languages flowed through Elijah's mind as he gazed at his last sight in this world, dust and red stones and bramble bushes covered with gray leaves.

Yeshuah, Isus, Yehoshua, Yasu, Jezu ufam tobie . . .

The audible click from the gun was not followed by an explosion.

"Bang-bang," said the man with the gun.

"Rest in peace," laughed the other.

They stood looking down at Elijah, smirking.

"The boss says to tell you this, old man: Because you're only a little fish, he's throwing you back into the water, alive."

With that, they got into the car and drove away.

For a time Elijah lay without moving, still bound, concentrating on breathing. When he could muster his strength, he got into a sitting position and then slowly rose to his feet. The plastic bands around his wrist were too hard to break, but he was able to stumble toward a dead tree. A snake slithered away from beneath it. He pushed his head carefully down on a twig, scratching his cheek, and forced the twig to slide under the scarf around his face. Dropping to his knees made the twig push the scarf up far enough to let him spew the ball from his mouth. Now he gulped air until his breathing eased and his heartbeat slowed.

When he was ready, he walked unsteadily back down the gravel road. Where it ended at another road, hard packed and well traveled, though for the moment deserted, he stood and waited. Minutes later, he saw a distant figure walking uphill from the direction of the city, a man in a djellaba moving at a leisurely pace, leaving a trail of dust in the air behind him. As he drew closer, the man waved to Elijah.

It was Enoch.

7

Riders in the Chariot

"Ooo, this is not a good thing," crooned Enoch as he sawed through the bindings with a piece of broken bottle found by the side of the road. "What happened?"

"I have had a rather difficult day."

"I can see you have, Bishop. There, now you are free. Rub those wrists and make the blood happy."

"Brother, how did you find me?"

"I was down in the city center waiting for you. I was sure you would come there. And then, when the thing on the mountain started up and all the people went crazy with cheering and you didn't come, I thought maybe you hadn't understood the message. And I could not go up the mountain alone because to give witness we must go together, right? Two witnesses are needed."

"Yes. But how—"

"As I was praying for you, in my thoughts I saw two mountains. One was the mountain where the liar is speaking. The other was across the valley from it, this one. And I knew in my heart that I should walk up this good mountain."

"And here you are."

"Here I am!" declared Enoch with a grin.

"Thanks be to God."

"*Allah hu akbar.*"

"God is indeed good."

Feeling dizzy, Elijah sat down on a rock. Enoch gave him water. When he had revived a little, Elijah said, "We must go now to the other mountain."

"Bishop, you don't look strong enough for that."

"We are running out of time, Brother. We must confront him now."

"God is master of time. And you need to rest."

"Yes, but our task is clearly before us, and we must not delay."

"*God* is master of time," Enoch repeated, with a tone that was both respectful of the bishop's office and mildly reprimanding.

"Besides, there is no place for us to rest," Elijah countered.

"We will have rest, but not in this barren place. Now we should walk down to the city. Maybe, if you are feeling well enough when we get there, we could try to walk up the evil mountain."

"Agreed, dear Enoch. So, let us begin."

During the hour of their descent, Elijah tried to get an explanation out of Enoch regarding his absence the previous days. Why had he not returned to the apartment? In answer, the brother related a convoluted story about his confusion when he realized Elijah had not come to the plaza of the Wall. At that point he left, intending to return to the apartment in Al Sheikh Jarrah, but about halfway there he thought he was being followed by two men on foot—both Jewish, both plainclothes. It came to him also that if they were to arrest him, or even simply to track him, it would be better not to lead them to the apartment. So he stopped at a grocery store and paid a little boy to deliver the message that he was going to Ramallah. He knew the city would be the site of the President's next major event, and he thought that Elijah would inevitably want to go there. He caught a bus to Ramallah, which his followers also caught. But he shook them off at the Qalandia checkpoint. After he was through the barrier, he hastened to lose himself in the crowd. In the city center, he happened to meet his friend Amal, who was in town trying to find his parish priest, who had disappeared. Amal urged Enoch to come with him to a place of safety, a farming community in the hills north of Ramallah.

"Did the boy give you the message?" asked Enoch. "Or did the angels guide you here?"

"I received the message. But I think the angels were also at work."

Elijah then recounted what had happened to him. Regarding Viktor-Petro he gave only a general picture, subtracting the man's name and the specifics of his sins. He said only, "He is a person who does very great evil. He regrets what he has done but sees no way out of it. I tried to speak to him about Christ's mercy."

"And he tried to kill you for it."

"It would seem so. But he did not kill me."

"This is true," said Enoch with a philosophical air then added with a whiff of irony, "This is a bonus."

"Are you never afraid, Brother?"

"I am always afraid, Bishop."

"Really? You never look it."

"*La taqlaq! La taqlaq!* Don't worry!—that's what I tell myself."

"And so you should. Jesus is with us."

"Always. If we are at a nice supper, he's there with us. If we are on the cross, he's on it with us."

"You are right, Brother. There are times when I forget this."

"Of course we forget. You and I, we are little donkeys. Sometimes we just carry what's on our backs, and we keep

our noses pointed ahead, and we put one foot in front
of the other across the desert. That's what donkeys are
supposed to do, right? And if we are carrying our Lady and
the baby Jesus and sometimes forget it, they understand."

"I believe they do. Should we pray?"

"A good idea."

Elijah had lost his rosary and everything else in his
missing knapsack, but Enoch had his bag, with water
bottles, bread, a string of large brown beads, and a breviary.
First, they prayed the Rosary as they walked along, asking
the Mother of God to intercede for their mission, to open
the path ahead of them. Then Enoch led midafternoon
prayer, holding the breviary before him and stumbling at
times on small rocks in the road and at other times over
some of the words.

As always, his whole heart is in it, mused Elijah.

By the time the road brought them lower in the hills
to the outcropping villages, they could hear an undulat-
ing rumble from across the valley, the crowd still erupting
in cheers. As they entered the city proper, loudspeakers
on street corners were broadcasting band music. Elijah
recognized the Israeli national anthem, "Hatikva" ("The
Hope"), and the Palestinian national anthem, "Fida'i"
("My Redemption"). As they reached the city center,
cars were already reversing out of the streets, and the
first streams of pedestrians were heading away from
the mountain in the direction of the southern highway.

Looking up at the heights, Elijah and Enoch saw a white
helicopter rising and veering toward Jerusalem.

"We are too late," said Elijah.

"*La taqlaq,*" said Enoch.

For an hour they waited at a corner near Holy Family
Church, where Enoch had arranged for a friend to meet
him after the ceremonies on the mountain.

"Did you think we would not be arrested while fulfilling our mission?" Elijah asked.

"It was my hope that we would not be arrested. A small hope, very small. But I thought we should have help, just in case the little birds escaped from the lion's mouth."

"Brother, we did not even enter the lion's mouth, and this is a grief to me."

"To be honest, Bishop, it is a relief to me. No, it is a relief *and* a grief. God has spared us for a better day."

"Yes, glory to his name. Today is the fifth day. Tomorrow our adversary goes to the Golan Heights to meet with the leaders of Israel and Syria for a permanent peace treaty. It is now clear that our task will be in Jerusalem, on the seventh or the eighth day."

"Then tomorrow we will rest."

Brother Enoch suddenly grinned and waved to a yellow minivan lurching down the street in their direction. As it pulled up to the curb and idled fitfully, Elijah noted the Arabic and Hebrew letters on its hood and side: Jericho First Fruits, surrounded by garishly painted figs, lemons, plums, oranges, and pomegranates. At the wheel sat a young Palestinian man in jeans and T-shirt, with a checkered baseball cap perched backward on his head.

"Get in, get in, get in," he shouted over the sputtering roar of the engine. Elijah climbed into the back, and Enoch took the front passenger seat.

Greetings without introductions were exchanged all around, but it was clear that Enoch knew the driver well enough to tease. The other played along easily, and Elijah wondered, as he had so often over the years, at the small one's tendency to levity in dangerous situations. Were they in danger? Perhaps not yet.

"We're going to stay with Amal's community tonight and tomorrow," Enoch shouted over his shoulder. "They're good people, you'll see."

"Our driver's name gives me hope," said Elijah.

The two in front laughed, for Amal means "hope" in Arabic.

"That's what my grandmother says," Amal shot back.

But the vehicle's broken muffler was too loud for further conversation.

Leaving the city behind, they headed north by secondary roads. Half an hour's drive brought them through variegated countryside of olive groves and dry terraced hills rising above small tracts of bottomland, green with farm plots and citrus orchards. A few kilometers past the town of Kafr Malik, they turned right onto a dirt road and went still higher into more rugged terrain. The region was relatively unpopulated, though flocks of sheep grazed on the brown grassy hillsides, and a few goats rummaged in the dusty roadside bushes. Between gaps in the hills, the great white wall of the Jordan Valley's eastern escarpment was now visible.

When the van turned onto a narrow lane of rough stones, it bounced and rattled for what seemed interminable minutes, until finally it came to a halt in a long, narrow vale, roughly ten acres in size. Its lower slopes were covered with grapevines and fruit trees of various kinds. The valley floor was dominated by garden plots, where half a dozen people were harvesting vegetables into wicker baskets.

Two cars and a pickup were parked in a yard before a single-story stone building roofed in red tile. Behind it a cluster of smaller houses sprouted, and beyond these rose an array of solar panels. To the left of the main building was a cement block structure that appeared to be a barn of sorts, for there were dozens of fruit bins stacked by its wide entrance.

Amal led them to the open doorway of the main building, where an orange and white cat lay sleeping on the step. From the interior came the smell of baking bread. Amal went inside, calling to someone.

"A safe place," said Enoch, pointing to a sign above the doorway. On it, beneath a symbol of the Jerusalem cross, was written "House of Reconciliation" in Hebrew and Arabic. Beneath these words was the Arabic word *Rahmah*, "mercy", in the sense of universal nurturing love. Then came the Hebrew word *Teshuvah*, "repentance", literally "turning to embrace each other".

"They don't know who you are," Enoch whispered to Elijah as they stepped into the front hallway. "Should we keep it that way?"

"Do you trust them?"

"This is where I lived after the destruction of Stella Maris."

"For now, it is better that my identity and our mission remain unknown."

"No problem. They accept anyone who comes, and today I'm bringing them a nice Jewish man to learn about their work—that's you."

Amal popped his head out of a doorway at the end of the hall and waved.

"Come," he called.

Enoch, followed by Elijah, went into a spacious kitchen where three young women were scrubbing vegetables. A fourth woman, corpulent and elderly, was up to her elbows in bread dough, which she was kneading on a stainless steel table. Loaves of baked bread were cooling on a sideboard.

"Enoch," said the older woman, "you bring us a new friend!"

"A good friend, Katé, a very good friend."

Katé appeared to be queen of the kitchen, for she gave the other women instructions as she washed her hands and arms at a sink and removed a large apron.

"Now, let us go into the garden and talk," she said. "Amal, dear one, go tell the boys in the barn we'll have tea soon."

She toddled out a back doorway onto a sunny patio, shaded with a grape arbor and furnished with three refectory tables and benches. At the head of each table were old wooden chairs, held together with wire and plywood patches.

"Sit down, sit down, sirs, here on the best seats," said the woman.

She and Elijah and Enoch drew three chairs together, facing each other.

"Enoch, sweetie, you are back sooner than we thought."

"Yes, Katé. And not alone, as you can see. Would it be possible for us to stay with you today and tomorrow?"

"Certainly. The guest room is empty. Why don't you go check it now and make sure there are towels and sheets."

Enoch jumped up to do as she had bidden.

Elijah noted that the woman exercised authority with affection. People obeyed her happily, it seemed.

Now she and Elijah regarded each other thoughtfully, without speaking. The woman was in her mid- to late seventies, with white hair and a dark, heavily lined Arab face, though her features were not exactly Palestinian. She wore a rusty-orange cotton dress that hung loosely from shoulder to ankle, with tortoise-shell glasses on a cord about her neck and large turquoise earrings. Her intelligent eyes lost their whimsical maternal look and settled into an unblinking gaze that probed him gently. Elijah returned the gaze, wondering what to make of her.

To his great surprise, she stood up, bent over, and put her arms around him, hugging him in a prolonged embrace. Embarrassed, at a loss for how to react, he smelled a curious mixture of baked bread, lily, and cinnamon. When she straightened, keeping her hands on his shoulders, he saw tears in her eyes. And then, to his astonishment, she knelt before him and bowed her head.

"Give me your blessing, O man of God," she said.

Elijah made the sign of the cross over her.

She nodded her thanks, and he helped her to her feet. When she had taken her seat again, she said, "Welcome to our house. It is a blessing to have you here."

"Do you know who I am?" Elijah asked.

"I do not know your name or why you are here," she replied, "but in the communion I know who you are."

"Who do you think I am?"

"You are one who bears many wounds for Jesus, and there is a grave task before you."

"Enoch has spoken of our mission, then?"

"Our little brother has told me nothing. But now I see many things I did not understand yesterday. Enoch is God's fool—and thus he is wise in his way, though not always prudent, I think. But that is the way of donkeys. I understand donkeys because I am one too.

"Oh, how beautiful is the heart of Jesus! How beautiful that he loves us in our foolishness, he who suffered so much for us. Now our poor world grows indifferent to what he gave, though not all. We still find many who are not blind."

"I see that you are not blind, madame."

"Oh, dear one, I am blind enough. Very blind, actually. But I have the privilege of being a mother."

"It is a very great thing to be a mother."

"And a very great thing to be a father. *You* are a father. Despite your kippah, I know that you are a priest. And something more. I see a shepherd of the flock of the Lord. Am I mistaken to see this?"

"No, you are not mistaken. I am a bishop."

She blinked and swallowed.

"Welcome, Bishop. You do not have to tell me your name. You need not tell me why you are here."

"I can tell you that I am here at the bidding of the Holy Father."

"You come from Rome, then?"

"From Rome by way of Ephesus. My name is Elijah."

"My name is Katherine Shafiq."

"You are not Palestinian."

"I am Egyptian."

"How did you come to live in Israel?"

"My late husband was Coptic Orthodox. Since my birth in Alexandria, I have always been a Coptic Catholic. For years I taught art history at Cairo University. After my husband was killed by radical Islamists in a massacre at his church, I was a broken person—really quite a mess, I was. I left the university, and later I taught in Italy for some years. There my daughter married a young Israeli student, and they moved to Israel. I could not bear to be so far from my grandchildren, so I came here too. Then I began to work for peace in this holy land, which, as you know, is an impossible task."

"Our Lord is the master of the impossible."

Katherine smiled broadly.

"Yes. That is why we live the impossible life here. See how he makes the desert bloom?"

"And the more difficult task, to make fruitful the desert in men's hearts."

"Exactly. Of course, everything you see around you here in this little valley is the fruit of uncountable sacrifices. They have been made by many lives given to Christ, to holy peace, not for the peace that the world offers. The need for sacrifice never ceases. Not until the end of the ages will this truth change."

"Does your family live here at the House of Reconciliation?"

"They have moved to America. So many young Israelis emigrate to America."

"And that is *your* sacrifice."

"Yes, my sacrifice is to be apart from them. But I offer my longing to God so that he can use it to bring others together."

"Do you have any harassment from the Israeli or Palestinian authorities?"

"Oh, a little from time to time. But the governments aren't the problem, really. I should say, not the source of the problem. The root is the fear in all hearts."

"Are you ever afraid?"

"Afraid? To be killed, to be arrested, to be constantly misunderstood—none of these frighten me. Only one thing do I fear, and that is my own heart's hankering for contentment, for a certain kind of happiness. I fear that one day I will say to myself, 'Listen, Katherine, you have done enough; now you can take a reward for yourself. Go and retire in California and enjoy your beloveds.' My son-in-law teaches at Berkeley. My grandchildren have surfboards and play electric guitars—the American dream, you know. But I worry a lot about those kids. They live on the computer all the time. They don't have any faith. Maybe if I go to California I can help them find it."

"Of course you worry about your children and your grandchildren. If I may be bold, lady, you need not fear your contradictory feelings. You know that our hearts are revealed in what we choose. You have looked at me and known me for what I am. I look at you, and I see a woman on a cross. But I also see that your dying here gives life to others. You have many, many children, I believe."

"Yes, Bishop Elijah. I have many children in spirit. I love them, and they love me. And in truth I am very happy. Happiness is not without sorrows, even great sorrows."

"You have joy."

"I have a joy beyond the world's measure." She laughed and wiped her eyes. "I also have flat feet, diabetes, and bad blood pressure. And I am quite grumpy in the morning before I take my coffee. Oh, look, here comes our tea!"

The kitchen girls, chatting among themselves, came onto the patio and began placing baskets of bread on the tables, along with plates of butter and cheeses, jam, and steaming teapots.

Groups of people entered the arbor at random, eyeing Elijah curiously and calling greetings to Katherine, some of them addressing her as Mother or Mom.

She returned each greeting with *Neshama*, "my soul", "my darling", as well as smiles, pats, and kisses.

Enoch returned and sat down with Katherine and Elijah at the end of the table.

"They are all followers of the Lord," she said quietly to Elijah. "May I introduce you by name?"

"If you are sure they can keep it confidential," Elijah replied.

"They can. Each in his way has suffered to arrive at this place; each has overcome the spirit of the world. And I know they would be so grateful if you would offer the Holy Sacrifice for us. Is it possible? Would you do it?"

"Of course I will. Later this evening, if you wish."

Katherine stood and made a small clap with her hands. Up and down the tables conversations ceased and expectant faces turned to her.

"A priceless gift comes to us today," she said. "Our visitor is a bishop whom the Lord has sent to stay awhile under our roof."

This was greeted by a few exclamations of thanks to God.

"His work is in the heart of the Lord," Katherine continued, "and the angels cover him with a veil of hiddenness for a time. Can we guard his secret?"

All heads nodded emphatically, and voices murmured agreement.

"Our guest is Bishop Elijah from Rome. He will offer Mass after chores tonight."

"I would be happy to hear confessions beforehand," Elijah said.

They thanked him with smiles or with words in various languages. Several stood up and came to him for personal introductions.

Among them were five Sabras who were Christian converts. "*Shalom aleikhem,*" they said as each in turn shook his hand. There were seven Palestinians, four of them born and raised as Melkite Catholics; the other three were catechumens preparing for baptism into the Roman Catholic Church. "*As-salaamu alaykum,*" they said, some of them kissing his hand.

Then came a French nun in her thirties, fresh faced and glowing, followed by an intense, middle-aged Irish woman. There was a tall Croatian man in his forties, a German woman in her late sixties, and a man in his fifties on leave from the American university where he taught theology. All of these were Catholics of various rites. A Turkish seminarian with the Orthodox Patriarchate of Constantinople also came forward to meet the bishop. The welcome was warm but brief because they all had to get back to their work.

"For the time being there are twenty-eight people in the community," Katherine said to Elijah. "Some live here permanently; others have come to give a month or a year of their lives. Not everyone has shown up for tea, but you'll meet the others at supper."

Katherine took Elijah to the chapel, an austere room capable of holding about thirty people. Its walls were mortared bricks, and the floor was flagged with uneven white stone. The ceiling was whitewashed cement with a round cupola above the small sanctuary and cedar altar. On the wall behind the altar hung an olive-wood crucifix and Byzantine icons of Christ and the Mother of God. There were no pews, only rough wooden benches.

A man and a woman were kneeling at the front, with a baby asleep in a basket beside them. A third adult sat in a wheelchair facing the tabernacle, which was a silver dove suspended from the ceiling behind the altar. The breast of the dove was open, revealing the Blessed Sacrament. A red vigil lamp burned in a wall niche beside it.

Katherine left Elijah there. He knelt and offered a prayer of thanks for these people and for this place where he might have a little respite, even if only for a short time. Feeling the terrible weakness of his age, he remembered that he had walked from Jerusalem that morning and later had walked down the mountain at Ramallah. The bread and cheese was all he had eaten since his meager breakfast. His hands began to tremble as he recalled that only a few hours earlier he had prepared himself for death, with a gun to his head. How was it possible that so much could be compressed into a single day?

He drifted down within himself, resting in stillness and the familiar sense of timelessness. The future was completely unknown to him, but it was enough to be here, now, waiting and empty. The presence in the tabernacle was with him. Everything—everything—was in God's hands.

Enoch came into the chapel and knelt beside Elijah for a few minutes. Then he shook Elijah's arm and said, "You need to lie down. I'll take you to your room."

The guest room was in one of the cottages behind the main building. It had two narrow beds and a sink with a single tap. A warm breeze came through the small open window, which offered a northern exposure with a view of a barren upper hillside. On the sill was a pot of purple hyacinth blooming out of season. On the wall facing the window hung a crucifix beside a small icon of the Lebanese Maronite hermit Saint Charbel Makhlouf. Elijah kissed the crucifix and the icon. Exhausted, he lay down on the bed, where he slept for two hours, until he was awakened by Amal, who had come to fetch him.

The evening meal was served in a large refectory off the kitchen. By the time Elijah arrived, the residents had already seated themselves at three long tables covered with flowered oilcloth. The walls were soft yellow, and the only decoration was a painting at the end of the room. Katherine came forward and took Elijah by the hand, leading him to an empty spot on a bench at the table beneath the painting. Glancing at its bright reds and golds, he saw the prophet Elijah being taken up into heaven in a fiery chariot, his cloak falling toward a man reaching upward to receive it—the prophet Elisha. Riding in the chariot with Elijah were numerous people of diverse ages and races, smiling and waving—a rather creative departure from the biblical theme.

"An unusual painting, Katherine," he said.

"I know. People often say it's not correct, according to Scripture."

"It seems not."

"Its title is *Because He Was Faithful*. Our dear friend Father Ephraim painted it when he was a young man. Look closely at the riders in the chariot."

Elijah noted that there were twelve little figures accompanying the prophet. One carried a radiant chalice, another a Bible; others carried crosses or instruments of martyrdom.

"Elijah the prophet was human like us," Katherine explained. "You remember how he grew weary and discouraged. Terrified actually. He was ready to give up; he wanted to die. Then the angel strengthened him, and he went on to do the amazing things."

"But there were no other people in the chariot when he was taken up. Clearly, the painting is an allegory."

"Yes, because he was faithful, many souls went to paradise. And he affected our salvation too."

Just then, the man in the wheelchair propelled himself into the room and found a place next to Elijah at the head of the table. He greeted Elijah with a garbled *salaam*. His face had been badly burned, and though it was now healed the scarring was severe. His legs had been amputated below the knees. Much of his scalp had been ravaged, though patches of bristling black hair testified to his youth. His bare forearms were also marked by burn scars, though he used them normally, extending his hand for a shake.

"Peace be upon you, little son," said Elijah in Arabic.

"And upon you, sir. My name is Ibrahim."

"Ibrahim," Elijah said.

At Katherine's request, Elijah stood and prayed the blessing over the meal, and then the hum of conversation and the clatter of utensils began.

As he filled his plate with steaming vegetables, Elijah felt suddenly indifferent to the food, for his heart was entirely transfixed by Ibrahim.

"Where are you from?" he asked.

"Iraq."

"Are you visiting here?"

"This is now my home. I was caught in the hell that came with ISIS, later the Islamic State, they called themselves. My family was Christian, and all are in paradise. I am the only survivor. Please, would you hear my confession?"

"Of course. We can meet in the chapel after supper."

Slowly, Elijah turned to his meal, but in his mind he saw a lamb bleeding upon an altar.

Across from him sat the Croatian, a gentle giant named Krešimir. The man understood none of the languages used around the tables but could converse in broken English. Elijah learned that he was a journalist and novelist from Bosnia-Herzegovina. He was also a publisher of Catholic reading materials, which had run him afoul of a jihadist terrorist group in Bosnia. He had been captured and held for ransom and then finally released in a prisoner exchange. Arriving in Croatia, he was arrested for "subversive activities", meaning his Catholic journalism. While awaiting trial, he was released on an exorbitant bail, raised by friends. Though it was a very large amount of money to lose, these friends urged him to go into hiding. But Krešimir wanted to stand trial, believing it crucial to bear witness to Christ publicly. Then, while praying, he had felt a strong prompting to go to the Holy Land.

"Why to the Holy Land?" Elijah asked.

"I don't know for sure," he replied. "I know only must come here to pray for return of Christ. I don't want to leave my homeland. If in prison, maybe even die, I offer to Jesus. But God wants me here, so I come. I am crazy maybe?"

"Not in the least," Elijah smiled.

"I am illegal person here. I hope is not scandal to you."

"I have my own problems with the law, Krešimir. You pray for the return of the Lord. Do you know the book of Revelation?"

The man seemed not to understand the question.

"The Apocalypse?"

"*Apokalipsa Svetog Ivana*? Yes, I think much about. I pray. *Antikrist* is growing power, yes?"

"I believe so."

Krešimir regarded Elijah thoughtfully, nodded, and dipped into his bowl of lentils with a spoon.

This time, in his mind's eye Elijah saw a noble and virtuous warrior riding a white horse.

To Krešimir's left sat the French nun, her work overalls replaced by a white habit. She left off her conversation with the person beside her and addressed Elijah in Hebrew:

"Welcome, dear Bishop. I am *Soeur* Marie-Thérèse. We are so happy to have you with us. We have not had the sacraments for the past two weeks."

"Do you have a resident priest?" he asked.

"Our chaplain, Father Ephraim, died six months ago. Since then, priests from Jerusalem or Ramallah take turns driving out here to offer Sunday Masses. But now they have stopped coming, and we have had no word from them."

"Has no one phoned to explain?"

"We have no cell phones and no landline into the valley. We rely on the old methods—post and word of mouth. Amal tells us that the parish in Ramallah is locked up and none of the parishioners know where the priests have gone. Do you know what is happening?"

"It appears that priests and leaders of religious orders have been apprehended or placed under house arrest. Parishes are closed. A man I spoke with in Jerusalem says that it may be a temporary situation, a measure by the government to minimize all potential public protest."

"And are Muslim spiritual leaders being arrested?"

"I do not know. My guess is that they are not, since the governments do not wish to provoke riots."

"And they know that Christians do not riot," she sighed. "This is about the events in Jerusalem, this President who is gaining so much influence, isn't it?"

"It is."

"I could not help overhearing Krešimir talking with you. He said *Apokalipsa* and *Antikrist*."

Elijah nodded. "What are your thoughts on the matter, Sister?"

"I have never been a person who focuses on the end times, Bishop. But in my prayer and meditations I see that much of what the prophets and our Lord foretold seems to be materializing before our eyes. I do not want to jump to conclusions, but ..."

"Do many in the community feel as you and Krešimir do?"

"I think all of us do, in our different ways. Some more than others. The lady from Ireland is very strong on this. Mother Katherine is cautious about private interpretation. She worries about us losing sight of our calling here."

"What is your calling?"

"We try to live the beatitudes. We are to be a living example of peace. Here, a very beautiful grace is given—the vocation to love. I love my brothers and sisters, even those who in my younger days I would have found extremely difficult to be around. Do you know what I mean?"

"You do not mean race and religion. You mean personalities and temperaments."

"Exactly." She smiled. "Exactly."

"You are a consecrated religious. How have you come to be apart from your community?"

"I am a member of an order from France. We are part contemplative, part active. Twelve years ago, our mother superior sent me to our convent in Beirut to work with the poorest of the Palestinians in the city. Eight years ago I became the superior of our house in Gaza City. No one harmed us, which surprised me because I expected to be killed in Gaza. We made dear friends there, despite the occasional outbursts of suspicion. Then I was sent to open a little house in Ramallah. Three years ago, the sisters were all called back to France, but the superior general of our order asked me to move to the House of Reconciliation for a time. She is a friend of Katherine's from her years in Cairo."

"Katherine is a friend to everyone," said a voice to Elijah's right. He now noticed the young man sitting beside him.

"Especially to those who bring her favorite espresso, Pasco," said Sister Marie-Thérèse, laughing.

"*Sì, sì, sì,* it's true. But how can anyone help loving me, gifts or no gifts! Excuse me, Bishop, I am Pasquale."

"I am happy to meet you, Pasquale," said Elijah in Italian. "Have you lived here long?"

With a flash of perfect white teeth and vivid dark eyes, Pasquale explained that he had been a "perpetual visitor" for years. He first met Katherine when he was a child, when she taught art history in Florence and became a close friend of his parents. For several years now, he had come in the summer months to help with the farming, and sometimes during the Christmas break. He was a professor of literature at the University of Florence and would be returning there in a few days for the autumn semester.

Elijah was surprised, because Pasquale could have been mistaken for a sixteen-year-old. But a closer look revealed a few grey hairs at the temples, a few wrinkles around the eyes whenever he smiled. As Pasquale went on, bantering with the sister and making the others around them laugh—even Ibrahim could not restrain a broken chortle—Elijah could see both his sparkling intelligence and a childlike heart.

"Enough, enough, *carissimo*," Katherine shouted. "Bishop needs to hear confessions. Let him finish his supper."

In a small room off the sanctuary, Elijah heard confessions. Many in the community availed themselves of the sacrament. Each penitent raised questions and asked for Elijah's advice, and thus he found himself giving a great deal more counsel than was usual for him.

Ibrahim's confession was the last before Mass. The quiet increased in Elijah as he listened to the young man's very simple presentation of his sins. Rare were the times when he had felt the presence of Christ within himself while hearing confessions. *In persona Christi* and *alter Christus* were foundational to him, and he had never experienced doubt about the efficacy of Christ's operating through his priesthood. Yet he had not, until now, sensed such fullness in it. When Ibrahim finished telling his sins through his burned mouth, Elijah gave him a penance, absolved him according to the ritual, and blessed him. For a minute or so, neither Ibrahim nor Elijah moved. Elijah searched for words of consolation and encouragement to give the young man, but found none. Instead he took Ibrahim's ravaged hand and held it. As he did so, he recalled the words of Saint Paul: "It is no longer I who live, but Christ lives in me." Ibrahim bent over in his wheelchair and kissed Elijah's right hand. Elijah bent and kissed the scars on Ibrahim's hands.

Ibrahim straightened and looked at Elijah. And there it was: the soul shining brightly through the young man's eyes, light streaming outward through the damaged flesh.

"How great are the glory and the love coming to you, Ibrahim," Elijah said. "Rejoice, for truly he is coming soon."

Ibrahim said simply, "*Shukran*, thank you" and wheeled himself out of the room.

More than thirty people crowded into the chapel, including a few local farmers and their families. Elijah offered Mass in the Latin rite. The first reading was from

the book of Ezekiel, the passage about the prophet's call to
be a "watchman" for God's people. He must speak words
of warning with the knowledge that few, if any, would
truly heed him:

> As for you, son of man, your people who talk together
> about you by the walls and at the doors of the houses,
> say to one another, each to his brother, "Come, and hear
> what the word is that comes forth from the LORD." And
> they come to you as people come, and they sit before you
> as my people, and they hear what you say but they will not
> do it; for with their lips they show much love, but their
> heart is set on their gain. And behold, you are to them like
> one who sings love songs with a beautiful voice and plays
> well on an instrument, for they hear what you say, but
> they will not do it. When this comes—and come it will!—
> then they will know that a prophet has been among them.

In his homily, Elijah spoke about the humanity of
prophets, their flaws, their emotional turbulence caused by
their tendency to fear. He described Ezekiel's seemingly
impossible task to inform a whole people that they were
about to be overcome and taken into slavery in exile.
There was Isaiah's terror in the face of an invading army
and Jeremiah's initial fear before the people. The prophet
Elijah had been discouraged under the threat of Jezebel,
had fled into the desert, and had prayed that God would
take his life. Indeed, in his dismay he had felt that he had
reached the very end, when in fact, with divine interven-
tion, the greater part of his work was about to begin.

During his homily, people listened raptly, with the
exception of a few babies and toddlers. Whenever the little
ones cried or made a distracting fuss, he merely paused,
smiling, hearing the sound of life and, God-willing, the
sound of the future.

The Gospel reading of the day had been an account of Jesus speaking to the apostles about their authority:

> Truly I tell you, whatever you bind on earth shall be bound in heaven, and whatever you loose on earth shall be loosed in heaven. Again, I say to you, if two of you agree on earth about anything they ask, it will be done for them by my Father in heaven. For where two or three are gathered in my name, there am I in the midst of them.

Elijah exhorted them to pray always, to pray together, and to pray especially in times when all hope seemed lost.

"Such times may soon be upon us," he concluded. "Indeed they have already begun in part. Soon the great dragon will make war upon all those who follow Jesus. The enemy will hate you and bring all manner of calumny against you because of his envy. Remember always that the One who is within you is infinitely greater than the dragon. Within you is the power of the Lamb who was slain and lives again. Yours is not strength as the world understands it, yet it is greater than all earthly powers.

"For a time, the enemy is masked and appears to the world as light, though he is darkness. When he reveals himself, his malice will be unleashed as never before. Take heart, beloveds, that great in your midst is the Holy One of Israel, our Savior Jesus. Like the prophets before you, like the apostles and saints, you will have fear, yet you will overcome this fear by his presence, by the power of the Blood of the Lamb. When you see the things that are about to happen, do not let yourself fall into despair. Look up! Look up, for your redemption is near at hand."

For an hour after Mass, Elijah heard more confessions. Finally, consoled but physically depleted, he made his way back to the guest room. There he found that Enoch was already sleeping. He lay down on his own bed and fell instantly asleep.

In the night, he stirred and awoke. Sitting upright in the darkness, he did not know what had roused him from his dreams. These had been pleasant: young again, he was walking in grassy pastures by the walls of a golden city, surrounded by children who danced and sang as they accompanied him on his journey. There was no sun in the blue sky above, for the sun—or a source of all light—was within the city.

Groggy, rubbing his eyes, he noted a gentle perfume in the air. The window was open, and he supposed the scent came from the hyacinth or from the garden below. As full consciousness returned he realized that the perfume was neither hyacinth nor any other familiar scent. The room glowed faintly in the light of a quarter moon, and with a skipped heartbeat he saw a form standing at the foot of the bed. It was a man looking at him.

"Who are you?" whispered Elijah, making the sign of the cross. Even as he began to pray the words of protection, he felt no hint of the unease one would feel in the presence of evil.

The figure did not answer. Instead he opened wide his arms in a cruciform gesture. In his right hand he held a small cross. Even in the dimness, Elijah saw that the man's face was old, with a long white beard, and he appeared to be wearing the robe and cowl of a monk. Now he held the cross toward Elijah. With his other hand he pointed to the window.

Elijah got up and looked out. The valley slumbered quietly in deep shadow, while above, the sky was full of stars. To his amazement, he saw a brilliant star displace itself from its position and plummet headlong toward the earth, followed by another, then another. More and more stars fell throughout the vast array—without pattern, now here, now there, small ones, large ones—until it seemed that a third of the lights in the heavens were cast down.

Shaken, Elijah stared at the phenomenon in wonderment until it suddenly ceased. Then, with a blink of his eyes, the sky was as it had been before, all the stars in their proper places. Turning to the monk, Elijah saw that he had gone.

8

The Cloud of Witnesses

Elijah offered Mass just before sunrise, with most of the community in attendance. Afterward, he remained in prayer as people left the chapel one by one. When he had completed his thanksgiving he sat in silence for a time, pondering the apparition he had had in the night—the monk, the cross, the falling stars.

Entering the refectory, he saw that only a few people were still at their breakfasts. From the kitchen came the clatter of dishes and the lighthearted chatter of young people working together. A young woman who had been clearing and wiping the empty tables brought Elijah a cup of black coffee and a plate of croissants, made in their very own ovens, she explained. Would the bishop like some boiled eggs and yogurt? He thanked her and declined, resolving to continue the minor fast he had begun a few days before.

Amal came through the room and stopped by Elijah's table to tell him that Enoch had gone with the men to milk the goats and sheep.

"We make ewe cheese," he said proudly. "It's a big part of our income. Can I bring you some?"

Elijah relented and said he would be happy to have a taste. Amal went away and returned shortly, bearing a plate loaded with strips of the yellow cheese. Elijah sampled a piece and praised it.

Amal removed his cap and sat down facing Elijah, watching him eat and delivering odds and ends of news: He was on his way to Ben Gurion to take some of the guests to their flights home. The American and the Italian were sorry to leave but had to return to their teaching at universities. The German lady's visa had run out, and she had to go back to her country. She ran a Catholic Internet site that was in trouble with her government, which was accusing her of hate crime.

"Hate crime?" Elijah asked.

"Her site says we must always love and befriend gay people but we must not be afraid to warn them about what the sin does to them ... and to the rest of us. Don't call it marriage, she says. Don't give children to gay couples for adoption; they need a mother and a father. That kind of thing. You know, questioning the gender revolution stuff. That lady is going to court when she gets home, probably to jail. I saw Katé hug her a long time. They were crying. Lots of crying here today, Bishop. The Turkish seminarian wants to stay, but Katé told him he has to continue his studies."

"And you, Amal?" Elijah asked. "Will you stay?"

"I have my mother and sister to look after in Ramallah, so I don't really live here. But I drive up most days to see how I can help. I work as a deliveryman for the cheese and the guests, and I make fruit and vegetable runs for other farms between Ramun and Shilo. Sometimes I get lucky and go over to Jericho for a bigger load."

"As a Christian, has it been difficult for you in Ramallah?"

"I was Muslim when my father was alive, when I was in diapers. We lived in Hebron then. When I was fourteen I crawled under the fence and didn't go back for a few years. I didn't believe in anything—no faith, no Allah, no God. I just worked the streets in Tel Aviv and lived in a squat—totally illegal, me staying there. I spent time in juvenile reformatory, and then they shipped me back to Hebron. I had trouble there too, because some tough guys thought I was informing for the Shabak."

"Shin Bet, internal security, you mean?"

"Yeah." Amal grimaced. "I wasn't informing, I was just a dumb kid. So I threw some stones and was part of demonstrations, and then they thought I was okay. I was so stupid in those years. I'm still stupid but getting smarter."

"And you became a Christian."

"Yeah, it started when a priest got me a job."

"How did you meet him?"

"I hit him with a stone in a protest march. Not a big stone. He started bleeding from his forehead and ran after me. I thought he was going to kill me. I was running hard, but he was young, kind of a good runner, and he was gaining on me. I was ready to hurt him bad if he caught me. When he grabbed me, all he did was hold me by the shirt and say, 'Do you really need to do this?', and I screamed in his face, 'Yeah, I really need to do this!' Then he said, 'Do you need a job? I can get you a job.' I needed a job badly, because of my mom and sister. And he did find me work. In Ramallah. That priest really bent my head, made me look at things different. I didn't become Christian then. But I watched him closely, and I saw he was different—different from everyone. He had some kind of strength nobody on any side has.

"Once, I asked him why he was helping me, the guy who hurt him, when there were hundreds of thousands of others just like me. He said, 'Amal, I try to help you *because* it was you who hurt me.' By then, he had got some of his friends to lend me money so I could buy an old van and start my transport business. I've paid it all off now. One day he asked me to drive up here to bring some building materials, the solar panels—that was about four years ago. I met Father Ephraim and Katé and the others. They made me feel welcome, and so did the Jews who were living here, and the other Palestinian brothers too. Then he got transferred, so I don't see him much anymore. I got baptized here in the chapel by Father Ephraim."

"At what point did you come to faith in Christ?"

"It wasn't the good people or the job or the van that opened my mind. They helped, but I started praying to Allah again, just on my own, the bits of prayers I remembered. Sometime later, in the middle of the night, I woke up in my room when someone called my name. It was a man's voice, not Mom's or Aleah's. I sat up in bed, and then I heard the voice again, very strong—*Amal! Amal!* I turned on the lamp, but there was nobody. The window was open, so I went to it, thinking someone was calling me from the street. When I looked out, the street was empty. In the sky above the city a huge cross of light suddenly appeared. It filled most of the sky. I saw all my sins. And somehow, I don't know how, I also felt the Lord's mercy for the first time. It was terrible and wonderful. Do you know what I mean?"

"I know what you mean."

"So, I started coming here a lot, and to the parish in Ramallah, asking questions. About a year later, I had my first confession—that confession took hours. Then, at Easter, I had my baptism and confirmation and first communion. It was so beautiful, so beautiful!"

"Did you have any trouble because of your conversion?" Elijah asked.

"Not much. We'd moved to Ramallah, where nobody knew our family, and no questions were asked when we just blended in with the Palestinian Catholics. So, that's the story of my life. Sorry to interrupt your coffee."

"I am very glad you did, Amal."

"I liked your sermon last night, Bishop. It made me think."

"About what, may I ask?"

"This boss of the world is making things happen, things my people have always longed for. Everyone in the city believes the time of suffering has come to an end. No more terrorists, no more intifada. Only peace! And now everyone will live together and be happy. I threw a lot of stones when I was younger, and I feel bad about it now. They say there will be no more stones, no more tear gas in our faces. No more kids' funerals. But I have a bad feeling about it. I think maybe he is not good, that man. It's crazy, I know. Maybe I'm crazy."

"You are not crazy, Amal. You can trust those instincts ... and pray."

"Okay, I will. I have to go now, Bishop. See you later, yes? *Ma'a salama*."

"*Ma'a salama*, Amal."

And out he went, baseball cap on backward, bare arms tattooed with the graphic history of his enthusiasms and mistakes.

Now Elijah was nearly alone in the room. A conversation in low voices was still underway between two people finishing up their lukewarm coffee. The Irish woman was sitting with her legs tightly crossed, her back bending forward toward one of the Israeli women. The Sabra was leaning back, legs relaxed, wearing overalls and a kerchief tied about her head. Her expression and body language were very much those of an educated Sabra of her generation, earnest, intelligent, and accustomed to skepticism. She was listening intently to the older woman, revealing none of her thoughts about what she was hearing. Curiously, both of them wore large medallions on cords about their necks. The Irish woman's was gold, the Israeli's was probably aluminum.

"The old graces aren't enough," said the Irish woman, fingering her own medallion. "If you take this and wear it, you'll have the mark of the Lord, and the angels will keep you invisible. The Antichrist won't even see you."

Elijah grew attentive.

"The bishop talked about faith last night," said the Israeli. "I think I'll stay with our Lady's Miraculous Medal." She touched the shining oval on her breast.

"Yes, of course. But God is giving special dispensations, new revelations to save all those he wants to bring through these times."

"And you believe your medal will do that?"

"The Blessed Virgin showed me the design in a vision, which is why I had it made. Millions of people are wearing it now all over the world."

"How much does it cost?"

"It's free. Jesus promised me that no one who wears it will be lost."

"Jesus promised you?"

"Yes, he did. Have you read any of my books?"

"I'm afraid I haven't," said the Israeli.

"Over the past few years I've been given very important messages from heaven, warning us about what's coming soon, what's already begun. They show us the way we'll get through it."

"I don't doubt that heaven is warning us, and I know that the Church has approved several visionaries and apparitions over the last century, and some in our own day. But not every voice and vision gets approved. Have yours been through discernment?"

The question was met with a pause as the Irish woman prepared her reply.

"There has been a lot of diabolical interference. The devil doesn't want these messages reaching people. Secret cabals within the Church have been blocking anything Jesus is doing that would save souls."

"I thought he already saved our souls on Calvary."

"Yes, but——"

"Can Jesus really be blocked?"

"People in positions of power can be corrupted, and *they* can block his words from being spread."

"Anyone can be corrupted. So can we, if we're not obedient."

"Yes, but what, really, is obedience? In times when authority is corrupted we have to rely completely on God's personal direction."

"And you're saying these messages give us the directives?"

"Yes."

"So, are you some kind of channel?"

"I am. Though I'm an unworthy servant, I'm protected from corruption because I've been chosen for my mission as message bearer for the Last Days. Please accept this medal of salvation. It will protect you from the Antichrist."

"Thanks, but our Lady's medal is enough for me."

"I understand how you feel, but that was given during the 1800s. We're now in the twenty-first century, and we're running out of time." The woman dug into her ample purse and withdrew a silver disk, which she slid across the table. "Please take one."

"All right."

"Will you wear it?"

"I'll pray and think about it."

"You can use the special prayers in the books, if you want. They were dictated by the Lord himself. Mrs. Safiq has several copies as well."

"I'll talk with her. Sorry, but I have to go to work now. The weeds in the garden never give up."

The Israeli drank the last of her cold coffee, shook the other woman's hand, and left.

As the Irish lady rose from the table and fussed in her purse, Elijah observed that she was, for her age, a very attractive person. She was barely fifty years old, though she could easily be mistaken for a younger woman, with streaked blond hair and a trim figure inside a white suit of fastidious tailoring. He also noted her pinched expression. When she turned to leave she noticed him, and her face instantly transformed. The sudden smile, the crinkling about the eyes, the tilt of the chin might have been genuine signs of pleasure to see him, but Elijah felt that he was about to be the recipient of practiced charm. He prayed for patience. And for discernment of spirits.

Asking if she might join him, she sat down at his table and began with a compliment. She told him how very deeply his homily had affected her, that he was a man of "profound spirituality", and that his wisdom was sorely needed in the Church at this time when so many shepherds were misleading their flocks.

"Wisdom is surely needed," Elijah replied. "We must, all of us, pray for it continually."

"Yes, absolutely," she replied, reaching across the table and putting her hand atop his. The gesture seemed innocent yet practiced. He withdrew his hand and smiled politely.

"These are evil times," she continued. "You are a person who sees through the deceptions spread by the devil and his minions. I am so grateful for what you said last night. It confirmed everything I've been saying in my own work."

"I understand that you have written a number of books."

"You've heard about me, then?"

"Not until coming here."

"To be more precise, they're really not *my* books. The words come to me in prayer, and sometimes in visions."

"What has brought you to the House of Reconciliation?"

"For years, friends of mine have urged me to visit. They felt that the community could benefit from the messages. The people here are kind and wonderful, but I regret to say I find they're not as open to revelation as they should be—as we all should be."

"Do you mean private revelation?"

"Well, yes. The events here in the Middle East are now at such a crucial stage. Our Lord instructed me to fulfill my mission and come here in order to bear witness against the Antichrist. Bishop, I feel sure that you know who the Antichrist is. Wouldn't you agree with me that this President who has come to Jerusalem is the long-prophesied Man of Sin?"

"He could be."

"He is the one. The Holy Trinity told me that he is the one."

"Perhaps."

"Perhaps? No, it's absolutely certain."

"How will you bear witness against him?"

"I will be broadcasting from Jerusalem during the pinnacle event on the Temple Mount, two days from now. The words of the Lord will confront him."

"Will you broadcast on radio or television?"

"Internet. My publishing staff will also be receiving my messages and transcribing them. We'll have millions of copies printed within days and couriered all over the world. And my websites will make streaming global web feeds in real time, as well as podcasts. We have millions of visitors daily, but for the coming events we will have tens of millions."

"Have you had no interruption of your services? I have heard that Catholic media are suffering great difficulties."

"Yes, they are, but I'm protected. These messages are protected by the angels."

"The materials you disseminate must cost a great deal."

"They cost a fortune to produce. That's why we ask a small donation from subscribers."

"I see."

The woman withdrew her hands to her lap, and her eyes became damp and luminous.

"You sound as if you have doubts," she said in the trembling tone of a wounded feminine heart.

"You know that the wisdom of the Church teaches us to exercise caution about private revelation."

Now her lips tightened, her eyes became firm.

"That's understandable," she said evenly. "Remember, though, Saint Paul writes that we must not despise prophecy, we must not quench the Spirit."

"He also writes that we must test every spirit behind a prophecy. These two guiding principles cannot be separated. Private revelations can help us understand the signs of the times, insofar as they lead us to greater trust in Christ's ultimate victory. At the same time, we must always exercise discernment regarding their origins."

"That sounds like fear to me. Are you afraid of what God has given me?"

"Not fearful, but cautious. I am as cautious about the signs and words that come to me as I am about yours. I think you understand the need for prudence."

"Of course. Absolutely. But in my mission, the caution, as you call it, is no longer needed. It has been confirmed again and again that my prophecies are accurate."

"Do your books foretell the future?"

"They give crucial information that the faithful will need in the coming days. The great persecution is almost upon us—it will fall upon us soon."

"Yes, the great persecution is near. The Bride of Christ is being prepared to meet the Bridegroom. But first she must be purified. And she will not be purified by simply escaping from the trials that are at hand."

"But this knowledge will guide people to special places. You can call it escaping, but the Lord told me he wants this. He wants to bring a chosen few through the persecution unscathed so that they can rebuild during the thousand years of peace that will follow."

"The Lord will save all those who accept his divine mercy. Many of them will be called to martyrdom, and great will be their glory in heaven."

"I agree with you. But my mission is to give directions to those who will be spared."

"If they make a donation, they will be spared?"

The woman jerked back as if stung. Her eyes grew cold, and her upper lip trembled. She did not reply, and she did not break his gaze.

Elijah saw that she was sincere in her beliefs, yet there had been mixed motives in the original inspiration of what she considered to be her mission. Hers was a personality he encountered from time to time, a certain warping of the feminine genius. She was not unlike Karin, though saturated in religious thought and devotion. The missing thing was humility. He also perceived a young girl experiencing rejection and abandonment. There was, however, no trauma such as Karin had suffered. No, her pain was more along the lines of the fear of being unloved, which had precipitated a *demand* for love and the will to make it happen. Though she was intelligent and beautiful in appearance, she had throughout her life chosen to be respected and loved by taking charge, by assuming responsibilities and labors that were not rightly hers. Much admiration and much material reward had come to her because of her success.

Within her faith was a profound argument with the authority of God, not outright rebellion but rather resentment—as if on a barely conscious level she believed that God did not rule the world and the Church properly; therefore, she must do what she could to set things straight. Her reputation as a spiritual woman had grown. She had heard voices, and lacking humble submission to a spiritual director and a bishop, she had simply proceeded to make her interior landscape visible to the world. Offering a route map through the apocalypse, her locutions and her fame grew exponentially among the many fearful souls who consumed her words and eagerly waited for more. And more did come. Thus, when financial affirmation came through her work, she interpreted it as providence enabling her to enlarge her enterprises.

"You have no love in your heart," the woman said authoritatively, breaking the silence. "I can see it in your eyes. You judge me."

"On the contrary, I love you as a father concerned about your immortal soul."

"You have made a very hasty judgment," she said in a small, hard voice, "a very unjust judgment, and you will answer to the Lord for it. On that day you will understand who I am in the Kingdom."

Elijah was quiet for a moment.

"I am sorry if I have offended you," he said. "Perhaps you can tell me more about your mission."

"Since you are a bishop and ... for the sake of confounding your unfair evaluation, I will tell you. It has been given to me to be the seventh trumpet of Revelation. It is my task to reveal the contents of the seven seals."

Elijah then said in a shaken voice:

"The Lamb of God is the one who opens the seven seals, and the trumpet is an angel."

"That is a symbol. I *know* I am the one referred to by that prophecy."

"My dear woman, you have become the victim of deception. Turn away from it, I beg you. Turn again in humility, and you will know the Lord's mercy. For your own sake and for the sake of countless children of God, cease now. Do not be an instrument of the deceiver any longer."

"Who is the deceiver? I say to you, Bishop, that *you* are the one resisting the will of the Lord and are in danger of committing the unforgivable sin."

"Daughter, I believe you are sincere."

"I am not your daughter."

"I say again, I believe you are sincere, but those who consider themselves to be recipients of extraordinary inspirations must regard them with extraordinary caution. Such interior movements can be the imaginings of the heart or of the subconscious, or worse."

"Mine are from God."

"Are you not aware that authentic visionaries, including saints, have warned that, as the time of Antichrist approaches, the world will become infested by a swarm of false revelations? The instruments of false prophecy would not knowingly cooperate with the devil."

"I am well aware of the prophecies. But I am assured by heaven of my own authenticity."

"The false prophets are also sure of theirs."

"I have nothing more to say to you. Indeed, you may be one of those who work for the False Prophet ... or *you* may be the False Prophet."

The woman rose from the table, her face tightening with bitterness.

"Woe to you," she said in a low, calm voice. "Woe to you."

Then, swinging her purse over her shoulder, she strode out of the room.

Elijah did not move for some time. At last he got up stiffly. He returned to the chapel, where he spent the rest of the morning.

At lunchtime in the refectory, he hoped to meet the woman again, to attempt a discussion wherein she might be able to engage in some needed self-questioning. He watched for her as the members of the community arrived one by one or in groups, but she did not come.

Finally, Katherine limped into the room, supporting herself with a cane. Elijah offered the blessing of the meal, and then he and Katherine sat down together beneath the fiery chariot.

"The Irish lady is not here for lunch," he said.

"Yes, the poor dear has left. She was going to leave tomorrow, but it seems she doesn't like us as much as she did in the beginning. She has a cell phone, so a taxi from Ramallah came to pick her up at about eleven o'clock."

"Is she on her way to Jerusalem?"

"That's what she said."

"We must pray for her."

"Oh, yes, much prayer, and maybe fasting."

"Have you had an opportunity to read her books?"

"I spent a sleepless night doing just that. She makes amazing claims. Also there is heresy woven like a thread into very good insights. It's like a stew of imaginings and evil inspirations, and some private revelations borrowed from others—some of them dubious, some authentic. All with plenty of devotional material to glue it together."

"Of course there would be. Satan is clever enough to know that devoted Christians would not be seduced by overt evil, and thus he proceeds subtly as he seeks to divide the Body of Christ."

"I thought it best to go around to all our people and ask them to give me any books or medals she left. Have you seen the medal?"

"Not closely."

"Interesting symbols, but like her books, they're a mixture of true and—"

"Misleading?"

"Yes, but I think the books are worse. Here, look at this."

Katherine removed one of the large medallions from her dress pocket and laid it on the table in front of Elijah. On one side was the Blessed Virgin in a traditional pose. On the other was the symbol of the Sacred Heart of Jesus and the initial *M* for the Blessed Virgin. Winding through both was a large serpent design.

When he saw it, Elijah startled.

Katherine pointed to the detail. "She says it's a letter *S*, for 'salvation'. Apparently this medal will save you."

"The *S* is so elongated, it looks more like a snake than a letter."

"Mmm, I thought the lines of the *M* crossing the *S* make it look more like a dollar sign. Depending on how you interpret it, I suppose it could be either or both."

"Supposedly, the woman designed it under heaven's instruction," Elijah mused. "One does not find this kind of ambiguity with genuine inspirations."

"In any event, the poor soul has gone. Let's hope it's an overactive imagination and she will wake up to the fact as soon as possible."

"I think it is more than imagination. Such false revelations have always arrived, to divide and confuse us, precisely at the moment when we need to be united in prayer, in proclaiming the truth in the face of the adversary."

"You're right," sighed Katherine shaking her head. "Nothing new about that."

They ate their lunch without further conversation, Elijah restricting himself to bread and thin soup. After the meal, they drank their coffee, still pensive.

"Why did the woman come here?" Elijah asked. "After all, she is rather famous and your community isn't well known."

"She planned to make a broadcast from the Holy Land, and we were a safe base for it. She brought a cameraman and another tech person. But I told them, no media here in our Lady's valley, and so the tech people went on to Jerusalem and are waiting for her there. But she stayed awhile, and I think it's a good sign that she did. There's some restlessness about her mission, deep down, and in this quiet place she recognized it. So, you see, maybe we're a little spring in the desert for the donkeys."

"For a beloved flock, Katherine."

"It's obvious she's not an evil person, but someone in need of serious spiritual help."

"Healing will also be needed, if she is to find self-honesty and repentance."

"I told her she can come back any time. 'But leave the technology and the books and medals at home,' I said. 'And bring some good work clothes for yourself too.' She didn't like that. She didn't say goodbye. Just drove away. Ah well . . ."

When the young people began cleaning and wiping off tables, Elijah asked Katherine if the community had any contingency plans in the event of persecution.

"Plans? No, Bishop. When it begins, we will continue with our work, laboring and praying. Praying especially for the conversion of souls. And if our daily sacrifices turn from white to red, then praise be to God. Of course, I remind the others that they must search their hearts and listen with docility to the Holy Spirit before choosing what to do, where to go, if they are called to go. I think some of them are going to get through it all, like seeds of a new springtime that will come after evil has exhausted itself. Others will shed their blood. Our task is not to save ourselves. No one can do that."

"Do you know what the Lord is asking of you personally?"

"As for me, Bishop, I think I will just stay put. For years I have invited my grandchildren to come and visit me here, but their parents always said it was too dangerous. I asked them, what is danger? Isn't spiritual danger a thousand times worse than bullets and bombs? But they just laughed when I said that."

"With such an adventurous grandmother, your grand-children will want to know you better someday."

"Well, I have hoped and prayed they would come to me here, even if only from curiosity. But I no longer pray for this."

"The spiritual danger is here, isn't it?"

"It has spread everywhere. But this man in Jerusalem. This week of darkness masquerading as light. What will come next? Now I am praying for my grandchildren to stay home. But I wonder, is it still possible they will find true faith there?"

"You know that God is always at work, Katherine—everywhere. Soon there will be undreamed of graces, lights, and words from heaven. If your family accepts what is shown them, they may become part of the remnant that will come through these times."

"That's what the Irish woman says," she sighed. "That's what makes it so hard, because these people always have something true to say, even if it's mixed with the poison. One drop of arsenic hidden in a glass of sweet orange juice doesn't make for a healthy drink. And there seem to be so many more of these poor visionaries, though, as you say, some are truly from God." She lowered her voice, just above a whisper. "For example, I know a stigmatist ..."

"Does she foretell the future?"

"She gives no details, no precise predictions, if that's what you mean. She just says we must stay awake and watch as the Lord commanded us to. And she says repent— all of us—turn away from anything God does not want. And we must fast and pray. She does say that a time of darkness is coming, though she doesn't describe it. We are not to put our trust in material things but to ask God for holy peace to secure our hearts. Peace that will prepare and sustain us when we are maligned and persecuted, and even killed for Christ and his Church. She emphasizes that we must forgive everything, everything and everyone. No defending ourselves in worldly ways. Let God be God. Not enough to fill a book, you see. Not even a pamphlet."

"Is the stigmatist here in the community?"

"No, she's in another country. She's quite anonymous, unavailable to the public—hidden, as we say. But under guidance from a wise director and happy to be obedient to her bishop.

"When she is suffering the Passion on Fridays, the Lord comes to her and sometimes speaks a word through her. I've been with her when it happens, and I've seen the holes appear in her hands and feet, her side, the blood flowing. It's not macabre, Bishop, as one might think, but simply intense, like labor." Katherine smiled. "Whenever the Lord speaks through her, it's very simple. He says do not fear but put on the whole armor of God. Repentance, sacraments, prayer, obedience. Love the Church with a great love and offer your sufferings for her purification and strengthening."

"Yes, a true message, a timeless one that grows more urgent in these days."

"And, Bishop Elijah," said Katherine widening her eyes significantly, "she also says that the time of Antichrist is near. It seems to me that you think so too."

"I believe so, Katherine."

"Well, it had to come sometime. God won't let evil go on devouring the good forever."

"Yes," Elijah nodded gently. "The apocalypse will be justice, and yet it will be an immense mercy to bring the reign of evil to an end. The Holy Father has said exactly that. And he is warning us to prepare for it spiritually."

"These visionaries who have become so visible all over the world, they really worry me. Some of them are even saying that we must not listen to the Holy Father, because he's an antipope, a false prophet. Then they go on to act as if *they* are the voice of the Almighty."

"Still, Katherine, there are authentic visionaries like your stigmatist who have received singular graces to help strengthen God's people."

"But many, many are not authentic. And so we get confusion among those who love the Lord the most."

"And more and more people of good faith relying on a diet of secret messages."

"I know," Katherine sighed. "I see the damage this does in people's lives. It makes an appetite, they become obsessive, they put their trust in—how do you call it?"

"Gnosis."

"Fortune-telling dipped in holy water, if you ask me."

"You are not far wrong, Katherine."

"Well, we had our Irish lady this week. Now, I really like Irish people, and they certainly have visions in that country, but not all of them are true. Mind you, they all know how to talk as if they are true, so it makes the weeding harder. A few of them have visited here, wanting to give talks. I never let them. I say that the Scriptures and the Church's teachings and our spiritual life are enough for us. This is the house of poor men. They are welcome to stay here if they are willing to dig gardens and clean toilets, same as the rest of us. I offer them our prayers, food, shelter, a community of love, but I do not give them an audience. Some of them bring technical devices so they can broadcast their messages to the world with a biblical backdrop, you see. I say no, and again no. That's always a good test." She chuckled.

"In what way?"

"Some just say, 'Okay, Katherine, how can I help? Give me a job.' They're the humble ones. Then there are the others; whenever I resist their plans, they're hurt at first, then they become manipulative, and finally they get angry."

"Angry?"

"Angry and accusing. They reproach me, at first with gentle voices. Oh, I know that kind of voice very well. They are like wolves in sheep's clothing. At some point this kind of 'sheep' becomes not so gentle. Their attitude begins to snarl a little, and they tell me I am resisting God's will. To resist *them*, you see, is to resist God himself. Hmm, very smelly, a very rotten fish. Then they go behind my back sowing seeds of division among the Lord's children who live here, saying I am trying to silence the voice of his prophets, that I cannot be trusted."

"It must be disheartening."

"It has been at times, but I'm beginning to see the pattern, and now I know what to do about it. Whenever it happens, I stand up in the dining hall after supper and clap my hands. Then I say to my children, 'Listen, beloveds, it is quite true that you cannot trust me. I'm a sinner. I'm a really dumb donkey. You should trust Our Lord Jesus and the Church he gave us. And now I am going to read you something.' You see, Bishop, I have made a collection of more than a hundred scripture passages dealing with false prophets and discernment of spirits. Actually I have a larger collection of writings from the saints on the same subjects. So I just continue reading from both. I don't accuse anyone. I just let the Lord's word do its work. Often our visionary guests leave the room before the end of my talk, and then they announce that they're going home. Amal enjoys driving them to Ben Gurion Airport. Poor souls."

"You are a wise mother, Katherine."

"Am I? No, no, Bishop, I am not wise. Oh, my nose can smell well enough, but you can't make a happy home out of a nose. A community like this needs a proper head. Father Ephraim was a real papa to us, but the Lord took him. We need a priest, not an old lady art historian. I'm not cut out for this."

"You must pray together for a wise shepherd, and one will be given. Until then, be patient, my sister."

Katherine lowered her eyes and sighed, her lips trembling. But she did not dwell overlong on her feelings. Standing, she said, "Let's go for a little walk."

She wanted to show him the outdoor bread oven being built in the yard behind the kitchen by a crew of both Palestinians and Israelis.

After that, Katherine and Elijah took a path between the small houses at the back of the main building.

"The dormitories are pretty simple, more shed than house," Katherine explained, "but we try to make them beautiful inside with enough shelter from the elements—the sun especially. There are two buildings for the men, two for women, and two more for families and guests. It can get crowded here, depending on the season, but it helps people learn to live together. Not always easy ..."

"Where do you live?"

"I used to have a bed in one of the women's dorms. But I snore loudly at night, and the girls asked me to take a room of my own. It's embarrassing, my personal luxury. Would you like to see it?"

Katherine led Elijah into one of the shed-like residences. As promised, it was simple: a rectangular dormitory with eight beds, four to a side, each with a night table. On the far wall was a crucifix and icons and a hanging red vigil lamp, and beneath them an overloaded bookcase. Art prints were taped to the cement-block walls here and there: Van Gogh's *Sunflowers*, Chagall's *Rabbi of Vitebsk*, and Giotto's *Flight into Egypt*. There was also a photograph of the Holy Father and another of the martyred Saint Teresa Benedicta, who had died in Auschwitz, the image taken when she was a young philosopher named Edith Stein.

"Now, my suite," said Katherine with a grand gesture. She opened a door at the end of the room, revealing an alcove barely large enough to hold its cot and bedside table. There was a reading lamp, a Bible, and a few other books. A knotted cord rosary lay neatly arranged on the pillow. On the walls were a Coptic icon of the crucifixion and a framed photograph of a Middle Eastern man—Katherine's deceased husband, Elijah supposed. In another photograph, a married couple posed with arms around two radiantly healthy teenagers in front of a white castle capped with sky-blue turrets and flying pennants.

"My family," said Katherine warmly.

Elijah nodded approval of her justifiable pride.

"The palace is remarkably preserved," he said. "Is it in Switzerland or Bavaria?"

"It is in Orlando, Florida," she replied with a certain dryness.

The only artwork in her room was a framed print of a painting by Fra Angelico: guardian angels in paradise, dancing hand in hand in a ring, rejoicing that their human charges had arrived there safely.

After that, Katherine and Elijah left the building and walked along a gravel pathway to a row of outdoor latrines and a series of compost heaps. Then they proceeded up a gentle slope to a round concrete cistern on the hillside.

"Our main water reservoir," she said. "Not much rain falls here, as you can guess."

"I wondered how you turned the valley green."

"We have a very deep well."

"Yes, you do," said Elijah, and she smiled.

He slept throughout the early afternoon and later walked alone in the hills. In a neighboring valley he came upon the community's pasture, an elongated finger of level land, about seven acres in total, with a trickle of brown water winding through it, permitting the growth of verdant grass. There were drier grasses and shrubs on the slopes. Here more than a hundred ewes and lambs grazed alongside a few goats with clanking neck bells. They were watched over by a Palestinian maiden and an Israeli youth. The young woman sat on a rock, playing a flute, and the young man stood nearby, listening to the sweet notes while keeping one eye on the flock. Elijah observed them for a while, moved by the beauty of the scene and by a sense of the continuity of time—the unceasing generations of shepherds in this land, including the one that brought forth David, the "least of the sons of Jesse". When the wind shifted, a black and white border collie at the boy's feet caught Elijah's scent and barked at him. The young people turned in his direction, and he waved. They waved back, and he walked on.

Elijah did not join the community for supper that evening. After begging some flatbread and a jar of water, he went out the back door of the kitchen and climbed the hill behind the cistern. At the height of its eastern flank he sat down and watched the shadows filling the valley as the sun fell into the west. He ate his small meal and recalled the many times he had climbed mountains. Foremost in his memory was beloved Carmel, even though he had more recently climbed to the shrine above Anna's farm in Umbria and in the hills beyond Ephesus. He and Ruth had often taken hikes during their courtship and marriage, seeking the high places where the air was clearer, where the contours of the land and of their life together were made distinct and known and loved. There were also the ascents on Masada and Tabor and Sinai—Horeb, the place of encounter—and Mount Zion in Jerusalem, where he would go tomorrow.

Elijah felt some apprehension, wondering if it would be his last ascent. If it proved to be the occasion of his arrest or death, he hoped for peace in the midst of it, to overcome fear with love. Praying now with great earnestness, he offered whatever was to come for the good of souls, for their awakening, their conversion. Indeed, he offered everything that he was and had been. He invoked protection on the little community in the valley below, and he asked for the graces each and all would need during the times to come. He hoped as well that the locked gates of men's hearts would open and that fathers would turn their hearts toward their children.

After the sun had set, Elijah stood and made his way downward in the dusk. The lights were on in the buildings, and sounds grew sharper in the cooling air: the bleats of sheep being herded into their pens for the night, the dog's bark, the single clang of a small bell, the tuning of a violin.

Planning an evening of prayer before the Blessed Sacrament, Elijah went into the refectory to find Enoch. He would invite the brother to join him for a vigil in preparation for

tomorrow's journey and would also suggest an early sleep.
Amal had promised to drive them to Jerusalem immediately after the predawn Mass.

He found Enoch helping a few of the men, folding up
tables and pushing benches against the walls. He was chattering happily as he worked, burbling with his inimitable
laughter—seemingly oblivious to the gravity of the task
facing them on the morrow. Elijah made the invitation,
and the brother assured him that he would join him soon.

Alone in the chapel, Elijah opened the doors in the breast
of the hanging dove and adored the Blessed Sacrament.
He knelt for a time, silence attentive to Silence. He felt
nothing but fatigue, and though he had hoped for the
strengthening provided by a little consolation, none came.
He knew that God very often did his deepest work in the
soul without any sensible manifestations. He was always at
work—always—and often most powerfully in those times
when his children felt abandoned, alone with impossible
responsibilities or afflictions.

Speak, Lord, your servant is listening.

Whenever his mind was drawn aside by distractions, he
returned his attention to the presence of Christ. It was
difficult not to think about all that had happened during
the previous days: his brush with death, the stories told to
him by Karin, Petro, Katherine, others. Then Ibrahim's
sufferings, the plague of false prophecy, his worry about
the Holy Father, a succession of images and words and
more images.

Here I am, Lord; I come to do your will.

Again and again he quieted his mind. Gradually the
sense of timelessness increased until he was able to rest,
asking nothing, hearing nothing. He remained in this
state until there was a burst of laughter in a nearby room.
Opening his eyes he found that Enoch was kneeling beside

him, gazing at the tabernacle with tears running down his cheeks.

Elijah put a hand on the brother's shoulder.

"Don't be afraid," he said.

"*La taqlaq*, Bishop," Enoch whispered with a nod. "I'm okay."

They prayed a Rosary together, then their Divine Office, and finally they rested, exchanging no more words.

Music roused them from their contemplation. Through the open doorway of the chapel came voices singing in unison and instruments—violin, harp, flute, and drum— struggling to achieve the same.

Discovering that there were no chapel doors to be closed, Elijah and Enoch glanced at each other and brought their time of prayer to an end. Elijah closed the tabernacle, then he and Enoch genuflected and went out to see what was happening in the refectory. There they found everyone gathered, as well as some local visitors, including half a dozen children ranging from toddlers to early teens. The electric lights were off, and the space glowed with candlelight and flickering lamps suspended from the ceiling. Along the walls trailed grapevines, from which hung stars made of gold and silver foil, cut like paper snowflakes.

With flowing movements, Amal approached Elijah and Enoch and welcomed them with a salutation in a high atonal chant. Grinning, Enoch replied in kind. Amal gave them glasses of fruit punch and danced away. They took the drinks gratefully, for the room was very warm and they had begun to sweat. Thankfully, all the windows were open, admitting currents of refreshing night air.

For the moment, most people's attention was on the musicians: a young Israeli woman strumming an antique harp, a white-bearded Palestinian plucking the strings

of a gourd-shaped oud, three children shaking tambou-
rines, and a boy thumbing a conical wooden drum with
a goatskin top. Two flautists and a violinist were playing
contrapuntal melodies.

Katherine was sitting on a chair on the other side of
the room, holding Ibrahim's hand, joking with him. Both
were laughing, the young man in his reserved manner and
Katherine with full employment of her ample frame
and rather raucous voice. She waved to Elijah, and then
her attention was pulled away by visitors claiming her with
greetings and kisses.

Now the musicians consulted, nodded at each other,
and began a gentle melody. Slowly it gained force and
volume, the rhythm steadily increasing. Four of the young
women stepped into an open space in the middle of the
room, joined hands, and formed a circle. Several men
linked hands and formed a wider circle around them. The
circles began to revolve. The movements were graceful,
the steps coordinated, though when children broke in to
join, there was some clumsiness as they tried to copy the
foot moves and keep up with the circles' reversing directions. Elijah recognized the Israeli *hora*.

As he watched, he remembered the last time he had
danced the hora—at a wedding with Ruth, the month
before her death. As always, he had been clumsy, stepped
on toes, too dignified for abandon, too intellectual for
the integration of mind and heart and soul and body. But
her love had guided him, sustained him, made him relax
enough to make an effort. He had also danced at their own
wedding a few years before that. He had danced for her
sake, for love's sake, hoping to leave the past behind. Or
had it been a barely conscious yearning to rediscover his
childhood and rebuild upon it, to make a happier future?
Throughout their short marriage they had lived in the

dance of love. But for him, an actual dance had been an act of endurance.

As a boy in Warsaw he had danced exultantly, his body spinning, his arms raised, his eyes closed, his tallith and earlocks flying in a crowd of men and youths. "You dance like a bird, Dovidl," his father once said, lifting him above the crowd. He had been completely free then, laughing and jubilant in an act of praise—for praise it was—David dancing before the Ark. Paradoxically he both rued that he could not yet grow a mustache and rejoiced in the feeling of early childhood, as if he were a toddler dancing before he could even talk.

There had been no self-consciousness then, no sober detachment, no hint of the Talmudic prodigy he would soon become. Or of the man without faith who would emerge after that period. Followed eventually by convert, then scholar and friar. Stage after stage, realm upon realm, nation after nation had been left behind, and what remained? He was still that starving boy curled in the fetal position, hiding in a sewer, knowing that his family and his world had been consumed by the fires of malice, seeing his beloveds rising as sparks and ashes from the smokestacks of Treblinka.

All of this came to Elijah as he watched the children and youths and older people, and he marveled at how their self-abandonment produced no discord but rather a mysterious harmony. Even their missteps and awkward lapses were concordant, for they combined with their trust and the music to create delight. If he had been a different kind of man, he might have longed to join them. It was enough to know that he, the child grown old, was firmly held in the hands of Christ—his wounds healed, his heart filled with faith and hope—and that sacrifice was now the form love took in his life. He would never dance again.

The musicians ended their piece, and the dancers lowered their arms from each other's shoulders and fell back in animated clusters, chatting, joking, all of them smiling. With hardly a break, the musicians struck up a new piece, this time the Palestinian *dabke*, dominated by flutes and drum and oud. Amal led the way. Leaping into the middle of the room, he flung his arms high and gave a number of shouts, as his feet and legs began the intricate steps. One of the Palestinian girls joined him and took his hand; then three of the Palestinian lads followed, after which all the children uninhibitedly scrambled to take part. Katherine came next, moving her body with elegance on surprisingly nimble feet. More and more people joined the line, which curved step by step around the room, while the flutes soared higher and the drumbeat was matched by hands clapping in time. One by one the Israelis joined, and then came Sister Marie-Thérèse and the giant Krešimir. Those who were new to the dance watched Amal for cues. Finally, Enoch jumped to the head of the line, taking Amal's hand and displacing him as leader. The brother now exhibited a side of himself that Elijah had never seen: warbling loudly as he pulled the line after him, he was simultaneously flamboyant with his flinging arms and concise in his mastery of his legs and feet. Slowly but surely he pulled them all into something like a circle hora, and then the dance became everything at once, without leader or choreography. Yet it was unified and coherent, the people moving of their own accord but mysteriously symphonic. Every arm was raised, bodies spinning slowly or swiftly according to their ages; they cried out and laughed and sang, and all the while the melody and beat continued without respite.

Finally, when the hora-dabke had run its course, people caught their breath and then moved to the refreshments table, where jars of punch and bottles of wine were available, along with bowls of fruit and plates of almond cookies, dates stuffed with goat cheese, and stacks of *halva* cakes.

Standing alone, Elijah observed with a smile the small one, Brother Ass, embracing some of the Palestinians and entertaining them with his dramatic flair. He glanced across the room to Ibrahim's wheelchair and saw the young man sitting by himself, his back bowed and head hanging. Sensing that he might be feeling particular sorrow over his inability to participate in the jubilation, Elijah crossed the room and sat on the empty chair beside him.

"*As salaamu alayka*, little son."

"*Wa alaikum assalaam*, Eminence."

"I am not an eminence, Ibrahim. That is a title for cardinals."

"Ah. What should I call you?"

"'Bishop' is good, for the word means 'shepherd'. Or Bishop Elijah."

"Bishop Elijah. May I tell you what I call you? I call you *Abi*. For me you are *Abouya Elias*. I am sorry if I am ... not respecting."

"By calling me 'Father', you give me great honor, Ibrahim."

"You were as a father to me in confession. I thank you for it. I was sad, and now I am not so sad."

"Is it very difficult to be in the chair when everyone is dancing?"

"When I was a little boy I danced a lot. And when I was a teenager really a lot. Especially at weddings. We danced the dabka too, a bit different from here. People always said I fly when I dance, like a bird. But I will never dance again."

"In paradise you will dance, Ibrahim. You will be whole again and beautiful, and you will fly as you dance."

Ibrahim gazed at Elijah without blinking. Then he turned his scarred face away and withdrew into silence.

Katherine, with flushed face and heaving chest, came to them carrying a brass tray with three glasses of wine.

"Our own vintage," she said. "Three years old, and the best we've ever made."

Ibrahim took a glass and gave a crooked smile of thanks. Elijah accepted a glass out of courtesy, sampled it, and was glad that he had. Katherine drank half of hers in a swallow.

"There, that's better," she exhaled with satisfaction. At that point the music began again, and people left the tables for the dance floor.

"Drink up, Ibrahim, drink up, because now you are going to dance with me," Katherine declared.

The young man looked at her sharply, furrowing his disfigured brow, his eyes watering.

"No," he murmured, shaking his head.

"What! You can't hurt my feelings like that! Please, won't you be kind to an old lady?"

She took one of his hands, but he pulled it free.

"In memory of your mother then?"

Ibrahim groaned and rolled his eyes.

"Come on, sweetie, you're so beautiful."

"Don't mock me."

"I'm not mocking you. I love you."

This was said so guilelessly, so vulnerably, that Ibrahim clamped his mouth shut and stared at her.

"All right," he said, relenting. "But it's going to look really ugly."

"I'm twice as ugly as you are, so don't be shy."

"Shy," he grumbled.

"Brakes off, handsome," she commanded, and he flicked the locks on his wheels. Taking his wrists in her firm grasp, she pulled his chair into the outer ring of the dancers and

let go of him. Now, she began to make lively steps around
him, clapping her hands in time to the music, throwing
her head back, tossing her white hair and earrings, her
orange dress billowing behind her. Frozen in the midst of
this display, Ibrahim looked trapped. Then suddenly he
began to shake with mirth and gave a loud bark of a laugh.
He grabbed his wheels and manipulated them in such a
way that they turned left and right and left in time to the
music, followed by a complete pirouette and then another
in the opposite direction. A beautiful girl kissed the top
of his head in passing. Back and forth went the chair, this
way and that, sometimes stopping when Ibrahim lifted his
arms and clapped his hands. Amal crouched close in front
of him and matched his every move, with peals of laughter,
and then went off to other spontaneous eruptions. And all
the while Elijah watched.

Perhaps because of the accumulated joy in the room,
or the ridiculousness, or perhaps a little influenced by the
wine, Elijah now got up from his observation post and
walked among the dancers. He gave no forethought to
this; he simply did it.

An island in the streams running past him, he closed his
eyes and remembered a little dancing boy in a city long
ago and far away, just before night fell on the world. He
raised his arms and began to sing a Yiddish song that no
one around him could hear. Moving with the rhythm of
that song, his body revolved slowly, and his arms swayed
as cypresses in a wind. His childhood trove of memories
opened: catching snowflakes on his tongue in Saski
Gardens, reaching for a summer star as if he could pluck
it and save it and love it and keep it. Then he was lifted
in his father's arms in a crowd of dancing men, lifted high
above their heads, and he was a bird. Then he was thirteen,
dancing at his bar mitzvah, and finally Ruth was dancing

with him on the day of their marriage, and their love was stronger than death. All of these blended into one timeless moment, and he let it take him.

Now he saw a cloud of witnesses above him, praying for those who danced below. And he saw the guardian angels too, dancing with them—and because they were beyond time, they were also dancing for him during the long desolate years when he could not. And he saw that what he had lost was not gone forever, for he danced in a single unity of past and present and future, a stream in the great river flowing from paradise.

When he opened his eyes he found himself hand in hand with Enoch and Katherine, and through them he was linked to the others. Ibrahim was facing him, looking up at him, his wheelchair immobile, his eyes full of the light Elijah had first seen during his confession. When the music ended and his voice could be heard, he said through his burned mouth:

"We are little children, *Abi.*"

9

The Wall of Tears

Waking before dawn, Elijah prayed for an hour, alone in the chapel. Then he heard the bleating of the sheep as their shepherds brought them out of the pens for their trek to the nearby pasture. He left the main building by its back entrance and followed the path to the hill overlooking the Jordan Valley. The sky paled as he climbed, and by the time he reached the highest vantage point, the first tint of rose was spreading across the horizon above the eastern escarpment. Lights from distant farms twinkled along the serpentine course of the river below.

Kneeling on the barren ground he invoked the graces of Christ's redemption on all the surrounding nations, and on all peoples. Standing again, he faced west, toward Nazareth, and quietly pondered the hidden years of Jesus. Turning toward northern Galilee he saw the public ministry, Cana and Capernaum, and then he gazed southward to the baptism at Hajalah ford. Beyond it in the southeast was the wilderness of Moab and the temptations in the desert. Finally, Elijah turned slowly toward Jerusalem and raised his arms in the priestly *orans* position.

"I am going to my death," he whispered.

Though he felt some fear, it was subsumed in the consolation of absolute abandonment.

"I give you everything," he said, and opened his arms in the form of a cross.

From this point onward, all that mattered was the faithful completion of his task. After that, in all probability he would be handed over to his enemies. Nothing would remain for him on this earth, only suffering, anguish, and death. There was a remote possibility that the walls of protection around the Man of Sin would be breached, or fall, and that he, Elijah, would be able to speak the words that the Holy Spirit would entrust to him. The words might even be heard. Yet he also knew that the mission was not so much about success but about whether he stood firm in obedience. It was the cross, rooted in the dust of the earth, watered by the blood of God's servants, the sign pointing to heaven, soaring upward into pure light.

Most of the community were present for the Mass. Elijah offered it for several intentions, especially for the confounding of the devil's plans, for the falling of fortress walls, seen and unseen, and for the conversion of souls.

His homily was brief, a simple exhortation that they all should keep in mind the words of the Lord regarding the latter days:

"For then there will be great tribulation, such as has not been from the beginning of the world until now. And unless those days be shortened, no living creature would be saved. But for the sake of the elect those days will be shortened.

"Then if anyone says to you, 'Behold, here is the Christ,' or 'There he is,' do not believe it. For false christs and false prophets will arise, and will show great signs and wonders, so as to lead astray, if possible, even the elect."

"Watch, therefore, for you do not know at what hour your Lord is to come."

At the close of Elijah's homily, he said, "Be vigilant, praying at all times." And his final words: "Stay awake and watch."

During the Consecration and Elevation, he silently offered his life in union with the sacrifice on the altar. At the conclusion and dismissal, he blessed the community, begging God to protect them and above all to keep them faithful until the end.

As if in farewell, Elijah kissed each of his vestments as he slowly removed them. He kissed the chalice and the altar. And then he knelt on the rough stone floor while, one by one, community members left for their breakfasts. After a time, he looked up and noticed that a bar of sunlight from one of the windows had moved a good way along the wall. A few people had remained in the chapel; they were immediately behind and on either side of him.

Enoch was to his right, still kneeling, eyes closed, his healed eye watering. Katherine was seated on a bench to his left, fingering her rosary. Beside her in the aisle, Ibrahim slumped in his wheelchair, chin on chest. Behind him, Krešimir and Sister Marie-Thérèse were also absorbed in their devotions.

"We will be leaving soon, Enoch," said Elijah. The brother opened his eyes, looked at the tabernacle, and nodded.

"Amal should be here shortly, to drive you to Qalandia," said Katherine. "May we pray with you?"

"I would be grateful," Elijah replied.

The others gathered around and laid their hands on the shoulders of the two men. For the most part, their prayers were silent, though Elijah could hear the name of Jesus on their lips in different languages. Each person seemed to experience the presence of God on a different level. Enoch and Ibrahim wept silently. Krešimir's face was impassive, solemn, profoundly recollected. Sister Marie-Thérèse beamed with joy. Katherine rocked as if she were a Jew praying at the Wailing Wall or a mother comforting a sleepless child. Upon all there descended a supernatural peace.

They rested in it for a time, until a car horn beeped insistently from the direction of the main entrance. Elijah stood and gave them his episcopal blessing, and they all went out.

Amal was waiting beside his van. The departure was simple—embraces, a few words of encouragement. But it seemed that in all eyes there was awareness of what lay ahead. Most of them knew nothing about the bishop's mission, but they had sensed its gravity.

The three men got into the van and took their seats. Katherine said to Elijah through the open window, "Come back to us. This is your home, if you need it."

"Thank you," he replied. "Pray for us."

"We will pray. What you are about to do is very great in the eyes of the Lord."

"It may well be, but we are very small. Too small for this task."

"And that is how it should be."

Amal gunned the engine, released the clutch, and the van lurched into motion. As they left the valley behind, Elijah noted that the noisy muffler had been repaired, but neither he nor Enoch nor the driver spoke. When the van turned off the farm lane onto the graded road leading in a westerly direction, the rattling and bumping ceased, and the hum of the engine took over. Amal, out of character, had not spoken a word, and Elijah supposed that the young man was feeling some worry over the journey. Beside him in the passenger seat, Enoch sat with shoulders hunched and face intent on the road ahead.

"*La taqlaq,*" said Elijah.

"*La taqlaq,*" Enoch murmured.

There were flocks of sheep on the passing hills and a few Arab shepherds. A child walked along the roadside, leading an old blind man by the hand. Amal was forced to brake when he came upon three stubborn donkeys blocking the road, refusing to move. He jumped out and insulted the beasts, pushing their hind ends, making them bray and kick. When they finally moved, he leaped back into the driver's seat and sped on before they changed their minds. Not long after, the van turned onto the paved road that led past Kafr Malik, increased speed, and headed south toward Ramallah.

They were about ten minutes north of the city when, for no apparent reason, Amal slowed the vehicle and pulled off onto the narrow strip of roadside gravel. Bowing his head, his hands gripping the wheel, he left the engine idling.

"Are you unwell, Amal?" asked Elijah.

"I'm okay." He cast a glance at Enoch and said, "Where are you from?"

"The Carmel at Haifa," the brother replied.

"I mean before that. Are you from Hebron?"

"I was born and raised in Hebron. Why?"

"We need to talk," murmured Amal. He turned off the engine and opened his door. Looking closely at Enoch, he gestured that the brother should follow him. Enoch climbed out of the van with a puzzled look and rustled through the dry grasses a few paces behind Amal. When they had reached a spot about twenty feet from the vehicle, Amal stopped and hung his head, facing Enoch.

Elijah could hear nothing of what was said. The discussion continued for a few minutes, with Amal's body language growing ever tenser. Enoch listened to him attentively but did not appear to be disturbed. At one point Amal put his hands over his face and bent as if carrying a heavy weight. Enoch threw his arms around the other and held him. Then both of them stepped back and shook hands. They returned to the van silently and took their seats without explanation, as if nothing had happened.

Elijah did not probe, but he did wonder if their driver was having second thoughts about taking them into Jerusalem. Amal turned the key in the ignition, and they drove on.

Ramallah appeared to be bustling with normal activity—if any day in the West Bank could be considered normal. The streets were busy with plenty of traffic and pedestrians. Everywhere, large posters advertised the event scheduled for the Temple Mount tomorrow—the eighth day, Dr. Abbas had called it. There would be no proclamation of today's private gathering of religious leaders at the Western Wall. Elijah knew only what the German archbishop had told him: that it would take place in the afternoon. If all went well at the barrier checkpoint, he and Enoch would arrive in Jerusalem before noon. Amal would bring them as close as possible to the Old City.

At Qalandia, they stopped the van and parked a few blocks from the checkpoint. Here Enoch got out. Amal's transport pass and Elijah's documents would probably bring them through without trouble, but they thought it would be best to take precautions. If authorities were searching for a Jew (or a Jewish Catholic) and a Palestinian traveling together, it would be best for Enoch and Elijah to separate before entering this bottleneck of scrutiny. Amal could be explained as a hired driver, but Enoch was a traveling companion, and that would draw attention.

The van was waved through after a brief examination of papers. On the other side of the barrier, Amal parked down the road among empty Jerusalem taxis and mini-buses, and there they waited. While passing through the checkpoint they had noticed a substantial crowd of Palestinians on foot and soldiers funneling them into a slow-moving line, carefully examining all who were seeking to enter Israel. Nevertheless, in due course, Elijah spotted Enoch walking blithely along the roadside in their direction.

The brother climbed into the van, and they continued on their way.

Within half an hour, Amal slowed and pulled over to the curb near the Damascus Gate. There Elijah and Enoch gave all their identification papers to him and asked that they be delivered to the House of Reconciliation for safe-keeping. Though Elijah realized that this would reduce the possibility of return to the West Bank, he hoped that, if he and Enoch were detained, it would also impede the means by which they could be identified as persons sought by international police and security agencies. The risks were great either way, with or without documents. In the end, Elijah thought that their identities belonged to God alone, and in this he would trust.

As they said their good-byes, Amal grabbed Enoch's arm and held it for a moment.

"Thank you," he said, in a manner very unlike that of the dancer he had been the night before.

Enoch merely grinned, pointed to his healed eye, and stepped out onto the sidewalk. He and Elijah stood side by side and waved as Amal gunned the engine, shot the clutch, and then eased back into traffic, leaving a trail of exhaust behind him.

Before the two friars turned toward the gate, they sat on a stone wall in the park, drank their bottled water, and ate a little bread for strength.

"Amal seemed worried when we stopped north of Ramallah," Elijah said. "Did he want to turn back?"

"No, no, Bishop, it was nothing like that."

"What was troubling him?"

"An old memory."

"Can you discuss it?"

"I think he would not mind. You see, about eight years ago—you remember that time I went to Hebron because my aunt had died? After the funeral some Muslim boys rioted at the church and pelted us with rocks. Amal was one of those boys, though I don't remember him. He was a young teenager then. He still feels bad about it."

"So you set his mind at rest?"

"I hope I did."

"Brother, I remember it was eight years ago you nearly lost your eye. It happened in Hebron, didn't it?"

"Yes, in Hebron."

"Someone drove you back to Stella Maris, and we took you directly to the hospital in Haifa. That's where Dr. Abbas saved your eye."

"But not my sight. Amal just told me that in Hebron he had thrown a jagged rock at a man in a brown robe coming out of the church beside the casket. The rock hit the man's eye, and he saw it bleed. He ran. Ever since then, and especially since his conversion, he has felt guilty that he may have blinded someone—or *half*-blinded."

"And he put two and two together during our drive today."

"Yes. He asked me to forgive him. So I did. A priceless gift, Bishop, a priceless gift. To have such an opportunity to forgive. And another gift, a greater one, because without that wound I never would have been healed by you in our Lady's cave at Ephesus."

"*God* healed you, Brother."

"Right. But you see what I mean."

"I see what you mean."

Enoch slapped his knees and stood abruptly.

"So, Bishop, no matter what happens to us, it is already a *beautiful* day!"

"A beautiful day," murmured Elijah with some reservation, appreciating the theological truth but conscious of how unbeautifully the day might end.

They went separately through the gate into the Old City, passing soldiers and plainclothes security without being stopped. Minutes later, they reunited in the square by the Church of the Holy Sepulcher. It was no more crowded than usual, a mixture of tourists and local residents, along with a number of cell phone users trying to find better reception in the open space.

As agreed, Elijah and Enoch did not approach each other and avoided eye contact. Enoch wore his brown djellaba and sandals and looked much like a number of Palestinian laborers they had passed. Elijah, wearing a small black kippah on his head and his tallith around his shoulders, circumspectly examined the square for surveillance cameras and noted one high on the wall above the church's entrance. It swiveled slowly, soundlessly on its axis, taking in a broad view of the scene below. As nearly as he could guess, the camera probably would not have been able to see his encounter with Father David. He now noted that the poster that had been torn off the doors had been replaced, along with a proliferation of similar posters on every wall of the square. He saw that the President's itinerary remained the same. According to the information, only a single event was yet to take place—tomorrow, the eighth day, on the Temple Mount. There was no mention of this afternoon's gathering at the Western Wall.

But when, exactly, would it take place? And how would he and Enoch penetrate the barriers that undoubtedly would be erected to protect its privacy?

Elijah left the square and retraced his steps northward toward the Damascus Gate. Coming to the Via Dolorosa, he turned right onto it. When he paused momentarily by a stall where religious curios were sold, he glanced over his shoulder and saw that Enoch meandered after him, keeping a distance of about ten paces and not once looking in his direction. Entering a shop that sold Jewish talliths, kippahs, and other religious apparel, Elijah lost himself in its narrow aisles, until he sensed the presence of Enoch at his elbow. The proprietor was busy haggling with customers, thus freeing them to share a whispered exchange.

"All this shopping and gaping at the sights," Enoch said. "Business as usual, very noisy—I can't think straight."

"Let us find a quiet place," Elijah murmured. "The Lord will lead us, if we are attentive."

Enoch was the first to leave the shop, followed by Elijah a minute later. The brother strolled toward the intersection of the next artery, El Wad ha-Gai, where they came upon soldiers wearing flak jackets and carrying automatic weapons, standing watch on each corner. Enoch stopped at a booth where drinks and snacks were sold. It was now midday, and the two friars mingled with the several people who were crowding close to buy their lunches. Some chatted as they waited to be served.

"Nothing is happening today," said a woman in English—an American accent. "Why so many soldiers?"

"It's always like this," said a Jewish matron.

"There's more and more security as you get closer to the Wall," said another. "Much more than usual."

"It must be the same all around the Temple Mount. They're getting ready for tomorrow."

"We should come early, honey," said the American woman to her male companion.

"Yeah, the news says they think half a million people will show up."

"My guess is you can't compress a quarter that number into the Old City."

"Well, everyone'll try to squeeze in, historic event and all that. Religious leaders from around the world, and the Israeli brass, plus the head honchos of eight Islamic nations—the okay ones and the bad guys too."

"Not to mention our own president and two former presidents, the prime minister of Britain, a member of the royal family, plus dozens of other heads of state. Russia and China too." The woman paused. "Get four falafel to go, wouldya, Brad? I'm starved. Make sure he's wearing latex gloves; otherwise don't buy it. And some iced tea."

Elijah and Enoch purchased bottles of water and then made their way through the crowd to a narrow side passage partway down the block. Entering it, they found a scattering of tourists peering into shop windows. There were no soldiers, and as far as Elijah could see, no other forms of surveillance. They prayed silently, then left the passage and merely followed a sense of the rightness of the choices that followed. Left, right, and left again, and so forth, walking thus through the maze of the quarter, moving ever closer to the Western Wall.

Elijah had presumed that he would enter the plaza through the tunnel of scholars, where the Haredim rented tables and prayer books to those wishing to pray at the site. He had passed this way several times over the years, and it seemed to him the best access point if one wanted to enter without too much notice. However, as he and Enoch approached it today, they found the route solidly blocked by more than a dozen soldiers and police, all with weapons in hand. Plainclothes security agents were also present, as well as more of their number circulating unobtrusively in the nearby streets.

Without haste, Elijah turned and walked away from the barrier, Enoch following as if unconnected to him. Thinking about the other access points, Elijah dismissed the main entrance at the Dung Gate, for he knew from experience that it was the most heavily guarded. It was also where he had been detained by security five days ago. This left two smaller entrances. He determined to proceed to the closest, the steps at the northwest corner of the plaza.

Here too he found the way heavily guarded and clogged by disappointed people being turned back, grumbling about the lack of an explanation for the blockade.

Elijah, with Enoch still trailing behind, tried yet a third way, and in the process discovered that all the entrances were blocked. However, it was not a complete loss, for he heard one guard say to another that his shift would be over at "1400 hours", an hour before "he" (whom the soldier left unnamed) would arrive by helicopter. Again they turned away, and for lack of another plan they put some distance between themselves and this last hope. When they found themselves alone in a cul-de-sac about three blocks from the plaza, they discussed what to do next. But neither of them knew of any other way to enter, and thus they prayed for light.

They waited. And while they waited they became confident that the Lord would open locked gates.

As Elijah continued to ask for divine assistance, there came into his mind the words, *This is the way you will go.*

Simultaneously Enoch said, "This is the way you will go" and then looked puzzled.

A moment later a twelve-year-old boy entered the cul-de-sac and came to a halt a few paces away, smiling at them. He did not appear to be from any recognizable race; indeed, his face seemed to be a blend of Middle Eastern peoples. He was dressed in a white shirt and trousers and was wearing sandals.

"This is the way you must go," he said in a calm, clear voice. He turned and walked out of the cul-de-sac. Instinctively Elijah and Enoch followed.

Within minutes the boy had led them by streets and alleys to a line of stone apartment buildings, which by Elijah's reckoning bordered the western side of the plaza. There were no passageways between the buildings.

Looking up, he could see armed guards standing on the flat rooftops. At ground level, four soldiers stood watch along the block. Elijah expected at any moment to be hailed by one of them and questioned, but the soldiers paid them no attention, thinking perhaps that they were local residents. The boy entered a building's front door, holding it open for Enoch and Elijah, and closed it behind them. Now they were in the base of a stairwell, congested by trash bins, a parked bicycle, and a baby carriage.

The boy walked to the end of the hall and opened the door of a storage closet beneath the stairs. He beckoned to the two men, and they entered it with him. Inside, they found a jumble of cleaning materials, mops, and buckets— and an opaque window. Elijah opened the window, letting in a rush of cool air, which winnowed through an exterior iron grid. Its bars were not embedded in the stone wall but hung as a single piece on hinges with a padlocked latch. Elijah jiggled the lock, and it clicked free. He pulled the grid inward on its squealing hinges and realized that the way was now open. Beyond was the plaza.

Elijah and Enoch stared at the boy, wondering.

"Pray to your Savior to unlock men's hearts," he said to them. "Pray that the sea will be parted, that you may speak the word you bear."

Elijah and Enoch nodded, their hearts beating hard, for they knew that the person before them was of a rank of beings who had not needed a savior. Material or immaterial, he was real.

Enoch reached out to touch him. The boy raised his hand to deflect him gently. He said:

"Fruitfulness is in the Father's hands, and its weight and measure are known to him alone."

He stepped out of the room and was gone from their sight.

Elijah and Enoch gazed at the empty space, until finally, still awestruck, Elijah turned to the window. Looking out, he saw that the building rose from a rocky outcropping of the ancient Upper City at the head of the valley of Tyropoeon, and that it was a good deal higher than the plaza floor. Yet the drop from the window was only three or four feet to a narrow shelf of natural stone, from which they could make their way downward on the rugged sloping surface. This path would bring them to the pavement below.

The section of the plaza closest to the Wall was now completely filled with rows of chairs arranged in concentric arcs, divided by a central aisle leading to a microphone and what looked to be a giant golden chalice, in which charcoal or wood was burning, tendrils of smoke rising from it. Behind it, workmen were busy positioning the last of dozens of pedestals that had been erected along the Wall. On the top of each was a large golden symbol representing one of the world's religions: a seated Buddha, a menorah, a dharma wheel, a lotus with a flame in it, a crescent moon with star, a yin-yang, and so forth—and near the left end of the line, a simple cross. Beside it was what Elijah first took to be a Star of David, the Magen, or shield, of David. Then he noticed a circle around the six-pointed star, which in occult symbology made it a hexagram surrounded by a magic ring of power. On the other side of the cross was a sculpture of a male goat rising or metamorphosing from the body of a fish. As symbol after symbol was raised, Elijah recognized few of them.

The upper section of the plaza, closest to where they stood, had been entirely cleared and taped off to make a landing pad for a helicopter—a relatively small helicopter, it would seem, for the space was not very large. Clearly, the President would land here and then be conducted to the far side of the plaza and the microphone in front of the Wall. The pad seemed the most likely place for them to confront him. Elijah estimated that it would take no more than a minute or two for Enoch and him to climb through the window onto the shelf and then descend to the pavement below. Between the base of the rocks and the landing pad there was a last barrier of waist-high sectional rails, but these offered no serious impediment; indeed the sections could be parted without great effort.

People were now entering the plaza's lower area and taking their seats or standing about in clusters, engaged in animated discussion. Some wore various ceremonial robes. Among these few dozen figures who had arrived early, Elijah noticed six cardinals and archbishops, identifiable at this distance by their soutanes and violet or crimson zucchettos. He especially noted a figure who seemed familiar to him—yes, it was Cardinal Vettore. There were also several Orthodox bishops and a patriarch in their distinctive headgear, carrying their staffs of office, the double serpent surmounted by a cross. Asian men came barefoot and wearing saffron robes. Others wore mulberry and bright orange. A tall personage, with a dazzling ornamental turban and wrapped entirely in white fabric, strode in and seated himself alone in the front row. Three Haredim in high fur hats and extralong talliths also seated themselves in the front row. There were imams and mullahs as well. Three women and a bearded man with long gray hair passed below the window with a slow, studied ballet-like gait. They were dressed in tight black bodysuits with silver symbols on their chests.

O Adam, O Eve, Elijah's soul cried as he raised his hands toward them in preparation for prayer, *how you have fallen!*

At the very moment when he began prayers rebuking evil spirits, the man and one of the women stopped and looked up at the window. For a few heartbeats they remained as if frozen, then smiled at Elijah—a leer from beyond the frontiers of natural vision. Turning their backs to him, they walked on, making their way through the growing crowd and taking seats in the second row, directly in front of the ram symbol. As Elijah continued the prayers of exorcism, he noticed that one of the black-clad women bent over suddenly. From this distance it appeared that she was convulsed with vomiting or dry heaves. One of the other women put an arm around her and hurriedly conducted her out of the plaza. The two others remained.

The presence of adverse spirits was growing more oppressive. Though the sky was cloudless and the bright autumn sun illuminated everything with crystalline clarity, the plaza was now covered by an unseen dome, filled with a thickening cloud of invisible darkness.

"I am afraid," Enoch whispered, choking on his words.

"It is the enemy," Elijah answered. "He knows we are here, Brother, and he will assault us. Let us pray together."

They knelt and prayed in the name of Jesus, calling upon the intercession of the Mother of God, the archangel Michael, and the saints. The oppression gradually receded from them. As Elijah and Enoch were relieved personally from demonic assault, the religious leaders of the world continued to stream toward the Wall. Doubtless, thought Elijah, the demons would not reveal themselves, nor would they oppress in such a way that participants in the religious gathering would feel fear or revulsion. No, these people's wills would be weakened and their feelings exalted, so that their minds could be seduced.

Enoch breathed more easily and sat down on the closet floor. Elijah sat too.

"It won't be long," he said.

"When do we go down to meet him, Bishop?"

"The moment we hear the helicopter approaching. All eyes will be on it, and then we will go through the window."

Even as he said it, he knew that this scenario was optimistic, for security forces were trained for precisely such moments, knowing they must keep their attention on the crowd and the environs. Elijah hoped that angels would distract them, diverting their eyes elsewhere for the short minute or so it would take Enoch and him to descend the rock to the landing pad. But one could not presume, only hope.

And if they failed? If they were caught and silenced before they delivered their message? Then the President would walk down the central aisle to the Wall, creating a watershed of history, declaring the end of all religious conflicts and divisions in the name of peace, as the Great Reconciler, the future leader of the world.

And if they delivered their message successfully, would it shake the President from his trajectory? Would it awaken any among the audience, revealing to them the peril? Elijah knew it was not his part to know the answers to these questions. The angel had said that fruitfulness was in the hands of God alone. Elijah's mission was to obey and not to count the cost. The truth must be spoken, even if no one listened, no one heard.

Going to the window, he surveyed the crowd. Almost all the seats were now filled, a few hundred people who exercised spiritual authority over vast multitudes—millions of souls. The evil spirits would be working on the participants, informing them that here, now, in this great man, was the last best hope of humanity—that he was, in effect, its savior. This day would be a prologue. Tomorrow on the Temple Mount above the Wall, the spiritual new world order would be proclaimed to all mankind.

As he waited for the sound of helicopter blades in the sky, the interior voice spoke to him one more time:

There are others.

Enoch turned to Elijah and said, "There are others."

"What do you mean, Brother?"

"I don't know, Bishop. I just heard it in my heart."

"So did I. Perhaps it is a reassurance for us. Do you remember when Dr. Abbas told us about the telephone calls? The cardinal prefect said the same thing. 'There are others,' he said. Though what it means, we really do not know."

"Are there other messengers?"

"I think so.... I hope so."

Elijah considered a chilling alternative. The *others* might mean other Antichrists. He recalled what Anna Benedetti had told him before her murder, how she had penetrated into the President's inner circles and met people who were on intimate terms with him, as equals. She had mentioned obscure names: Abaddon, Mago, Architetto. The last was the President himself, the architect of the emerging new world order, the Plan, as they called it. But who were the others? Was Mago—the "magician"—the false prophet foretold in the book of Revelation? Or was *he* the Antichrist and the President the false prophet? And who was the man named Abaddon—the "destroyer"—obviously named for the demon who held the key to the abyss? What were their roles? And what would they do when the entire world came under their power?

Elijah pondered all of this, noting as he did that a dozen plainclothes security men had moved into position around the landing pad. At the near end of the central aisle leading to the Wall, six men and women gathered in preparation for welcoming the President.

The hum of an approaching aircraft could now be heard. Elijah looked up, and there over the Mount of Olives appeared a small white helicopter. It circled the Temple Mount at an altitude of a thousand feet and then paused to hover high above the landing pad. The hundreds of people below rose to their feet, eyes upward, their cheers and applause erupting. The helicopter slowly began to descend.

Elijah removed the tallith and kippah. He exposed his brown scapular. Then he blessed Enoch and made the sign of the cross on his own forehead, lips, and heart.

"Now we go," he said.

Enoch was through the window first, Elijah after him as swiftly as his aged body would permit. As they paused side by side on the stone shelf, the helicopter touched down. The hum of its engine was cut, and the blades slowed their revolutions while the two friars carefully picked their way downward on the uneven rocks. Hoping against hope that they would remain unseen, they arrived at the pavement just as the blades came to a halt and the welcoming party moved forward to the portal on the other side of the vessel.

Enoch and Elijah were now at the rail barriers. They had neither time nor thought to spare for wondering if they had been spotted. The roar of the crowd was tumultuous, and there was much movement in the enthusiastic audience, as many people left their places to throng closer to the aisle, jostling and holding up cameras. Some were rushing toward the pad, only to be held back by security guards.

Enoch pushed the rail section open, allowing them to pass through, still unseen. Then several things happened at once:

Just as they were about to walk swiftly across the pad to confront the President, a young man ran out of the crowd waving a bare white cross and yelling "Antichrist, Antichrist, Antichrist!" He would have made it to the edge of the pad had he not tripped. Guards threw themselves on him, covering his body in case of an explosive vest, and others surrounded the President to shield him. The man with the cross was wrestled into immobility, handcuffed, and carried off still shouting, "Abomination, abomination, abomination!" until he was silenced by a hand across his mouth.

During the few seconds of this demonstration, an elderly bearded man, barefoot and dressed only in a sackcloth robe, had stepped out of the crowd on the other side, lifting high a bronze Byzantine cross. He got as close as ten feet to the President and cried out in Greek, "*Anathema, anathema, anathema!*" The guards near him overpowered and disabled him. He too was dragged away.

While all of this occurred, Enoch and Elijah rounded the nose of the helicopter and saw the President ringed by bodyguards. The man was frowning but not unduly disturbed. If anything, he appeared to be mildly amused.

Enoch and Elijah raised their arms in the *orans* position—and had it not been for the fact that it was also the universal gesture of surrender, they would have been immediately shot, for the security people had drawn their weapons, preparing to fire. In the confusion of noise and mayhem around the helicopter, the President did not at first notice the two friars. But then Enoch lunged forward and shouted in Arabic, "May Jesus Christ rebuke you, Satan!" Immediately guards fired into the brother's chest. Blood spurted from Enoch's body and he fell, crying out once more, "*Yasu*," the name of Jesus.

Simultaneously, with his arms still raised, Elijah's voice boomed,

"Repent, Man of Sin!"

The President had turned to stare at this latest outbreak of disorder. Now he was visibly shaken, his face gripped by sudden fear. As if he and Elijah were alone in the universe, they faced each other across an abyss, though they were but a few feet apart. It was no more than an instant of suspended time, yet within it the final confrontation was made visible. In Elijah's face there was authority beyond all worldly power. In the President's there was the shock of recognition.

Elijah cried out, "Turn now, for you are dust, and into dust you will return!"

Paralyzed, terrified, his face flaming red, the President opened his mouth to make a retort, but from it there issued nothing. Through his eyes, the hidden spirit that controlled the man roared—a torrent of violent malice, of fire without light, of absolute hatred.

Suddenly the President convulsed, and from his mouth there erupted an unearthly scream.

Calm and fearless, Elijah addressed the spirit:

"He who is faithful and true, the Word of God made flesh, the King of kings and Lord of lords rebukes you, and on the day of his coming he shall destroy you with a breath of his mouth!"

Upon his final word, time accelerated and motion returned to the world. Elijah was wrestled to the ground by the police, while a phalanx of bodyguards forcibly conducted the President in the opposite direction, toward the group of dignitaries waiting to greet him.

Elijah was half-carried, half-dragged to the steps leading out of the northwest corner of plaza. He heard voices shouting, "Terrorists, fundamentalists, fanatics!"

He was struck hard in the face, and his nose began to bleed; his arms were twisted behind his back and his wrists cuffed with bands that bit into his flesh. At the top of the steps, the guards stripped him in search of concealed weapons. They tore off his cloth scapular, yanking so hard that the cord cut his neck. Then they dragged him naked along the cobbled street toward the Via Dolorosa, where they thrust him into a waiting police van. Enoch's body was thrown in beside him.

"My brother is dead," Elijah whispered as the last of the small one's blood drained away.

Just before the van doors closed, Elijah heard the voice of the President, broadcast by loudspeakers, echoing against the Wall and the city streets:

"A minor disturbance, my friends, a reminder for us, a symptom of all that humanity must leave behind. Be at peace, for this is a Day of Joy."

10

Intifada

He could see nothing now. There was a black bag over his head. Held upright by guards tightly gripping his arms, he stumbled along, trying to pray, trying to collect his thoughts, trying to prepare. The guards cursed him and struck him on the back of his head as they dragged him through echoing hallways and down a series of stone steps. The air around him grew chilly.

They shoved him onto a cold metal chair, secured his arms behind its back, and strapped his ankles to its legs. The bag was pulled off his head, and he was slapped hard in the face once more. Then they left him.

He was alone in a small, windowless room with concrete walls. The chair on which he sat was bolted to the cement floor. Near his bare feet, wisps of vapor rose from a rusty floor drain. The room smelled of disinfectant, barely masking older scents of blood, vomit, urine, feces.

Facing him was a desk with two chairs behind it. Time passed with agonizing slowness—was it minutes or hours?

Two men entered the room and seated themselves, placing notepads and a small recording device on the desk. One of the men was older, in his sixties, the other in his midthirties. Their faces were businesslike. They stared at him, frowning. Remembering his early years in Israeli Intelligence, Elijah knew what their techniques would likely be. He had never been an interrogator, but he had witnessed things and knew what to expect. One of them might play the friendly encourager, the other the role of tormentor. The carrot and the stick. But in the end they both wanted the same thing: information.

"Who are you?" asked the younger man.

Elijah did not answer.

"Why were you in the plaza?"

"I was there to deliver a message," Elijah said.

"A message written in semtex?"

"No, in words."

"You were there to kill the President."

"No, I was not. I wish him life."

"And the Palestinian? You worked together, didn't you?"

"A friend. He was a man of peace."

"His name?"

"Enoch."

"Enoch what?"

"Enoch Mika'il al-Dura."

"Is he Hamas?"

"No. He rejected violence."

"That's what you all say. Out on the street you do something different."

"There was no duplicity in him. He was a Christian religious brother."

"From where?" asked the elder interrogator.

"Mount Carmel, Haifa. Stella Maris Monastery."

"That place was destroyed. Who do you really work for? Who sent you?"

"God sent us."

"Yes, yes, like all terrorists—*God* sent you."

"We were sent to bring a word of warning," Elijah gasped, spitting blood. "And to pray for the liberation of this man."

"Liberate the President?" said one of the interrogators in a mocking tone.

"An exhortation to repentance," Elijah added.

"Repentance? What is that?"

"A change of heart."

"So you wanted to stop him from bringing peace to the world?"

Barely able to keep his eyelids open, Elijah formed broken words:

"A false peace. I hoped to call him to another way."

"Don't you agree with what happened in Ramallah, the Golan, Beirut, Tehran? Your own leaders have welcomed it, signed the treaties. Why are your Palestinian factions still fighting against it and against each other? What faction do you belong to?"

Elijah shook his head.

"Are you Shi'ite or Sunni? Are you resurgent ISIS? Do you still dream of a caliphate?"

With great effort: "I am not a Palestinian. I am not an Islamic activist. I am a Christian and a citizen of Israel, and so was Enoch."

"Where are your papers? Only terrorists leave home without identification."

"We went to the plaza in our basic humanity. That was all we needed."

"No, that is *not* all you needed. Not in this country. Not in any country. What was your comrade screaming at the President?"

"In the name of Christ he rebuked the evil spirits that control the President and his circle."

"Evil spirits? What are you babbling about? In the name of Christ? You expect us to believe that?"

Elijah paused before answering. "No."

"Then why say it?"

"It must be spoken, even if no one listens, or hears."

"I'll ask you one more time. If you don't give us the truth, we take you to another level of interrogation."

"I am a Catholic priest. I am a Jew by birth and a Catholic by conviction."

They pondered this for some moments.

"What's that supposed to mean?" the younger asked.

Elijah did not respond.

"You were working with a terrorist cell, and something went wrong with your plans," said the older interrogator. "What went wrong?"

"I do not know what you mean."

"You do know. You know exactly what we mean. You and the other members of your cell conspired to kill him."

"I was involved with no people other than my friend. Neither of us carried weapons of any kind."

"The two other fanatics, the ones carrying crosses— they were part of your cell."

"My friend and I acted alone. I do not know to whom you are referring. Were they carrying weapons?"

The interrogators looked at each other and then fell silent. One impatiently tapped the pad before him with a pencil.

"Combined, the four of you were to create a distraction at the helicopter so that your coconspirators could assassinate him. Long-range snipers, right? Why didn't they shoot?"

"I know of no snipers."

"They're planning to try again tomorrow, aren't they?" said the other. "Will it be a suicide bomb on the Temple Mount? Will it be handguns at close range? Or a sniper?"

"I know nothing of any such plans."

"Don't lie to us. We already know your plans."

"You cannot know this, because it is simply untrue."

"Give us their names and locations, and we will be lenient with you."

"I have no such information."

"This is your last chance. If you refuse to assist us, you leave us no choice; you force us to use pressure."

"You mean torture."

"We have laws in this country," said the elder. "This is a civilized nation. We do not use torture."

"You rewrite laws with euphemisms. As a priest, I have buried some of your recipients of pressure. I have seen their bodies and what was done to them in your prisons."

"Propaganda. What is your name? Where do you come from?"

Elijah now realized that if he told them his name, it would be checked with police and intelligence files, and he would be identified as a fugitive from justice, the man accused of murdering a Supreme Court judge in Italy. The resulting legal processes and the scandal in the world media would further defame the Church. The President wanted him declared guilty, and the President would have his way. No, the President wanted him dead.

To give them his assumed name—the one on the Vatican passport—would only delay his identification.

"My name is unimportant," he said.

"It is very important to us."

"My name is my own and is known to the Lord."

"Known to the Lord," the older one mimicked. "Who is your Lord, then?"

"Jesus Christ."

Unblinking, the interrogators stared at him.

"You are a Christian Zionist. A prophet with a machine gun. Are you an American?"

"I am none of these. I am a Roman Catholic priest and a citizen of Israel."

"And you have provided no proof of either claim."

"I have done no wrong. I have harmed no one."

"But you and your fellow conspirators intended to."

"No," Elijah groaned. "No."

"Then your coconspirators did?"

"I know of none."

"You're a Settler, aren't you?" said the elder. "You don't like the peace treaty. You hate Arabs."

"I am not a Settler. I do not hate Arabs. My friend whom you killed is an Arab."

"Then you hate Jews; you hate Israel."

"I do not hate Israel. I am a Jew, and the Jewish people are my people. We are the firstborn of the Lord."

"We?"

"Yes, *we*. You do not have understanding of the New Covenant. Yet you are beloved."

They stared at Elijah, bemused, shaking their heads.

"*Sh'ma Yisrael, Adonai eloheinu, Adonai echad ...*" Elijah whispered.

"Impressive," said the younger. "Where did you learn a Hebrew prayer?"

"I learned it from my father when I was a child, and from the Torah."

"And you think this makes you a good citizen?"

Elijah recalled the night in 1943 when he was saved from the SS by Pawel Tarnowski, at a time when Jews did not torment Jews, when Jews did not kill other Jews. When Nazis and their allies did such things.

"*Un az du vest kumen iber a groysn fayer,*" he sighed, "*far groys tsores zoltsu zikh nit farbrenen.*"

"What language is that?" asked the younger.

"It's Yiddish," said the elder. "'If you should come across a great fire, do not burn for sorrow.' It's a song they sang in the Warsaw ghetto. A lament for those who perished."

"Who are you, old man?" demanded the younger.

"He is obviously a Polish Jew. Not many of them are left now."

"Is he a fanatic, or is it dementia?"

"Is there a difference?"

But the question was rhetorical.

"Your name, old man. This is your last chance. Tell us your name."

"Dovidl," Elijah breathed and hung his head.

"You bring this on yourself," said the younger interrogator. "We're not going to let you and your gang kill any more people. You're going to talk *now*, or you force us to continue to the next level."

"I have told you all I know," sighed Elijah.

Both men stood and lit cigarettes, gazing down at the prisoner as if he were a specimen in a cage.

"I forgive you," he whispered.

"What?" said one of the men.

"I forgive you."

They rolled their eyes and left the room.

Minutes or hours? It was minutes felt as hours. With his cold, aching body constrained, his muscles cramped and screamed in protest. Though immobilized, he was short of breath. He could feel his heart beating too rapidly, then giving odd thumps followed by pauses.

Someone entered the room. He felt fingers on one of his wrists, a pressure band on his arm, a stethoscope on his chest and back.

"The heart is weak," said a disembodied voice. "Don't go too far."

The metal door closed with a bang.

"Your name!" a voice shouted, with a blow to his upper arm, making him cry out.

"Whom were you working with?"

Another blow, then another—ribs, shins, the back of his skull.

"What are they planning for tomorrow? Tell us! Talk!"

The clicking of a cigarette lighter, the faint smell of petrol, a hissing sound, and the strong smell of propane. Then the audible gush of an ignited blowtorch.

"Fire," said the voice. "Tell us the truth, or you will feel this fire."

"Praise be to Jesus Christ," Elijah groaned.

A needle of blue flame penetrated his chest. He screamed. Daggers of heat stabbed his feet and his hands. Then the breath of the dragon roared in his ears and the tips of his ears burst into flame and the hair on his head went up in smoke. He screamed and screamed.

It went on and on.

Fragments of thought blew through his mind: The name, the name, the Holy Name, and his own name, his many names, and everything was burning from the outside into the center.

He opened his mouth to speak but only cries came out, and in his mind's eye he saw his lifeless body thrown onto a heap of other naked bodies, then carried to an oven and thrust into its mouth as the gas burners were ignited.

There was water somewhere in what followed, cold water. There was a band on his arm, the pressure increasing, and he thought it was the armband he had worn in the ghetto, and still wore, the yellow star becoming the cross of Christ, and then the star again. And all the while, the sound of a rapping toy drum, pausing and uneven.

Then silence. He could see little now, for there was blood in his eyes. There were people milling about. His flesh smelled burnt, and he was naked and ashamed. Then he was unbound. He would have fallen to the floor and poured his life down the drain, but he was lifted up and carried by strong hands, and he knew that everything was now over. The pit or the crematorium.

Only upon awakening did he realize that he had slipped from their grasp by the collapse of consciousness, freed by a burnt fuse in his mind, a wire pulled from its terminal. Where was he now? Was this a pause between strokes of pain? Still, the Holy Name had not been taken from him, and in the sanctuary of his heart he kissed the wounds of Christ. He could do no more than this. *It is so small*, he thought, *but I give it to you.*

Someone had wiped the blood from his face, and he could see well enough from one eye. The other was swollen and fused shut. He was lying on his back, on a cot in a cell or a bare room. This place was warm and dry. As long as he did not move, he did not feel the agony. He was clothed again—his own clothing, black trousers, white shirt, one arm soaked with Enoch's blood, or was it his own blood? His feet were bare, inflamed, blistered in some places, bleeding in others. His hands too. When he turned his head a little, he noticed his sandals set neatly by the bed.

Now his thoughts steadied, and full consciousness returned.

Seated on a wooden chair at the foot of the bed was a very old man. He wore a business suit and tie and shiny new shoes. He leaned forward, supporting his upper body with both hands firmly gripping a cane. His hands were crippled, deformed by arthritis. His hands and the bare dome of his skull were covered with liver spots. His eyes were faded blue, set in wrinkled pouches that spoke of aeons of anxiety and fatigue. There was no humor in them.

"So good to see you, David," said the man in a rasping whisper.

"Who are you?" asked Elijah, his own voice cracked and hoarse.

"And just in time, I see."

"Where am I?"

"You're in Maskobiyeh, the Shin Bet interrogation center in West Jerusalem. It looks as if you've already been interrogated. Well, they were in a hurry. I do apologize."

"Who are you?" Elijah asked again.

"Don't you remember me?"

"No."

"We worked together a long time ago. In another lifetime, it seems."

"When?"

"When we were colleagues. When we were friends."

"I do not remember you."

"The years pass swiftly. For both of us there have been so many people, so many decades—and governments."

"Why do you call me David?"

"You were David in those years. The sixties, the Eichmann trial. The journeys and campaigns, the rallies. Remember New York?"

"New York?"

"I think you would remember, if you gave it some thought. Cast your mind back to an old woman in Manhattan who brought you a message and a medal. A Polish war medal thrown from a train headed to Auschwitz."

"Who are you?" Elijah croaked.

"I'm Lev."

"Lev?"

"Yes. Do you remember me now?"

"I remember you. Why are you here?"

"I still enjoy certain privileges—honorary and emeritus, of course. Years ago I was the minister of the interior."

"Yes, I read about it."

"I was also deputy director of Shin Bet for a time, though this was not public knowledge. Also some special projects with Mossad. At one point I was in line to run for prime minister."

"I read about that too."

"Then you also read that the people threw us out of office. Ancient history, very ancient. I am retired now but not forgotten."

"I did not recognize you."

"Understandably. But I recognize *you*. Not long ago, your aging face was on the front pages of European newspapers—a new name, of course, the one you assumed when you became a monk. A strange life you've had, David. Very strange. You might have become prime minister one day, if you hadn't thrown it all away. You would have won the country easily and done so much good—so much good."

"I would also have done so much evil, Lev. You cannot imagine. You do not understand."

"So, after all these years, you're still set on your course. I don't suppose you're actually a murderer? No, I think not. But it's very clear that you have enemies."

"I am not a murderer."

"Are you feeling any discomfort? Is the morphine still working? I made them inject it as soon as I arrived."

"Do they know who I am?"

"The lads from Shin Bet? No, they have no idea."

"But how? How did you know I was here?"

"I will fill in the details presently."

"Why have you come?"

"Not for old time's sake. And, at the risk of repeating myself, I must say I arrived in the nick of time. Even as we speak, security people from the President's party are at headquarters, meeting with the director. They want you handed over to them. They won't say why."

"The President wants me dead."

"Does he? Why would he?"

"He is the one who arranged the murder I am accused of. That, and other murders. I saw the evidence, and I know his guilt."

Lev looked dubious.

"Well, be that as it may, the director grows uncooperative whenever anyone tries to give him orders. He doesn't like to be pressured, not even by the future leader of the world. He is also somewhat suspicious about their intense need to take into custody an old man who made a religious fuss in the middle of their grand event."

"How do you know all this?"

"The director is a friend of mine, a protégé of sorts. We spoke by phone a few minutes ago. As soon as he is finished talking to the President's men—and enjoying their disappointment—he will call the head of Maskobiyeh and tell him to release you. We are waiting for an ambulance to arrive, and it will bring you to any place you want to go."

"The President knows it was I who confronted him in the plaza. Why isn't he unmasking me to the director?"

"If he wants to deal with you personally, he wouldn't want Israel holding on to you. By law, Israel would have to hand you over to the Italians."

"He wants me silenced forever, Lev, and as soon as possible."

"If so, it's reason enough for you to remain nameless as far as Israel is concerned, just another harmless religious fanatic. There were a few others in the plaza, you realize."

"Where is the body of my friend Enoch? The man who was killed by security."

"He is in cold storage."

"Can you give me his body? I want to bring him with me for burial."

"It can be arranged. Now, listen to me. Stop talking and rest. They say your heart is in bad shape. Also you've had burns and a few hits to the head. A concussion even."

With the unburned part of his hands, his fingertips, Elijah touched his forehead and his ears, wincing.

Despite his longing to drop away into the morphine's embrace, he persisted:

"Why are you helping me, Lev? Don't you believe in the President and his agenda?"

Lev frowned. "In some ways I am sympathetic. I want peace. Everyone wants peace. But I've learned things along the way. You don't deal with the dark side of human nature for as long as I have without developing radar. That man wants power. He's the ultimate humanitarian, of course, but he wants power so badly it makes me wonder why. Also, I don't want to see Israel dissolve. We might gain a little and lose too much."

"What would you lose?"

"Our identity, forged in the fires of the Shoah. Go farther back, and you get Sinai and Mount Zion. Four thousand years of slowly emerging identity. All his rhetoric about preserving diversity and strengthening identities is just that—rhetoric. Everything would be absorbed into the new global monoculture."

"And you would resist?"

"As much as I could. As much as Israel could. But everyone's in love with him, you see. Our people are presently enthralled by him and can't wait to give him our sovereignty on a platter. But I smell another *führer*. A sanitized one perhaps, but—Don't look at me that way."

"What way?"

"You're hoping I've become religious. Well, I haven't. I was an atheist when we knew each other, and I'm still an atheist."

They fell silent, pondering each other across a chasm. And yet to Elijah the gap did not seem as wide as Lev supposed.

"The Palestinians have a good word, Lev."

"What word is that?"

"*Intifada.* 'The shaking off.'"

"You call that a good word? The two main intifadas were a disaster for everyone. A lot of people died, Israelis and Palestinians—mostly Palestinians."

"The whole world needs an intifada, Lev. We need to shake off the cloud of deception so we can see and move again."

"Are there that many stones in the world?"

"I do not mean with weapons. If we can't shake it off by ourselves, then the shaking will come from another source."

"What source? Russia? China?"

Elijah said nothing.

"God, you mean."

"Yes, from God. Mankind needs to be shaken out of its illusions."

"Illusions are in the eye of the beholder. We all have illusions. *You* have illusions."

There was a rap at the door. A Shin Bet agent entered the room and nodded respectfully to Lev.

"The director says we're to release him. An ambulance is here. We'll take him out through the back exit."

"Good," said Lev, slowly rising to his feet with the help of his cane.

A gurney was wheeled in, and two orderlies in medical uniform shifted Elijah's body onto it. When he cried out in pain, one of the medical staff injected him with a syringe of morphine.

Lev limped along beside the gurney as it rolled down a hallway toward a set of double doors.

"Lev, you still haven't told me how you knew I was here."

"A friend of mine informed me. A friend of the President's too, apparently. She's also a friend of the prime minister's."

"A woman?"

"Yes, an Austrian who lives in Israel. She was in the plaza and saw the whole thing. Somehow she knows who you are, knows everything, in fact. She phoned me right away and told me the various versions of your name, and that you were an innocent man whom the President wants to subtract from the social equation."

"Karin."

"Yes, Karin. I'm surprised you know the lady. Whether the part about him wanting to kill you is true or not, I do owe her some favors. I was fairly sure you would be brought here for the first stage of interrogation. I came as fast as I could. Please forgive my regrettable delay. Before I could arrive, they took you to the second or third stage, because they are desperate to stop anything that might cause problems tomorrow. I will chew some ears off before I've finished, but for now we need to get you out of here. Where do you want to go?"

"The West Bank. Is it possible?"

"Certainly. This is a Ministry ambulance—our driver, our medical staff. Very discreet gentlemen with all the necessary passes."

"I don't know the address, but the people who will shelter me live on a farm just north of Kafr Malik."

"There are hundreds of farms in that region. A name?"

"The House of Reconciliation."

Lev took an apparatus from his jacket pocket and tapped on its miniature keyboard with his gnarled fingers.

"Yes, here it is. A humanitarian project, nonpolitical, interracial cooperation. Harmless people, according to both Israeli and Palestinian state security. We keep an eye on them, it seems, but they are low on the watch list."

"Can you promise me they won't be harmed?"

"Promise?" Lev frowned. "Promises in this country? All I can promise you is that you were never here in our little institution. We have no idea who you are and where you've gone. Good enough?"

"Thank you."

Lev went forward to speak with the driver, while the attendants transferred Elijah onto a stretcher and slid it through the rear doorway of the ambulance. Lev came back and stood for a moment, gazing somberly at Elijah.

"Too many years, David," he said.

"Too many. But I hope we will meet again."

"We won't meet again. And, as I mentioned, you were never here."

"Lev?"

"Yes."

"Soon—in a day or a week or a year from now—two men will arrive in Jerusalem. They will come in the power of God, and everyone will see them. They will be two witnesses, testifying against this new *führer*. Listen to them."

"You want me to listen to them? . . . Just listen to them?"

"For the sake of the whole household of Israel, listen to them."

Lev stared unblinkingly at Elijah, weighing what he had said, revealing nothing. He nodded briefly and stepped aside, for a body bag had arrived and was being loaded into the ambulance. Elijah looked down at the long plastic sack stretched out beside him. The back doors closed, and he covered his face with his burned hands.

11

The Cloak

He awoke in a room with a window. As consciousness returned, he felt that it was very important, this window. To look out, to gaze upward into infinity. The sky was black, filled with stars, all of them in their proper places. They were singing an eternal song. They were beyond the reach of fallen man. They were the watching lights of paradise, and soon he would pass through them into joy.

The pain in all his limbs was severe, the burning of his ears, hands, and feet especially, and the hole in his chest a constant fire. By the glow of a nightlight he noticed bandages on his extremities. His damaged eye now opened, and he could see blurred images through it.

People came and went. They spoke with him, administered medicine. He was ill, feverish sometimes, chilled at other times. For the most part, someone was always with him, seated on a chair by his side, reading or praying or, during his lucid moments, talking to him soothingly. He could not always hear what they said. His mind wandered.

Whenever he was alone grief threatened to overwhelm him. He grieved for the loss of his friend, and he grieved over the follies of mankind, the repeated choice for falsehood, generation after generation, as men preferred darkness to light, the mystery of iniquity to the long, hard labors of love. And there was another grief embedded within it: He had failed in his mission.

"Has the Man of Sin spoken?" Elijah croaked through his infected throat.

"He is speaking at this moment, in Jerusalem." It was Katherine's voice. He opened his eyes, turning to look at her.

"We must pray!" Elijah cried out. "We must stop him!"

"We are all praying," she said. "Please do not thrash around, dear Bishop. Your wounds are bleeding again. And your heart—"

"I have failed, Katherine! I have failed! I did not stop him in time!"

"Shhh, shhh. Be still now."

"I was not good enough!"

"Trust in the Lord, my friend. Trust. We cannot know all the ways of divine providence."

"My little brother is dead! I have killed him," he raved. "In my pride I have killed him, for I thought we were the two witnesses."

"Be still, be still."

He slept for a time, and later the sounds of murmured discussion woke him, new people standing close by.

"His heart is giving up," said a voice that Elijah recognized but could not place. "Keep him comfortable and rested."

"The pain comes and goes. Sometimes it is extreme."

"The morphine drip will help. Don't let him pull out the needle in his delirium."

"I'm a nurse. I'll be here until the end."

"*Merci, ma Soeur.*"

"*Merci, Docteur* Abbas. Should I tell him about the funeral?"

"If he is lucid, you may tell him. He will want to attend, of course, but it is impossible."

"The priest you brought should anoint the bishop. He needs the last sacrament."

"Yes, in a moment. Then the young father will offer the funeral Mass for Brother. I must take him back to Lod as soon as possible. His flight is tonight."

Elijah was relieved—the doctor was still free. He tried to reach out to him, but his arm was bound by the needle and tube, and by his weakness.

"Tarek," he breathed.

Dr. Abbas put a hand gently on Elijah's shoulder.

"I am here."

"Tarek, Gabriel prays for you."

"I know he does. He is praying for you too, and for all of us."

"We can open the locked cage together, but we cannot do it alone."

The doctor said nothing, though his hand did not move from the dying man's shoulder.

Elijah closed his eyes and rested.

Later, another voice recited the prayers of anointing over him, and a bedside candle burned brightly, its sweet beeswax illuminating as it was consumed.

When Elijah tried to confess his sins to the priest, he felt confused. What was a fault, what was a sin? There was pride. There was lack of trust. There had been anger. Was it choice? Was it feelings only? He no longer knew.

"Just be a very little child," said the priest. "You are in the hands of God. Always you are in the hands of God. He works everything to the good for those who love him."

Absolution, then peace. Now he saw the priest more clearly.

"It is you, true son."

"Do you remember me, Bishop?"

"We met by the tomb."

"Yes, we did. I won't forget what you said to me that night."

"I cannot remember it."

"You gave me hope and courage. You helped me to see that crucified love is the strongest thing on earth."

"And you have brought the Lord to me."

"He is with you."

Father David gave Elijah Holy Communion, and the sweet fire of Christ entered him, making the dagger of pain caused by the blowtorch lose its power to derange and cast down. The presence did not take away the pain but gave the consolation that made it bearable.

"Now I have to go, Bishop," said the priest. "I'm offering the funeral Mass for your friend Brother Enoch."

"Enoch Mika'il is his name."

"I know. I'm very sorry you can't concelebrate, but you will be with us in spirit. Can you pray the Mass in your heart?"

"I will. Where will you bury him?"

"On a hill above the sheep pasture. Facing east."

"The night is almost ended, then?"

"The night must still run its course."

"An hour and two hours and a half hour?"

"Yes. It has begun. The devil will rage because his time is short, but he is defeated by the Blood of the Lamb."

"*Satana, Agni sanguine victus es!*" Elijah whispered.

"Keep praying against the evil one, Bishop. Please keep praying—we need you now more than ever."

"I will pray."

He slept again. He dreamed of a golden city and a Child in white robes coming forth from it to take his hand and guide him home. The Child's hands and feet were pierced with terrible wounds. The bearded monk was there too, waiting for him at the gates. Also John of the Cross and Teresa Benedicta and others. Many, many others.

When he opened his eyes, Katherine tried to spoon-feed him warm broth and tiny bits of bread. He was, for a moment, nothing more than a small bird in a nest. He turned his head away and asked for water.

"May I give him the water?" asked a woman's voice. He could see her shape standing beside Katherine, but he could not see her face, for the night was in the window and the lamp was off—there was only candlelight.

"All right," said Katherine. "Be careful of his wounds. Krešimir, you lift him."

A giant came forward and put his arms under Elijah's shoulders and raised his upper body. The woman in shadow drew a chair to the side of the bed and sat down. Gently, gently, she put the lip of a glass of water to his mouth. He drank and was laid back, the giant lowering him onto the pillow.

The woman took one of Elijah's bandaged hands in both of hers, tentatively, delicately.

"May I have a moment alone with him?" she asked.

The others paused, then left the room.

"Do you know me, David Schäfer?"

"I know your voice," he said. "It was long ago. I saw you suffering, alone in the world. I would have protected you, but I could not."

"You have protected me. More than you realize."

"He did not destroy you, Karin."

"He tried. And he came very close. He would have made me the very instrument of my own death."

"He will not cease trying to destroy you."

"I know it. But now I also know there's something bigger than him in the world."

"And above. This is sure and true."

"For you, maybe."

"For *you*, Karin. The One who loves you would have died for you alone."

She did not reply, yet she did not let go of his hand.

"I would have been a father to you, Karin. I would have given my life in exchange for what happened to you. If I could, I would go back and step between you and that man on the day of darkness, by the water, the horses, the knife. I would have blocked the lie he put into you."

"Yes, I know you would have. I saw you do it in Jerusalem."

For a time he said nothing.

"It's too late for me now," said the woman. "But at least I know there's something stronger than evil."

"It is not too late," he said. "You are not alone. Never again—never again—must you feel alone."

"I'm not sure what I'll feel tomorrow, or where I'll be. I only know that today I'm different. As I watched you and your friend confront the President, I saw the most powerful man in the world become terrified. Never in my life have I seen him afraid of anything. He wasn't afraid of being wounded or killed. He was afraid of *you*—of your presence."

"I would have freed him, if he could have accepted it."

"Freed him? He doesn't want what you have to offer. He wants you *gone*. All of you. If you only knew the vitriol he's spewing against your people now—in the most reasonable tones, the most elegant language. With the media calling him the Father of All Peoples, this man who hates you so much."

"He is of the spirit of the Destroyer."

"I know he is. It was you—you who have no power, without weapons or networks of alliance, without wealth—it was you who revealed the limits of his power. You who have been a friend to me."

"I do not understand."

"You were more than a friend—you were a father. I assure you, you have become a father to me."

"If this is true, it is because I am a small sign of the Father of us all."

She did not reply.

"Karin, has the President discovered that you were the one who freed me from prison?" he asked.

"He may or may not know. It doesn't matter."

"But it does matter. If he finds out, he will want to punish you for it. You must leave the country quickly. You must find sanctuary somewhere in the world."

"You mean hide? Why should I hide?"

"If you fall into his hands, he will torment and destroy you."

"*You* did not hide."

"That was my task."

"And what is *my* task? I have spent a lifetime hiding. I have lived in a palace of lies. I have been the queen of lies. Now it must end."

"You cannot do it on your own."

"I know I can't. You have shown me this."

"If you are determined to remain in Israel, stay awhile with Katherine. She will help you. You can trust her."

"She has already asked me to stay."

"Does anyone else know where you are?"

"The people who live here, but my name means nothing to them. I dismissed my driver and guards and drove myself. No one followed. Only Lev knows, since he gave me directions."

"Lev knows where you are! Karin, you must leave!"

"No, I think I'll stay. Besides, something has happened to him."

"Oh, no, the President discovered—"

"Nothing like that. It was something you said to him in the prison. He wouldn't tell me what, but I can promise you he's not going to give us away."

"Are you so sure?"

"I'm sure. He's very shaken. You changed him too."

"If that is so, it wasn't I. The truth woke him."

Was it hours later, or was it days? Time was a river that carried him along, swimming or floating, though at times his mind sank into deep waters, only to rise again, gathering small portions of thought:

Is this what it is to die? Is it drowning, this sinking down? Or am I rising? I do not know the way, O Lord. I do not know the way!

He saw the depths and the surface waves, the currents converging or parting, swift and silent or turbulent. There were riptides and calm, and demons that appeared, seeking to make him deny his faith. But with each assault he became a child again and turned to his Father. He saw that angels were also with him, fighting for him.

Sometimes he saw the marvels of beauty in mankind, at other times its perils—the seductive vices and the virtues with repellent features. All of these were present, dwelling together within these waters. Souls were in chains or flying—or drowning, like him. And others were rising through the fires of purgation to the light.

Now he saw demons blinding millions of souls who were rewarded with pleasures and reassurance, for the way home was the long, hard path, and the gate to the path was narrow. The gate was not locked, but few would choose it, for the truth had been degraded wherever it was not denied altogether. Darkness was called light, and light called darkness. Good was called evil, and evil good.

In distress for all these souls, Elijah wrestled and offered and wrestled again and again. Was it minutes, was it hours and days, or was it years he suffered for them?

Only yesterday I was a child, dancing, he thought. *And after that, I danced in an attic in the City of Night, under the heel of the devil. I danced and sang and praised in the pit of disaster, with the three young men in the furnace of affliction and in the tomb of degradation. And you brought me forth. Later, you loved me when there was no love within me. Why are you silent now? Why do you not speak to me? Oh, when can I see your hidden face, O Lord? When can I come to you? Do you hear me? Are you there?*

Demons were present again—rising to engulf everything, sucking it down into the eternal abyss. The demons fought against him, and the unseen angels fought for him.

I am far from you, and alone, and all those whom I loved have been murdered by the one who brought death into the world. And all that you gave me to do in this world has come to nothing.

His soul's anguish over, he will see the light, said a voice speaking beyond the realm of human speech.

"There is a struggle," said a woman's voice. "He seems to sleep, but he is agitated."

"Death is very near. We must pray for him."

"He is a holy man; he is a saint. God will not let him be harmed."

"Even so, it is his last battle, and we must pray for him."

Elijah tried to tell them that he was not a saint, but the words would no longer come from his mouth, and he could not move his body. He tried to open his eyes, but they too were failing. His soul cried out to the people in the room, though they could not hear:

I am not holy! I am a poor man! I have failed at everything!

Yet as they prayed for him, the black current subsided and dropped away, and the demons were beaten back for a time. Yet the way of unknowing, the *nada*, continued.

He slept until there were new voices in the room.

"Behold the sea of humanity, the creatures most blessed and yet most capable of destroying," said a man.

"The consequences of their unbelief are hidden from their eyes and will bring calamity upon them," said another.

"Yet among them are the islands where love remains."

"For the children of light will not vanish from the earth."

"And here is the obedient one."

"In the furnace of affliction he has been tried."

"These wounds he bore for the sake of the Lamb."

"And for the purification and strengthening of many."

"He has borne the words that were sweet to the tongue and bitter to the stomach."

"He has spoken them truly and rightly and in season."

"So that wisdom may be justified and the Father's will be made manifest."

"His part is fulfilled."

"Now he may rest."

But who are you? Elijah's soul cried. And in the realm beyond all human speech they heard him.

"Open your eyes, beloved shepherd."

Elijah opened his eyes, and now he could see, though dimly as through a darkened glass. Two men stood close by his bed. One placed a hand on Elijah's chest, a warm hand, flesh and blood.

"We are the sent," he said. "What you have begun, we will complete."

I thought I was to be a witness. My brother is dead. They killed him. We were to be the two witnesses.

"You are indeed witness and sign of contradiction," said the other.

But we failed. We did not fulfill the prophecy.

"It was not your labor to fulfill the prophecy."

Who are you? he asked them again.

And the first answered:

"From the fiery chariot the prophet gave his cloak unto Elisha, and the double portion of prophecy and works of great wonder to glorify the Lord before men."

Then the second spoke:

"Dipped in the Blood of the Lamb, the cloak is now given to all who would follow him in spirit and truth."

"A small piece of the cloak is to be for each, as a larger portion was yours and your brother's."

"And great portions to the children of the Cross throughout the world."

"And a great portion to the whole household of Israel, which is beguiled by the deceiver yet is soon to be shaken and will awaken to bear witness."

"And a portion to the Gentiles who sleep in ignorance, though some will open their eyes and give witness with their blood, to glorify the Lamb who was slain and lives again."

"And a portion to the Gentiles who have known him and denied him in apostasy, though some will repent."

"And when we two have completed our testimony, the beast that ascends from the bottomless pit will make war against us and slay us, and our bodies will lie in the street of the city where our Lord was crucified."

It is you! Elijah breathed, his heart beating with wonder and fear.

Both men stretched forth their arms and laid their hands on his head.

"Be at peace, beloved servant. The victory is near."

Peace entered him with their touch. He closed his eyes again and slept.

When he awoke, a gentle breeze was coming through the open window. He heard the chirping of birds and the conversation of the children of God at work in the garden below. There were sheep on the hills. A shepherd walked with them.

Close beside the bed, Ibrahim sat in his wheelchair. He watched Elijah without turning away or dropping his eyes, without shame for his scars and mutilations. He was a man fully awake, restful yet attentive. Elijah looked back in the same way. No words were needed.

He desired to raise his hand and bless Ibrahim with the sign of the cross, but his body would not respond.

It is finished, he thought as his heartbeat slowed and began to fail.

And as the light of this world faded from his eyes, the last thing he saw was Ibrahim smiling at him. He saw the Christ of the burnt men.

"Now, *Abi*," said the boy. "Now you will fly."

And I took the little scroll from the hand of the angel and ate it; it was sweet as honey in my mouth, but when I had eaten it my stomach was made bitter. And I was told, "You must again prophesy about many peoples and nations and tongues and kings."

Then I was given a measuring rod like a staff, and I was told: "Rise and measure the temple of God and the altar and those who worship there, but do not measure the court outside the temple; leave that out, for it is given over to the nations, and they will trample over the holy city for forty-two months. And I will grant my two witnesses power to prophesy for one thousand two hundred and sixty days, clothed in sackcloth."

These are the two olive trees and the two lampstands which stand before the Lord of the earth. And if any one would harm them, fire pours from their mouth and consumes their foes; if any one would harm them, thus he is doomed to be killed. They have power to shut the sky, that no rain may fall during the days of their prophesying, and they have power over the waters to turn them into blood, and to afflict the earth with every plague, as often as they desire.

And when they have finished their testimony, the beast that ascends from the bottomless pit will make war upon them and conquer them and kill them, and their dead bodies will lie in the street of the great city, which is allegorically called Sodom and Egypt, where their Lord was crucified. For three days and a half men from the peoples and tribes and tongues and nations gaze at their dead bodies and refuse to let them be placed in a tomb, and those who dwell on the earth will rejoice over them and make merry and exchange presents, because these two prophets had been a torment to those who dwell on the earth. But after the three and a half days a breath of life from God entered them, and they stood up on their feet, and great fear fell on those who saw them. Then they heard a loud voice from heaven saying to them, "Come up here!" And in the sight of their foes they went up to heaven in a cloud. And at that hour there was a great earthquake, and a tenth of the city fell; seven thousand people were killed in the earthquake, and the rest were terrified and gave glory to the God of heaven.

(Revelation 10:10—11:13)